Praise for *Mistletoe Season*

"'Say No to Mistletoe' has everything you could want in a holiday romance—a hilarious underdog heroine, a hero with a heart as good as his looks, and a charming small-town setting. A perfectly delightful story, as sweet and satisfying as a Christmas cookie."

—Marie Bostwick, *New York Times* and *USA TODAY* bestselling author of *Esme Cahill Fails Spectacularly*

"Whenever I'm needing a charming, festive story, I reach for those by Sheila Roberts, and 'Say No to Mistletoe' was exactly as promised!"

—Melissa Ferguson, author of *How to Plot a Payback*

"A sweet love story wrapped in all the holiday feels. 'Return to Mistletoe' is the perfect feel-good escape that will leave you humming your favorite Christmas songs."

—Rachel Magee, author of *It's All Relative*

"Pepper Basham's 'A Mistletoe Prince' will sweep you away on a joyfully jerky journey of a royal romance that despite the ups and downs is going to delight you more than the best kiss under mistletoe and leave you smiling. This story has all the feels, a wonderful southern mountain setting, is chock-full of royally funny mishaps and so many oh-my-gosh-that-would-so-happen-to-me's that you will believe there's a chance your prince might just be under the tree on Christmas morning. Dear Santa, bring me a prince just like Arran!"

—Nancy Naigle, *USA TODAY* and ECPA bestselling author

"Funny, tender, and oh-so-sweet. 'A Mistletoe Prince' is the royal Christmas romance I've been waiting for!"

—Teri Wilson, *USA TODAY* bestselling author

T0191121

Mistletoe Season

Other Books by the Authors

Sheila Roberts

Stand-Alone Novels
Bikini Season
Love in Bloom
Angel Lane
Small Change
The Best Life Book Club

Life in Icicle Falls Series
Welcome to Icicle Falls
Sweet Dreams on Center Street (formerly *Better Than Chocolate*)
Romance on Mountain View Road (formerly *What She Wants*)
Merry Ex-mas
The Cottage on Juniper Ridge
The Tea Shop on Lavender Lane
The Lodge on Holly Road
Starting Over on Blackberry Lane
A Wedding on Primrose Street
Christmas on Candy Cane Lane
Home on Apple Blossom Road
Christmas in Icicle Falls

Moonlight Harbor Series
Sand Dollar Lane
Welcome to Moonlight Harbor
Winter at the Beach
The Summer Retreat
Beachside Beginnings
Sunset on Moonlight Beach
Mermaid Beach

Stand-Alone Christmas Books
On Strike for Christmas
The Snow Globe
The Nine Lives of Christmas
Three Christmas Wishes

Christmas from the Heart
One Charmed Christmas
A Little Christmas Spirit
The Twelve Months of Christmas

E-BOOK ONLY
All I Want for Christmas
A Carol Christmas
A Very Holly Christmas
Tourist Trap
The Valentine Games

NONFICTION
How to Live Large on a Small Budget (e-book only)
Old Is Not a Four-Letter Word
Unexpected Journey

KATHLEEN FULLER

THE MAPLE FALLS ROMANCE NOVELS
Hooked on You
Much Ado About a Latte
Sold on Love
Two to Tango

THE AMISH OF MARIGOLD NOVELS
The Courtship Plan
The Proposal Plot
The Marriage Pact (available May 2025)

THE AMISH MAIL-ORDER BRIDE NOVELS
A Double Dose of Love
Matched and Married
Love in Plain Sight

THE AMISH BRIDES OF BIRCH CREEK NOVELS
The Teacher's Bride
The Farmer's Bride
The Innkeeper's Bride

THE AMISH LETTERS NOVELS
Written in Love
The Promise of a Letter
Words from the Heart

THE AMISH OF BIRCH CREEK NOVELS
A Reluctant Bride
An Unbroken Heart
A Love Made New

THE MIDDLEFIELD AMISH NOVELS
A Faith of Her Own

THE MIDDLEFIELD FAMILY NOVELS
Treasuring Emma
Faithful to Laura
Letters to Katie

THE HEARTS OF MIDDLEFIELD NOVELS
A Man of His Word
An Honest Love
A Hand to Hold

STORY COLLECTIONS
An Amish Family
Amish Generations

STORIES
A Common Thread included in *An Amish Quilting Bee*
A Heart Full of Love included in *An Amish Cradle*
A Lesson on Love included in *An Amish Schoolroom*
He Loves Me; He Loves Me Not included in *This Time Around*
Love's Solid Foundation included in *An Amish Barn Raising*
Sleigh Bells Ring included in *Amish Christmas Miracles*
Wreathed in Joy included in *An Amish Christmas Wedding*
Amish Generations: Four Stories
Reeling in Love included in *An Amish Picnic*
Melting Hearts included in *An Amish Christmas Bakery*

PEPPER BASHAM

CONTEMPORARY ROMANCE

STAND-ALONE NOVELS

MITCHELL'S CROSSROADS SERIES

A PLEASANT GAP ROMANCE SERIES

NOVELLAS

Mistletoe Season

Three *Christmas* Stories

SHEILA
ROBERTS

KATHLEEN
FULLER

PEPPER
BASHAM

THOMAS NELSON
Since 1798

Published in Nashville, Tennessee, by Thomas Nelson. Thomas Nelson is a registered trademark of HarperCollins Christian Publishing, Inc.

Thomas Nelson titles may be purchased in bulk for educational, business, fundraising, or sales promotional use. For information, please email SpecialMarkets@ThomasNelson.com.

Scripture quotations are taken from the Holy Bible, New International Version®, NIV®. Copyright ©1973, 1978, 1984, 2011 by Biblica, Inc.® Used by permission of Zondervan. All rights reserved worldwide. www.Zondervan.com. The "NIV" and "New International Version" are trademarks registered in the United States Patent and Trademark Office by Biblica, Inc.®

ISBN 978-0-8407-1681-1 (TP)

ISBN 978-0-8407-1682-8 (epub)

ISBN 978-0-8407-1683-5 (audio download)

Library of Congress Cataloging-in-Publication Data

CIP is available upon request

Printed in the United States of America

24 25 26 27 28 LBC 5 4 3 2 1

Contents

RETURN TO MISTLETOE

Kathleen Fuller

To James. I love you.

ONE

Emmy Banks hummed along to a cheery Christmas carol playing through the speakers as she hung a third sprig of mistletoe over the doorway of her antique shop, Mistletoe Antiques. She clasped her hands together and tilted her head. "Maybe one more—"

"Three isn't enough, Mom?"

She glanced at Carina, who was standing behind a glass display case that doubled as a checkout counter. "There's never enough mistletoe in Mistletoe, Missouri," Emmy told her daughter.

Carina groaned. But she was smiling, her plum lipstick contrasting beautifully with her mahogany skin. She started unpacking a box of old books that had been dropped off earlier that morning. Emmy joined her, turning up the volume on her phone. Another Christmas hymn sang through the three Bluetooth speakers strategically placed around Emmy's shop.

"Christmas carols too?" Carina asked.

"It's December 1! Most places have been playing carols since before Thanksgiving." Emmy slipped on her purple glasses with sparkly rhinestones on the arms, and picked up the pile of receipts next to the cash register. Just because she needed reading glasses at forty-one years old, those glasses didn't have to be boring, and she had several pairs in different colors and styles. "When did you become a scrooge, Carina?"

"I'm not a scrooge." She pulled out a worn book with a brown frayed cover and brushed off the dust. "But by the time the Christmas season is in full swing, I'm a little tired of hearing the music."

Emmy never was. She wouldn't mind listening to Christmas carols and enjoying holiday decorations year-round. In fact, she had a fully adorned fake tree in her apartment living room that she meant to take down two years ago, but she kept it displayed because it was so festive. Dusting the tree was a pain, but worth it. During the summer, she even organized holiday movie watch parties in the small café in the back of the store—one movie every Thursday night. She also sold quite a few early Christmas gifts on those nights.

"Don't forget, we're decorating the store tomorrow night after we close," she said to Carina.

Her daughter winced. "Sorry, Mom. I've got a date."

Emmy peered at her over her glasses. "With Jeremy?"

Carina smiled shyly. "Yes. We're going bowling."

"How *romantic*." Emmy snickered and grabbed her accounting ledger and calculator. Ever since they opened the shop five years ago, Carina had tried to convince her to computerize the records. Emmy refused. She enjoyed the physical action of entering numbers on paper and tabulating them with her slim Sinclair Cambridge, a vintage calculator from the seventies she'd picked up at one of the many estate sales she loved to frequent.

Carina scoffed. "I think bowling is very romantic."

"But you're a terrible bowler," Emmy pointed out. "And I mean that in the best way."

"Oh, I'm awful, all right. But Jeremy doesn't know that." She sighed, hugging the book to her chest. "And when he finds out, he'll have to give me *personal* coaching."

Laughing, Emmy slid past Carina. "Just don't let him get too *personal*."

"Mom," Carina said, rolling her eyes. "I'm twenty-one years old. I can handle myself."

Emmy kissed her daughter's cheek. "I know you can. I should probably tell Jeremy to watch out."

Carina gave her a good-natured grin and looked at the front of the book. "Marshall Blankenship?"

"Author or title?" Emmy snatched a pencil off the counter and tucked it behind her ear.

"Author."

"Doesn't ring a bell," she said. "You'll have to look him up. I'll be in the café if you need me."

"Oh wait," Carina said, pulling out her phone. "We need today's selfie."

Emmy put her arm around Carina and pressed her cheek against her daughter's as Carina held up the camera and they both smiled. For a split second Emmy saw their images on the phone screen— her own fair skin and short, straight blond hair a stark contrast to Carina's dark complexion and short braids.

"Perfect!" Carina tapped on the screen to post the image on their social media platforms. Then she held out the phone to Emmy to show her the pic. "You look so cute, Mom."

"And you're gorgeous. I really should talk to Jeremy—"

"*Mom*," Carina warned.

"Just kidding." Emmy chuckled as she made her way down an aisle consisting mostly of décor items—baskets, metal signs, small lamps, and miscellaneous bric-a-brac—to the café area. There was a self-serve coffee and hot chocolate station on a long counter, along with snacks, all available for a voluntary donation. Near the station were several shelves of classic books, along with a few vintage volumes. Last year Emmy had set up the small book section, and she had started taking orders for both old and new books a few months ago. She set her things on one of the four round, blond oak wooden tables and fixed herself a cup of cinnamon hot chocolate.

As she toggled the hot water carafe and placed her cup under the spout, an unexpected memory surfaced. Or rather, a person—her ex-boyfriend, Josh Whitfield. When they had started working together to bring Mistletoe Antiques to fruition, he had been against the idea of providing refreshments on the honor system, insisting no one would put money in the kitty for plain coffee and a cookie or pastry.

"Maybe not in the big city of St. Louis," Emmy had said, getting in a friendly dig at his hometown. "But things are different in Mistletoe." She brushed his carrot-colored bangs to the side and put her arms around his neck. "Trust me," she whispered. "Everyone will pay their fair share."

He drew her close. "We're really going to do this, aren't we?"

"Yes." She started to smile but saw a flash of doubt in his sea-blue eyes. Their grand opening was the next day, and even though they were still bringing in antiques to sell, she was certain they had enough inventory to open their doors. But this was her dream, not his, even though he'd supported it 100 percent . . . or at least he seemed to. "It's what you want, right?"

"Right," he said. Maybe a bit too quickly. Then he kissed her, and for several lingering moments of bliss, she forgot where she was.

And that had been her weakness—whenever she saw a red flag with Josh, he'd seemed to know what she was thinking. He would distract her with loving words, searing kisses, and promises of their future together. But none of it was true. Two weeks after the shop opened, he'd skipped town with most of her money and all of her dignity.

Hot water stung her hand and dragged her out of her reverie. She quickly let go of the toggle. The cup had overflowed, and she cleaned up the mess, salvaged what she could of her hot chocolate, and sat down at the table. Better to think about accounting than her catastrophic love life.

For the next hour she sipped hot chocolate, crunched numbers, and balanced her ledger. Due to hard work and careful spending, she'd recouped some of what Josh had taken from her, but there wasn't much room for margin. Most months there wasn't any margin at all.

She finished calculating the last of the receipts when her phone buzzed. She glanced at the screen and saw Sheryl Covington's name pop up. Emmy quickly answered it. "Hey," she said to her childhood friend and part-time employee, although Sheryl worked more for her love of antiques and people than for money. Her husband, Ben, made a comfortable living as an architect. "How's Cancún?"

"Tropical paradise. Not a snowflake in sight."

Emmy couldn't imagine Christmas without snow. "No mistletoe either?"

"Oh, there's plenty of that, along with Christmas lights on palm trees. They even have little green and red umbrellas in the fruity drinks. Very festive. I can't believe today is our last day. We've had an amazing vacation."

"Uh-huh." Emmy glanced at her pitiful bottom line. She wouldn't be taking a vacation anytime soon.

"Uh-oh," Sheryl said.

"Uh-oh, what?"

"You're balancing the books, aren't you? I still think you should take Josh to court for stealing your money."

Emmy scowled. Not this again. "If I did, I'd have to admit to the world I have awful taste in men."

"No, you're just too kindhearted. And Josh is a grade A jerk."

"It's not so bad. I'll earn everything back . . . in five or six years."

"But—"

"I'll be fine, Sheryl. Don't worry about me or the shop."

"You're my best friend," she said, speaking over her rowdy kids in the background. "I can't help but worry. But I do love your positive attitude."

Emmy smiled at the compliment. She was an eternal optimist, and that had helped her through some rough times, including Josh's deception and desertion.

"Boys," Sheryl said sternly to her children. "Settle down, or we're going back to the hotel room." After they quickly quieted, she said, "Can you do me a favor?"

"Sure."

"I've been trying to get ahold of the rental place so I can reserve tables and chairs. We keep missing each other. Do you mind taking care of that?"

"Not at all."

"Thank you." Sheryl's voice was heavy with relief. "That's one thing off my list, but I'm sure I'll add ten others later. It's going to be a challenge keeping Mom's surprise party a secret from her for two weeks. I still can't believe she's turning seventy."

"We all know Maggie is twenty-five at heart. Have you heard from Kieran yet?"

"My one and only brother who hasn't stepped foot in Mistletoe since he graduated? Of course not. I don't expect him to show up now. Oh, he sure does promise to, but something always comes up."

Emmy didn't miss the bitterness in her voice.

"Ben's waving me over. It's snorkel time. Gotta run, er, *swim*. Thanks again, Emmy. See you Thursday."

Smiling, Emmy shut off her phone. She and Carina were the shop's only full-time employees, and Sheryl typically worked one or two days a week. December was their busiest month of the year, and when Sheryl returned, she would work four days a week until Christmas.

Business was slow today, but it was Monday, and everyone was getting back into the groove of life after Thanksgiving and Black Friday shopping. It wouldn't be long before things picked up again, especially after Jingle Fest next Saturday. The annual Christmas festival was in the larger town of Bird Valley about twenty minutes away from Mistletoe. Every year Emmy looked forward to the festival and took the opportunity to pass out 10 percent off coupons to her shop. She'd learned never to let a business opportunity go to waste.

She closed her ledger and shoved her pencil behind her ear, gathered up her paperwork and calculator, and went to the front counter. Two customers were browsing the aisles of antiques while Carina was helping another customer in the vintage book section of the shop. As Emmy knelt and tucked her accounting materials into a lockbox, she heard the bell above the front door jingle. She shoved the box on the shelf underneath the counter and stood as Cal, the postman, dropped off a package and a short stack of mail on the counter.

"Mornin', Emmy." Cal adjusted his mailbag over his shoulder, his nose and cheeks red from the cold. "How are you doing today?"

"Can't complain." She smiled and swiftly went through the envelopes. Two were bills she could deal with later, and the rest was junk mail she would shred and add to the large bag of shredded paper upstairs in her apartment. Once it was full, she would take the bag to the Mistletoe Animal Shelter. "Help yourself to some coffee," she said, setting down the mail and moving the package closer to her.

"Thanks, Emmy, but I gotta run. You know how it is during the holidays. Got a lot of Christmas cards to deliver." He nodded at her and disappeared out the door.

Emmy waved as Cal passed by the picture window, then checked the return address on the package. Oh good, the ornaments had arrived. She glanced at Carina, who was talking to Mrs. Beasley a few feet away, her back to her mother. Emmy grabbed the package and crouched down again, eagerly opening it.

She'd ordered several sets of wooden heart-shaped ornaments to sell at the shop, with classic book titles printed on them, along with three specialty ornaments that were decorated like Fabergé eggs for Carina, Sheryl, and Sheryl's mother, Maggie. She'd already sent her parents their present—a small photo album filled with pictures of her, Carina, and her parents' friends in Mistletoe, along with a written recap of the year. She had started creating the yearly photo album when her mother and father had moved to Tampa ten years ago, although they usually returned to Mistletoe at least once every other year.

Her grin faded as she pulled out the ornaments. The books were so tiny, she could barely read the titles on them. Definitely not what was advertised. And when she saw the Fabergé-inspired ones, her heart sank. All three were broken.

Emmy shut the box and checked her email receipt from the company on her cell. Fortunately, they had a return policy. She pressed the tape back onto the box and stood. "I'm running to the post office for a minute," she said to Carina as she put on her coat and gloves, grabbed the defective merchandise, and left the shop.

Crisp Ozark Mountain air chilled her cheeks as she stopped in front of the building next door to hers. The For Sale sign was still in the window and had been for the past six years. It was the only empty building on Chestnut Lane, Mistletoe's main downtown street.

She stared at the sign. Now that Mistletoe Antiques had been in business for a few years, she wanted to follow her other dream—to open a real café. Mistletoe hadn't had a coffee shop since Sips and Such on the next street over had closed its doors two years ago. This building would be perfect, but she didn't have the funds. *I would, if Josh hadn't . . .*

Shaking her head, she frowned. Bad enough she'd thought about him once today. Twice was too much. She spun around—and knocked into what felt like a solid wall.

"Whoa, lass."

"I'm sor—" Emmy's jaw dropped. In front of her was the most gorgeous man she'd ever seen. Thick midnight-black hair, deep-set brown eyes, salt-and-pepper whiskers . . . *sigh*. And was that an Irish accent she'd heard? Her stomach wigwagged. That was the only way she could define the odd sensation. It wasn't a flutter. Or a flitter. Weird. She hadn't experienced a wigwag since . . . no. It couldn't be—

"Emmy?" he said, dropping his hands and taking a step back, surprise on his face. "Emmy Banks?"

"Kieran?"

He grinned and held out his arms.

When Emmy didn't make a move to hug him, Kieran O'Neill wondered if he was being too familiar. After all, he hadn't seen her since he left Mistletoe right after high school. She'd been a cute girl back then with her heart-shaped face, long, wavy blond hair, and malachite-green eyes. Now it was cut in a short pixie style that really suited her.

Then he realized she was carrying a box and couldn't hug him even if she wanted to. "Can I help you with that?"

She glanced at the box. "It's not too heavy. I was just taking it to the post office."

"Headin' that way myself." He reached for the box. "Let me give you a hand."

Emmy hesitated, then gave him the package. She was right; it was fairly light. Still, he couldn't abide her carrying it while his hands were empty.

"Thanks," she said as they walked in step down the sidewalk. "I was just talking to Sheryl. She said you weren't coming home."

"She doesn't know I'm here. I decided to surprise her and Mum.

Can't miss her seventieth birthday celebration." Especially since he missed the fiftieth and sixtieth ones, and he felt plenty of guilt over those.

"Did you know Sheryl's in Cancún?"

He nodded. "From her Instagram, it looks like they're having a great time."

"She'll be so glad to see you." Emmy put her hands in her pockets. "She's always showing me pictures of your adventures. Have you finished renovating the castle?"

"Aye."

Emmy glanced at him. "Nice Irish accent."

"Twenty-four years in Ireland will do that to a lad."

"I do detect some southern drawl mixed in." She grinned. "It makes you sound a little exotic."

"That would be a *wee* bit exotic, lass." He chuckled as her smile widened and they continued walking. He glanced down at her again. He wasn't all that tall, about five eight, but she barely reached his shoulder. "Anyway, back to the castle. Took me over fifteen years, but it's finally done."

"Wow. I didn't realize you'd owned it that long," she said. "What's it like, living in a castle?"

He tapped his fingers against the box. "Well, for fourteen and a half years it was unlivable. The six months I did live there . . . let's just say it wasn't exactly cozy. So I sold it."

Her head jerked toward him. "Why? It's been in your family for four hundred years."

"Four hundred and fifty, to be exact, although it's changed hands over the last thirty." Kieran shrugged. "Turned out there was a reason the O'Neills didn't want it. Living in a castle isn't practical, and it's expensive. When I got an offer from a hotel chain, I didn't hesitate to sell."

She sidestepped an uneven crack in the sidewalk. "But you put so much time and effort into it."

"And money." A whole lot of money, even though he did much of the work himself, which was why it had taken him so long to renovate it. He was proud of the restoration, but he didn't regret unloading it. Actually, it felt like a huge burden was lifted off his shoulders.

"Do Sheryl and your mom know?"

"Not yet . . . That would be another surprise." He just hoped they wouldn't be too upset about it. His mother in particular had been excited that Kieran had bought the castle, although she was a little less impressed when she had spent two drafty weeks living there last year. Castles certainly weren't for everyone.

He and Emmy turned the corner onto Evergreen Way. Although it had been more than two decades since he'd last been here, the downtown area still looked the same at Christmas, with thousands of twinkling lights hanging on every building, window, and streetlamp. Wreaths were everywhere, and of course sprigs of mistletoe hung from all the doorways. As they passed the Mistletoe Diner, a couple stopped for a quick kiss before leaving the eatery. There was probably more kissing in Mistletoe during Christmas than in any other town in the country. *No, make that the world*, he thought as he spied another couple giving each other a peck.

"I wasn't surprised when Sheryl told me about the castle," Emmy continued. "Or that you moved to Ireland after backpacking through Europe for a year."

"Two years, actually," he said.

"That's right." She glanced at him. "You were always the adventurous type. Remember the time—"

"I got caught skinny-dipping in the Mistletoe water tank?" At her nod, he gave her a sheepish grin. He would never live that down.

"Number one on my wall of shame. I was such an idiot for taking that dare. I learned my lesson."

"No more skinny-dipping?"

"Not in water tanks, anyway."

She laughed. "Still naughty, I see."

"I prefer *cheeky*." They stopped in front of the post office.

"I can take it from here." She lifted the box out of his hands. "Thanks for the help."

Kieran looked at her. "It's good to see you, Emmy."

She smiled. "Good to see you too. I'm glad you were able to come for Maggie's birthday. I know it'll mean a lot to her."

He nodded, although that didn't help his guilt. What kind of son didn't visit his mother for twenty-six years? Even though he'd flown his mum, along with Sheryl and her husband and kids, over to Ireland several times, he'd always been too busy to come back to Mistletoe. Correction—he'd never wanted to come back.

"See you around, Kieran." Emmy wiggled her fingers at him and went inside the post office.

Even though she couldn't see him, he waved back, then turned and walked in the opposite direction. In truth he hadn't been heading her way, but the post office wasn't that far—nothing in Mistletoe was *far*—and it was good to visit with her for a wee bit.

He turned onto Chestnut Lane to finish his initial errand, picking up two poinsettia plants from Mistletoe Florist. When he was growing up here, he'd always thought it was cheesy that everything was named after the town or was Christmas themed. As an adult, though, he got it. Mistletoe was a charming Christmas destination for people visiting southern Missouri, and with very little industry in the area, tourism was important.

After picking up the flowers, he headed to his compact rental car and got inside, then drove to his mother's, battling an attack of nerves the entire way. He wasn't sure what to expect when he arrived at his childhood home. When his father passed away shortly before Kieran's fifteenth birthday, he remembered several good-intentioned people telling his mother she should sell the house and find something smaller. But she had steadfastly refused. Just as Kieran steadfastly chickened out at the last minute when he'd thought about returning to Mistletoe.

Fifteen minutes later he arrived, pulled into the driveway, and turned off the engine. The outside of the house hadn't changed much, except that the window shutters were now a warm brown instead of stone gray. His stomach churned as memories flooded him, mostly of his father—how they used to play catch in the front yard, how every spring he cleaned out the flower beds for Mum so she could focus on planting her flowers, how every month he and Kieran washed and waxed the cars. There were bad memories too, like the chewing out Dad gave him after the water tower stunt, and the two months' grounding he'd gotten for it. Three months after that, his father had died from lung cancer that was detected too late.

He took a deep breath and got out of the car, shoving down the painful thoughts as he went to the other side to get the poinsettias. He'd get his bag out of the trunk later. The red petals and green leaves rustled in their pots as he moved. Inhaling a deep breath, he rang the doorbell. It seemed odd not to just walk into the house. But it wasn't his house anymore.

The door opened and his mother appeared, her gray hair cut even shorter than Emmy's. She was dressed in a bright red sweater and forest-green slacks. Her blue eyes widened. "Kieran?"

"Hi, Mum." He smiled.

She rushed to hug him, then noticed the poinsettias. "You remembered," she said as she took them from him, tears in her eyes and her smile growing larger. "I can't believe you're here."

A lump formed in his throat at seeing her joy.

"Let's go inside where it's warm."

He followed, and when he stepped through the door, the spicy scent of fruitcake baking hit his nose. His mother was the only person he knew who enjoyed baking and eating it. "How many loaves of fruitcake are you making this year?" he asked as they walked into a modest living room filled to the brim with Christmas décor.

"Thirty. I'm just finishing up the last batch." She set the poinsettias on the credenza. "There. Now the room is complete." She turned and threw her arms around him. "I'm so glad you're home, son."

Kieran hugged her tight. When he let her go, he kept his arm around her shoulders as they looked at the pretty red flowers. "Dad never forgot, did he?"

"Not a single time. Since our first Christmas, he always brought me two poinsettias. I kept up the tradition after he passed, and now your sister does the same at her house."

Kieran nodded, but he'd had no idea Sheryl bought poinsettias for her own home. He was so out of touch with his family's rituals, and since he left Mistletoe, he'd been too busy to create any of his own.

Mum wiped her cheek with her fingers. "After so many years, I can't believe both my children are home for Christmas. If only your father . . ."

He drew her close. "He's here with us in spirit."

"That he is." She turned to him with a bright smile. "No need to be melancholy. How about a glass of warm apple cider?"

Glad for the reprieve, he said, "Sounds delicious."

Soon they were seated at the kitchen table, which was covered in a red, green, and black plaid tablecloth, mugs of sweet cinnamon cider in front of them. His mother put a Christmas-themed plate of sliced fruitcake in the middle of the table. Kieran tried not to blanch.

"When did you arrive?" Mum asked, sitting down across from him.

He took a sip of the cider. "I landed in St. Louis around midnight last night. I just stayed in one of the hotel airports, then rented a car and drove here this morning."

"You must be exhausted from all the traveling."

"The jet lag hasn't set in yet."

"Where did you get the poinsettias?" She tore off a corner of fruitcake and popped it into her mouth.

"Mistletoe Florist."

"So you've been downtown already." She smiled. "See anything interesting?"

"I ran into Emmy Banks."

Mum grinned. "Your senior prom date."

He recognized the gleam in his mother's eyes. She had the same look when she suggested he ask Emmy to prom after his date canceled three days before the event.

"It's wonderful she and Siobhan have been friends for so long."

"Still can't bring yourself to call her 'Sheryl'?"

She lifted her chin. "Her name is Siobhan."

"Not the easiest to spell. Or pronounce." He'd lucked out with "Kieran." Most people knew how to pronounce it, although he did have to spell it out quite often.

"But it's a lovely name, just like she is. Speaking of lovely . . ." She snuck another nibble of cake. "What did you and Emmy talk about?"

"She was running an errand, so we didn't have much time to catch up." In fact, he was realizing that he'd talked about himself the whole time. She hadn't said anything about herself.

"I'm sure you'll have plenty of opportunities to talk to her."

Kieran shook his head, half grinning. "Don't get any ideas, Mum."

"*Moi*? I never get ideas."

"You've been planning my future marriage since I was old enough to date."

"A pointless endeavor, thank you very much." She leaned back in the chair. "At least I thought you'd meet a sweet lass in Ballyton."

"Here we go."

"And what's wrong with wanting my son to be happily married? You're nearing forty-four, Kieran. Are you ever going to settle down? Never mind, I already know the answer."

"Which is?"

"'My life is fine the way it is,'" she said, her imitation of him startlingly accurate.

"Because it's true."

The landline phone on the wall near the fridge rang. "Hold that thought," Mum said, getting up from her seat. "Wait, *change* that thought." She grinned and answered the phone. "Oh, hello, Pearl! Merry Christmas to you too. How are things in Kansas City?"

His mother's conversation with her friend disappeared as he thought about Emmy again. More particularly, prom night. He'd been irritated when his date had called and told him she had to cancel—mostly because he'd already bought the tickets, not because they were romantically involved. At first it had been a little awkward when his mother had suggested asking Emmy. She was a sophomore and his kid sister's best friend. He was sure she'd say no. But to his surprise she'd said yes.

At first he was just glad he had a date. Emmy had always been bookish and a little shy. But she was also nice, and they had a great time at the dance. Then the unexpected happened when he took her home and walked her to the front porch.

He suddenly, and inexplicably, had wanted to kiss her.

Thankfully he regained his senses and told her good night, quickly climbed into his mother's Grand Cherokee, and peeled out of her driveway, bewildered by his sudden urge. He'd never thought of her as anything but Sheryl's friend, and even during the prom the thought of kissing her had never entered his mind. He chalked it up to two things—being grateful he didn't have to go to the prom on his own and ending up having a blast with her at the dance. He kind of owed her for being such a good sport about being a last-minute replacement.

But he didn't feel obligated to kiss her. She had looked so pretty that night, especially under the soft glow of the porch light. Her long blond hair was loosely gathered up with clips and pins, and several long strands framed her face. The blue satin dress she wore had sheer short sleeves, a modest neckline, and flared out from the waist, the hem just touching her knee.

He'd wanted to kiss her, just like he'd wanted to ask her to slow dance, only to chicken out each time. Emmy was a friend, and she probably would have shoved him away if he had tried kissing her. He didn't want a great night to end on a sour note.

After the prom he didn't see her much, mostly because he was focused on school and working to save up for his trip to Europe. He'd only planned to stay abroad a year . . . and that had turned into twenty-six. When he left Mistletoe, he didn't give the town, or Emmy Banks, more than a second thought.

He sure was thinking about her now.

TWO

As Emmy expected, on Tuesday the shop was busy all day long. By closing time, she was tired. Even Carina looked a little weary, but she had her date with Jeremy to look forward to, so she perked up toward the end of her shift. Normally Emmy loved decorating the store for Christmas, but considering her current fatigue level, it would be a chore. Still, when Carina offered to cancel her date and stay and help, Emmy refused.

"Absolutely not," she said, practically shoving her daughter out the door. She flipped the Open sign to Closed and faced the tower of decorations in front of the counter.

Carina had brought down the ten bins of decorations Emmy kept stored in her 1940s-era apartment. It was a cozy, old-fashioned two-bedroom that was a product of its time, down to the radiator heating. Emmy didn't mind living there. One, it saved her money on rent because she owned the building. And two, she had less than a two-minute commute to work.

But there were times she was a little lonely, especially after Carina moved out five months ago. Now she lived in a rental house with two of her friends from high school. She wasn't far, just on the other side of Mistletoe, only a fifteen-minute drive away. Still, Emmy had to hide her tears when Carina had left, feeling more than a little selfish about wishing her daughter would stay.

Emmy shook off the memory. What was it about Christmas that always had her thinking about the past? Particularly the painful memories? Yesterday she not only thought about Josh—ugh!—but after her run-in with Kieran O'Neill, she couldn't stop thinking about him either. Or her wigwagging stomach.

She walked to the stack of décor bins and opened one. It was filled with garland. She picked up the silver garland on the top, looped it around her neck, and unpacked the rest of the box while "Rocking Around the Christmas Tree" played in the background. But her mind was still on Kieran. How in the world could he be so good-looking at forty-three years old, while she resembled a dimpled potato? She'd always had a roundish figure, and no amount of diet and exercise except for near starvation could change that, and she had tried everything over the years. But while she might be round, she was in good shape and watched what she ate . . . most of the time. Christmas was always a weakness.

Kieran was my weakness too.

She stared at the string of garland in her hand. Even Sheryl didn't know how deep Emmy's crush on her brother had been. When he'd asked her to his senior prom, she didn't believe he was serious. It was only when he admitted he couldn't find another date on short notice that she agreed to go.

"You're a good friend," he'd said. And if she had any doubt about how completely in the friend zone she was, he'd even given her the clichéd light punch on the shoulder.

Still, they'd had a great time, despite him leaving her alone several times to dance with other girls, and that included all the slow dances. Again, no problem. She knew her place. She was just glad to be there.

Yet something had changed when he dropped her off at home. She expected him to simply let her out of his car in the driveway, but he walked her to the porch instead. He even lingered there, devastatingly handsome in his white shirt and gold vest with a real bow tie, not a clip-on. He'd left his black jacket in the car, and his tie was undone and hanging loosely around his unbuttoned collar. He'd worn his thick black hair long back then, almost shoulder length. He literally could have been a romance cover model if he'd wanted to.

"Hope you had a good time," he'd said, soft light glowing on his face and highlighting his constant five o'clock shadow.

"I did." She smiled, telling him the truth. "Thanks for letting me be your date."

He tilted his head, his dark eyes turning smoky. "Thanks for letting me take you."

She couldn't respond, standing like a statue while trying to focus on what he was saying, not on the weird and pleasant feeling that he might, just *might*, kiss her. She had no idea why, only that her stomach was wigging and wagging like a sailboat in an ocean storm. At this point a peck on the cheek would do.

Suddenly he backed away. "See ya on Monday."

Before she could say a word, he was already in his mom's Grand Cherokee and revving the engine. A second later he was peeling out of her driveway.

Emmy's cheeks flamed. That was almost twenty-six years ago, and she felt a little foolish about assuming he would kiss her. Clearly that had been more hope than reality. And afterward nothing had changed between them. She was Sheryl's friend, and he was about to graduate high school. Shortly after that, he left Mistletoe and the country.

She touched her hot face and shook her head. What was the big deal? Everyone had high school crushes. They were a rite of adolescent passage. It wasn't like she'd mourned over Kieran like he was a lost love. *At least not for too long.*

"Get back to work," she muttered, forcing herself to focus on the daunting task in front of her. She had to finish decorating before tomorrow, or else she would be super behind. Emmy turned up the music and set out to enjoy herself. Two minutes later Mariah

Carey's singular voice belting "All I Want for Christmas Is You" played through the shop. She almost had to laugh at the irony. There was a time when all she wanted was Kieran. *Not anymore.*

And even if she did, there was zero chance he would want her. He was adventurous, and she liked being at home. She'd never leave Mistletoe for anything other than a vacation, and he couldn't wait to get out of the country. They were too different. For all she knew he already had a girlfriend, or even a wife, although Sheryl probably would have said something to Emmy about having a sister-in-law. Kieran had always been out of her league and mostly out of her life. That would never change.

By Tuesday evening, Kieran needed a break.

As expected, he spent most of the day with his mother. She was the main reason he'd returned to Mistletoe, and he planned to spend as much time with her as possible. Although she was almost seventy, she was as active as ever.

He accompanied her to her weekly Tuesday morning breakfast at the Mistletoe Diner, where she met with members of her bridge club, every one of them female and a senior citizen. Over tea, French toast, and grits—he hadn't had grits since he'd left town—he caught up on local gossip and the ladies' maladies. The list was extensive and, unfortunately, detailed. Obviously, there was an age where collective commiseration with friends trumped discretion.

Afterward he took Mum to the mall, about an hour away, so she could shop for Christmas presents for his nephews, and he picked up a few things to add to the gifts he'd brought them from Ireland. Then it was back to the house so she could have lunch and watch her soap operas.

Mum was dozing off in the middle of the last show when her

landline rang. His mother had a cell phone, but she rarely kept it charged. She stirred a little in her recliner as he quietly rose from the sofa to answer it in the kitchen. "Hello?"

"Kieran?" Sheryl's voice came through the antiquated receiver.

He braced himself, not sure if she would be happy that he was in Mistletoe or mad that he kept it from her. "Hi, Sheryl."

"Kieran Connor O'Neill! How dare you not tell me you were coming home?"

He pulled the receiver away from his ear. He'd gotten his fair share of her hot Irish temper over the years, and most of the time he deserved it. "I wanted to surprise you and Mum," he said, lowering his voice. "She's asleep right now."

"Oh, I forgot *Reckless and Yearning* was on right now. I was just calling to let her know our flight was delayed out of Cancún so we won't be home until late tonight."

"Sorry about that."

"It's all right. The boys are so tired from vacation, they're falling asleep in the waiting area. And by 'boys' I also mean Ben."

Kieran grinned, imagining his nephews and brother-in-law sprawled and snoring in their chairs.

"I can't believe you finally came home," she said, her voice a little thick. "I didn't think you'd ever step foot in Mistletoe again."

He didn't either. But after the initial barrage of memories, he was settling in. Funny how quickly he was starting to feel at home when he'd been gone so long.

"Why?" she asked.

"Why what?"

"Why are you here?"

Kieran rubbed the back of his neck. "I didn't want to miss Mum's seventieth birthday."

"How did you find out about the party?"

"Party?"

"Yes," she said, sounding hurried. "We're starting to board, so I have to go. The party is a surprise, so don't spill the beans."

"I won't—"

"See you tomorrow."

She clicked off, and Kieran hung up the phone. He smiled. A surprise birthday party for Mom sounded like a fun time.

After talking to Sheryl, he went back to the living room just as Mum woke up. Had she heard him talking to Sheryl?

But all she said was, "Ready for bingo?"

His mother might be raring to go, but Kieran wasn't. "I think I'll beg off tonight. I'm terrible at bingo."

She eyed him through her small silver-framed glasses. "When was the last time you played?"

"Uh . . ." He had no idea. Probably when he was a kid. He'd never been a fan of bingo even then.

"I'll give you a night off." She got up from the chair and patted his shoulder. "You're free to join me and Betsy for supper, though. St. Agnes Church always provides a delicious meal before the games start."

He considered it for a minute, then shook his head. No offense to the good people at St. Agnes, but he'd had his fill of social activities for the day. "I'll make a sandwich here."

"Suit yourself." She grinned. "Hope I didn't wear you out too much, son."

"I can barely keep up with ya," he said, only half joking. Truth be told, he wasn't used to the hustle and bustle, not to mention all the people. Some of them he knew, particularly at the diner. But at the mall he didn't recognize anyone.

He'd always considered himself an extrovert, but Castle O'Neill had been situated in a small hamlet in Cork with a tiny population, probably less than Mistletoe. During his travels in the UK and Europe, he went at his own slower pace.

But less than an hour after Mum left, Kieran was second-guessing himself. Not about bingo but about the meal. A sandwich didn't appeal, and when he searched through his mother's pantry and fridge, he didn't find much to eat. What he did find was Mum's schedule on the side of the fridge, and from the looks of it she ate out more than she dined in.

He got in the car and headed for the diner again. He'd learned from one of Mum's friends that the eatery had changed hands a few times over the years, but the menu was basically the same as it had been when he was a kid.

When he walked inside, the restaurant wasn't busy, and he was directed by a sign near the door to seat himself. He picked a table near the middle of the diner.

"I heard you were back in town."

He looked up and saw the waitress, a thin woman with bright red lipstick and his mother's energy level. Obviously she knew him, but he had no idea who she was. He glanced at her name tag and gaped. "Cindy?"

"Yep." She handed him a menu and grinned. "Bet you didn't think I'd still be working here."

He sure didn't. "How long?"

"Thirty years." She pointed with pride at a little gold apple pin on the white lapel of her pale blue uniform. "Thirty looong years."

"Congratulations." Kieran took the menu. "Guess I shouldn't be surprised that word gets around."

"That's life in a small town. Everyone knows everybody's business. I'll be back in a sec to get your order."

"Thanks." He perused the menu, and he was suddenly hit with nostalgia again. When his father was alive, his family went to the diner together on Friday evenings for the Mistletoe Friday Fish Fry. Those were some of his favorite times with Dad. They both loved fish and would often try to outeat each other, with Kieran losing until seventh grade, when he'd had a growth spurt and ate almost everything in sight. Good times. He'd had many of them growing up.

Cindy appeared again, pulling a pencil from her cloud of faded red hair and poising it over a small pad. "What'll you have?"

It wasn't Friday, but he decided to order the fish and chips anyway. After she left, his phone buzzed, and he pulled out his cell to look at the screen. Sheryl again, only this time she was texting him.

Sheryl: Now that you're back, I'm going to put you to work.

Kieran: I'm at your service.

He read as his always-organized sister outlined her plans and gave him party prep tasks, which were mostly picking up stuff and keeping Mum occupied, and he'd already planned to do the latter. The hardest part would be keeping the party a secret.

Sheryl: Emmy volunteered to help decorate the community center with us the night before.

His attention perked up at Emmy's name. He'd continued to think about her off and on last night. And a few times today too. He kept remembering her smile before she went into the post office. Warm, bright, and still pretty.

Sheryl stopped texting, and Kieran put his phone back in his pocket as Cindy showed up with his food. The diner fare was as tasty as he remembered, almost rivaling the fish and chips he'd eaten in Ireland and Great Britain over the years. During his meal, his former junior high school history teacher stopped by the table to exchange pleasantries. Kieran tried not to marvel at how old she was, which reminded him of how old *he* was. "Time flying" wasn't just a cliché; it was the truth.

He paid his bill, left the diner, and walked out into a brightly lit downtown Mistletoe. Kieran paused, marveling at the shiny, picturesque display that would rival any TV Christmas movie. He'd seen the decorations during the day, but they didn't compare to the sparkling splendor he was witnessing now.

Abandoning his plan to return home, he stuck his hands into the pockets of his coat and strolled down the street, enjoying the Christmas cheer. A few people were walking around downtown, but the diner was the only business open after five.

He passed by a building with a For Sale sign in the window, then stopped at the end of the street in front of Mistletoe Antiques. He had developed an affinity for antiques when he was refurbishing the castle.

The sign on the door said Closed, but the lights were on, and he couldn't resist peering through the large picture window in front of the shop. To his surprise he saw Emmy Banks pulling Christmas decorations out of a plastic bin, silver garland draped around her neck. Almost two hours past closing time, and she was still working.

She was removing the Christmas decorations in a deliberate manner, and a stack of similar bins sat nearby. From his vantage point it didn't look like there were any decorations in the shop, so he reckoned she was in the midst of bedecking her store. As he looked inside, he didn't see anyone else there. Perhaps she could use some help. He knocked on the window.

Emmy startled, putting her hand over her chest.

"Sorry, lass," he said, unsure if she could hear him through the glass. He jabbed his thumb toward the door.

Her eyes grew wide for a moment, then she stood and went to the door. "Hi," she said, appearing a little confused. "Did Sheryl send you?"

"Nay, why?"

"She works here." Emmy frowned, hugging her shoulders. "Didn't she tell you?"

Kieran remembered her mentioning in the past that she worked at a store, but he didn't recall the name or where it was.

"Is there something I can help you with?" Emmy asked.

He could see her breath as she talked, and she was wearing an emerald-green cardigan and slim black pants. Definitely not enough protection from the cold. "I was out for a walk and . . . Do you need some help?" At her bewildered look he added, "I noticed you gettin' the Christmas decorations out."

She glanced over her shoulder and then back at him again. "I'm running a little late this year. But I've got it all handled."

"Ah. Well then." His ego pricked a little, and that was puzzling. It wasn't like he'd asked her out and she turned him down. Wait. Was she married? He hadn't noticed a ring on her hand. Then again, he hadn't exactly looked. But if she did have a husband, the bloke might not appreciate Kieran being alone with Emmy, even though they were . . . friends. Or had been. "Guess I'll see you later, then." He turned to walk away.

"Kieran?"

He faced her again.

"How about some hot chocolate before you go? It's so cold out tonight."

He smiled. "That would be grand, lass. Real grand."

THREE

A short while later, Kieran and Emmy were in the café area of the shop, two mugs of hot chocolate in front of them. "Are you sure I'm not keepin' you?" he asked.

"I needed a break." She sat back in the chair. "I can't believe Sheryl didn't tell you about my shop."

"This is your place?" At her nod he added, "Don't go blamin' her. I'm sure she told me, just as sure as I am that I forgot."

"Or you weren't paying attention."

Busted. "Guess you know me pretty well."

"I also know Sheryl. She can get pretty far into the weeds when she talks." She lifted her mug and took a sip.

Kieran's gaze went to her left hand. No ring. That didn't mean anything, although Emmy had always been the more traditional type compared to their peers back in school. He would have expected her to wear one if she were married.

"I see you finally cut your hair," Emmy said, setting down the mug.

"Yep. Mum always hated it long. She actually cried when she saw my short hair when she visited at Christmas five years ago. I told her it was one of her birthday presents." He crossed his ankle over his knee. "I remember you having long blond hair."

She self-consciously touched the side of her pixie cut. "I got rid of that years ago. Too much trouble."

Inexplicably he couldn't take his eyes off her. A pair of green-framed glasses that matched her cardigan rested atop her head, and she wore a white turtleneck underneath her sweater. There was nothing extraordinary about her outfit. But there was something about *her* that made him pay attention. His pulse started to pitter-patter, throwing him off guard.

"How long are you planning to stay in Mistletoe?" Emmy asked.

Grateful for the distraction, he said, "Till the twenty-third."

Her brow lifted. "You're not staying for Christmas?"

Kieran shook his head. "I've got an investment opportunity back in Ireland. Dublin area this time. I'm supposed to sign the papers on the twenty-sixth, and with weather being unpredictable and all that . . ." He paused at her frown. "I don't have a choice. It's the perfect deal for me to invest the profit I made from the castle."

"Are you buying another one?"

"Nope. A very contemporary apartment complex. As soon as I settle things there, I'll come back for another visit." But even as the words came out of his mouth, he knew the possibility was slim. From her expression, he could see she didn't believe him either.

A switch of topic was in order. "Catch me up on what you've been doing," he said. "Have you lived here the whole time?"

Emmy tapped her finger against the Styrofoam cup. "Yes. My junior and senior year I worked at Preston's General Store."

"Which used to be here," he said, tapping his index finger on the table. "What happened to it?"

"Six years ago the Prestons retired and sold the building. I turned the lower level into the store, and I live in the apartment upstairs. It's not as exciting as owning a castle."

"No less impressive," he said, sipping the hot chocolate.

"Several years ago, I started watching those antique and picker shows on TV. That piqued my interest. Carina loves to go shopping and picking with me too. She's my daughter, and the assistant manager in my store."

Ah. So she was married or had been married before. He wasn't sure how he felt about that.

With a smirk she added, "I take it Sheryl never mentioned her to you either."

He really needed to pay more attention to his sister's conversations.

"Let me give you a tour," Emmy said, rising from her chair. She grabbed her cup and led him around the store. He was impressed with the variety and quality of antiques she had acquired, particularly the Irish glassware displayed in a locked curio cabinet near the front counter.

"I had no idea you liked Irish glass," he said, turning to her.

"I didn't either until I found some at an estate sale in St. Louis. Now it's my pride and joy." She turned to him. "What's Ireland like?"

As Emmy waited for Kieran to answer her question, she tried not to stare at him . . . and failed. When he'd knocked on her window, her brain had short-circuited, and not because he'd startled her. Kieran O'Neill as a teenager had been a cute guy, and she hadn't been the only girl smitten with him.

But adult Kieran? He was all *man*. He'd taken off his black coat and left it in the café area, but he was still wearing his charcoal-gray scarf and a heather-colored pullover. The combination looked very, *very* nice. She noticed the strands of silver highlighting his black hair and whiskers, and the charming crinkles in the corners of his eyes when he smiled. He didn't look old. He looked distinguished. Ruggedly distinguished, if that was a thing.

He'd also surprised her by offering to help her decorate, and when she said no, she thought that would be the end of it and he'd be on his way. And then the strangest thing happened. He seemed . . . disappointed. Or she thought he was. Either way it didn't seem right to send him off into the cold without a warm drink. At least that's what she told herself.

As he continued to gaze at the glassware, she wondered if he had heard her question. Finally, he said, "Ireland is green, lass," he said with a chuckle. "Very green. And beautiful. The history is so rich, and at times, filled with woe. The Irish people are strong. And stubborn, to be quite honest. They're also friendly and know how to enjoy themselves."

Emmy listened as he continued to talk about the country he clearly loved and where he obviously wanted to stay. Otherwise, he wouldn't be buying an investment property in Dublin. That drove home the point that even if he had returned her feelings in high school, a romantic relationship never would have worked out. She should be thankful they never went down that path.

But as she listened to his deep voice, with his light Irish accent, she couldn't help but wonder one thing. *What would it have been like to kiss Kieran O'Neill?*

Emmy blinked, brushing off the thought.

He walked over to the Christmas bins and picked up one of the Santa hats lying at the top. He put it on his head at a jaunty angle and turned to her. "Aye? Or nay?"

She tried to keep her composure. He managed to make even a cheap felt hat look good. "You're missing the beard and belly."

"Give me a few years, and I'll have both." He grinned as he took off the hat and set it on the counter.

Emmy was sure that even with a pot belly and a long beard, he would still be good-looking.

"I'll have to come back when you're open and do some more exploring," he said as they walked back to the front counter. He set his empty cup next to hers and glanced at the bins again. "Are you certain you don't need a hand, lass? Or is your husband comin' by later?"

His question caught her off guard. "I'm not married." She grabbed one of the bins off the stack and put it on the floor, the silver garland around her neck rustling as she moved.

"I see. Then perhaps Carina—"

"She's on a date."

Kieran rubbed his stubbly chin. "Looks like a big job for one person."

She took off the lid. "I'm sure you've got better things to do than stringing up lights."

He walked over to her. "Mum's at bingo, so as it turns out, I'm free for the evenin.'"

She glanced at the clock. Wow, she'd spent the last hour talking to Kieran, but it seemed like only a few minutes. Now she was more behind than before. "Well . . . I guess I could use the help."

He slipped off his scarf and set it on the counter next to the cups. "I'm at your beck and call, boss."

She chuckled. "You can start by putting lights in the window. There are clips inside the bin."

For the next hour they worked as Christmas music continued to play quietly over the speakers. Emmy set out vintage mini Christmas trees all over the antique shop while Kieran strung more lights along the shelves. Once that was done, she looked at the largest bin, filled with knickknacks she'd collected over the years. "Just one more left," she said as she lifted the lid.

Kieran glanced over at her. "It's been a long time since I've set out Christmas decorations." He paused. "Actually, I don't think I ever have. Not for myself, anyway. I've helped friends do theirs, but never my own."

"Not even in your castle?" she asked.

"There was no need. I rented a cottage for a long time before I was able to move in. I kept telling myself I would buy a tree and some ornaments. I just never got around to it. I suppose if I'd had a wife, she would have seen to it."

"You never married either?"

He shook his head, pulling out a box of vintage glass ornaments. "Came close a time or two, but it was never the right time. Or the right person."

Emmy nodded. "Same here." She pushed Josh from her thoughts. She didn't want the bad memories intruding now, or ever.

The front door opened and Carina walked in, Jeremy in tow, both bundled up for the cold weather. She stopped, giving a quizzical glance at Kieran, then at Emmy. "Are we interrupting something?" she asked, covertly tilting her head in Kieran's direction.

"No," Emmy said. "This is Kieran O'Neill, Sheryl's brother and an old friend from high school."

"Emphasis on *old*." Kieran held out his hand to Carina.

"Oh right. Sheryl's mentioned you a few times."

"Uh-oh," he said. "Whatever she told you, I plead the Fifth."

Carina laughed as she shook his hand. Emmy expected him to look shocked, as most people did when they found out she and Carina were mother and daughter. If he was, he didn't show it.

"I thought you two were on a date," Emmy said.

"We were." Carina smiled at Jeremy and moved closer to him. "The bowling alley is closed for repairs."

"The roof over Lanes 1 to 6 caved in last night," he added. "They'll be shut down for a few days."

"Oh no," Emmy said. "I'm sorry to hear that."

"So we figured we'd come here and help you decorate." Carina glanced at Kieran again. "But maybe we're not needed now."

"There's still plenty to do," Emmy said. She watched as Kieran shook Jeremy's hand. Carina's boyfriend was a good-looking kid.

His brown skin was several shades lighter than Carina's, his tight black curls were in a buzz cut, and he was well over six feet tall.

"Nice to meet you, lad," Kieran said.

"You're not from here, are you?" Jeremy asked.

"Yes and no," Kieran said with a small smile. "It's a long story, that."

"Ooh," Carina said, taking off her coat. "I'd love to hear it—"

"Some other time." Emmy put her arm around her daughter and guided her toward the opposite side of the shop.

Kieran shrugged at Jeremy. Quite the abrupt exit, but Emmy was right. There was still a lot of work to be done. He and Jeremy followed mother and daughter.

Now that he'd met Carina, Kieran was full of questions. The two women couldn't have looked more different from each other. Emmy was fair-skinned and blond, Carina dark-skinned with short, black twisted braids. Had Sheryl ever told him about Emmy's daughter? Again, he wasn't sure, and he had to admit that it wasn't just because he'd tuned out his sister's incessant talking. Once he left Mistletoe, he had little interest in what was going on in his hometown. But now wasn't the time to ply Emmy with questions. It was bad enough she knew how clueless he was about Mistletoe.

The next hour flew by as everyone pitched in to decorate. More than once Kieran saw Carina and Jeremy casually move over to the mistletoe sprigs hanging in the shop to sneak a kiss or two. If Emmy noticed, she didn't let on. The two seemed smitten with each other, that was for sure.

As Kieran hung tiny gold and silver ornaments on the pencil-style tree in the corner of the store, he stole a few glances at Emmy. She hadn't taken off the silver garland and he wondered if she'd forgotten she was wearing it. Holly berry crystal earrings winked from her small earlobes as she hummed along with the music and set up a book tree in the middle of a round, antique side table near the front door. She was even more fetching than she had been on prom night.

He glanced at the hanging mistletoe again. *What would it be like to kiss Emmy now?*

Nay, he shouldn't be thinking that. Last thing he needed was to start a romance with anyone while he was in Mistletoe. He would only have to end it when he left.

It was almost ten by the time every nook and cranny in the store was covered in sparkly Christmas adornments. Carina and Jeremy picked up their coats from the rack near the front door. "Y'all up for some Chinese food?" Carina said as she pulled her hat from one of the coat pockets.

"Not tonight," Emmy said.

"Rain check for me too." Kieran grabbed his coat and put it on.

"Okay." Jeremy opened the door. "See you later."

Emmy waved as the couple left. Then she sighed. "I think they might be getting serious," she said. "At least they better be, considering how many times they kissed under the mistletoe."

He wrapped his scarf around his neck. "You saw that too?"

"How could I miss it?" She moved toward the coatrack and started to pick up the last garment hanging from one of the hooks, a yellow drawstring hoodie jacket.

Kieran intercepted and pointed to the garland around her neck. "You plan on takin' that home with you?"

She glanced at her chest. "I completely forgot I had this on. I was just looking for a place to put it when I was unpacking the bins." She started to pull it over her neck, but it was tangled up.

He gently removed her hands from the garland and untwisted it until it could be easily removed.

"Thanks," she said, her gaze on his as he handed her the garland. Then she glanced up. They were standing only a few inches from another sprig of mistletoe. The stuff was all over the place.

She moved away as fast as he did, cementing the fact that she wasn't attracted to him. And although that was a good thing since he wasn't interested in a romantic entanglement, he couldn't help but feel disappointed.

Emmy hurried back to the coatrack. She grabbed her jacket and shoved it on.

"Is that all you wore today?" At her nod he said, "It won't keep you warm, lass. Not on a cold one like tonight."

"I'll be fine. I live in the apartment upstairs. The entrance is between my shop and the building next door."

"The one that's for sale, right?"

She nodded and turned off several lights until only two of them remained on, leaving her expression shadowed. "It's been on the market for years. When I purchased this building, I was hoping to buy it shortly after I started my shop, but . . ." She waved her hand, brushing off the rest of her words, and opened the door. Cold air rushed inside.

They stepped onto the stoop in front of the store, and he waited for her to lock up, then walked her to the door leading to her apartment. It couldn't have been more than ten steps.

"Thank for your help with the decorations," she said. "Even with Carina and Jeremy's assistance, I would still be working if it wasn't for you."

"My pleasure. I got to see what I've been missing all these years. Christmas decorating, I mean."

They stared at each other for a long moment. She took a halting step toward him. Paused. Then she hugged him.

Surprised, his arms went around her. Even though it was a friendly hug, he couldn't help but notice how nicely she fit in his embrace, the top of her head fitting under his chin. She smelled like Christmas—a mix of cinnamon and vanilla. Although he wasn't tense, he felt his muscles relax as warmth flowed through him.

Emmy moved away, not looking at him this time. "Good night, Kieran." Then she disappeared inside the building.

He stared at the door and smiled. "Good night, lass."

FOUR

The next morning Emmy was running late for work for the first time since she'd opened Mistletoe Antiques. After she and Kieran went their separate ways the night before, she had difficulty sleeping. All she could think about was her impulsive decision to hug him, and how amazing it felt to be in his strong arms. She had no idea why she hugged him, just that a simple thank-you for doing so much work didn't seem adequate. Trouble was, the moment she was in his arms, she didn't want to let go.

Even as she hastily brushed her teeth, she could still feel the softness of his sweater against her cheek, the oaky scent of his cologne. *Sigh.*

Emmy put on an ugly Christmas sweater from her extensive collection, white jeans, and her white tennis shoes and rushed downstairs, then realized she'd forgotten her jacket when she opened the door to the outside. *Get it together!* Why was she letting a simple, *platonic* hug turn her upside down? A few flakes of snow floated in the icy air as she pulled her keys out of her purse and went to unlock the door. Before she could insert the key in the lock, the door flew open and Carina yanked her inside.

"I've been waiting half an hour for you to show up," Carina said, grinning as she shut the door. She turned and faced Emmy. "*Old* high school friend, huh? I don't even have current friends as hot as Kieran."

Emmy straightened, trying to get her bearings. "Jeremy is a handsome young man."

Carina paused, a dreamy expression on her face. Then she smirked. "He's cute. But Kieran? Hubba-hubba."

Laughing, Emmy went to the counter. "What?"

"Isn't that what y'all said back in the day?"

"In your grandmother's day, maybe."

The door chimed and Sheryl came in. "Brrr. I want to go back to Cancún already."

Emmy looked at her, surprised, then turned to Sheryl. "What are you doing here? You're not scheduled until tomorrow."

She slumped against the counter, a weary expression on her face. "I came here for a vacation from my vacation. Don't get me wrong, I love my boys, but I need a little break. So what did I miss while I was gone?"

"You never said your brother was so *fine*," Carina said.

Sheryl frowned. "I guess. He's always had the girls chasing after him, that's for sure."

"Including Mom?"

Emmy quickly grabbed her phone and pulled up her Christmas playlist. When she glanced up, she saw Sheryl looking at her with interest.

"They did go to prom together," Sheryl finally said.

"Really?" Carina leaned her chin on her hand. "Do tell."

"There's nothing to tell, and we have to get to work," Emmy said quickly. She had to shut this conversation down pronto.

Carina held up her hands. "I'm not the one who was late this morning. Did something happen between you and Kieran after we left?"

"Kieran was here?" Sheryl said, sounding surprised.

"He came last night to help decorate," Carina supplied.

"Oh *really*. Funny, he didn't mention he was doing that when I texted him yesterday."

"Look, nothing happened," Emmy said, exasperated. "We just

said goodbye and he left." She made sure not to mention the hug. They were already jumping to enough conclusions.

Carina turned to Sheryl. "Is he single?"

"Very." She grinned.

"Stop it." Emmy scowled at her friend. "Your brother has never been interested in me."

"Oh, I don't know about that," Carina said. "He sure was watching you last night. With *interest*."

A shiver ran down Emmy's spine. *He was watching me?* "How would you know? You were busy kissing Jeremy every chance you got."

Carina's mouth formed an O. "You saw us?"

"You weren't exactly discreet."

Sheryl slipped off her coat, revealing a black-and-white buffalo plaid flannel shirt. "Wow, I really did miss out on all the fun."

"There was no fun!" Emmy insisted. At Carina's skeptical glance she added, "I mean, it was fun decorating for Christmas. That's all."

The door opened and Mrs. Lawson walked in. Saved by a customer. Emmy walked over to her. "Get to work," she muttered to Carina and Sheryl as she made her way to speak to Mrs. Lawson.

But when she glanced over her shoulder at the two women, they were whispering. Then giggling. *Great. Just great.*

After Mrs. Lawson left the store with a large bag full of vintage Christmas gifts, Emmy was relieved to see Sheryl speaking with another customer, and Carina was nowhere in sight. Finally, a reprieve. She circled the purchase amount on the merchant copy of Mrs. Lawson's receipt and put it in the small box next to the manual cash register. She had made sure to have a credit card machine. It was impossible to do business without one.

Business was brisk until noon. Emmy was in the café area, sipping on honey tea and looking for estate sales in the Classified section of the *Mistletoe Gazette* when Carina appeared. "Go ahead and take your lunch," she said, not looking up from the phone.

"I will." Carina slid onto the seat across from her. "I have a few more questions, though."

Emmy inwardly groaned and set down the paper. "I assume they aren't about work, right?"

"Correct." She grinned, a playful glint in her eyes. "Just how good of friends were you and Kieran?"

Knowing her daughter wouldn't let the subject go, Emmy said, "We were friendly friends."

"I don't even know what that means." Carina leaned closer. "Did you have a crush on him?"

"No," Emmy mumbled, then winced at the wave of guilt washing over her. She never lied to Carina—not purposefully, anyway—and here she was telling a big bald-faced one. From her doubtful expression Emmy could tell she didn't believe her.

"Then why did you go to prom with him?"

"He needed a date, and I was available." She quickly explained the circumstances. "He graduated a few weeks later and left for Ireland a while after. Until the other day I hadn't seen or heard from him in more than two decades. Sheryl would mention what he was up to occasionally, but that's it."

"You saw him the other day?" Carina's brow lifted. "When? Where?"

"On the way to the post office." She gathered up the newspaper. "There's nothing between me and Kieran. There never will be."

"But—"

"Take your lunch." She hadn't been this stern with her daughter in years, but she was tired of the inquisition.

Carina stood, looking contrite. "Yes, ma'am. Do you want me to get you anything?"

"No, thank you."

After she left, Emmy removed her reading glasses and rubbed her eyes. She was grateful Carina hadn't called her out on her lie, and she wished she could've been honest with her about her crush on Kieran. She knew what her daughter was up to. It had been five years since Josh dumped her, and Carina hadn't brought up the subject of Emmy dating again until lately. Not a full-court press, but just a hint here or a suggestion there that she should wade into the romance pool.

No. Way. She'd had zero luck with men. First there was Kieran, but he didn't count because it was high school. Then there were two relationships in college that hadn't worked out, and by the time she was thirty-one she had adopted Carina, and her personal life had gone by the wayside for a while. Then she met Josh and had fallen in love. Looking back, the red flags had been there, but she'd ignored them. Loneliness undermined common sense. She wasn't going to let that happen again.

As she headed for the front of the store, she heard Sheryl talking, and she assumed it was a customer. But when she looked up, she stopped.

Kieran.

"Oh hi, Emmy!" Sheryl held a plastic-wrapped brown loaf that resembled one of Maggie's infamous fruitcake loaves.

Emmy wilted a little inside. Every year Maggie gave her fruitcake, and every year she tried it and didn't like it. It seemed a waste of ingredients, and two years ago Emmy had cut the cake in slices, wrapped them in cling film, and put them in the café. They stayed there until New Year's. Apparently, none of her customers liked fruitcake either.

"And look who just happened to stop by," Sheryl said, her voice higher and brighter than Emmy had ever heard it.

Kieran turned around and said in his deep, lyrical voice, "Hello, lass."

She put her hand over her stomach. *Wig. Wag.*

Although he had wanted to explore the store some more—and see Emmy again—Kieran hadn't expected it to be so soon, or at Sheryl's request. Around nine-thirty that morning she had called Mum, and knowing his sister, he figured the conversation would be long. He'd taken the opportunity to go for a quick run around the neighborhood, even though it was lightly snowing. Like the rest of Mistletoe, the houses and streets hadn't changed much, and it was very different from Ballyton and other places in Ireland and Europe. He'd been in Mistletoe less than a week, and he kept expecting the culture shock to hit. Instead, being back home felt like slipping into a well-worn, comfortable pair of old shoes.

When he got back home, he was surprised when his mother had canceled the day's plans and gave him a list of errands. He wiped the perspiration off his forehead with the cuff of his sweatshirt as he studied the list.

Pick up milk, eggs, butter, and eggnog from Mistletoe Grocery.
Mail Christmas cards at the Mistletoe Post Office.
Deliver fruitcake to the following people and businesses:

He stopped reading at the last entry on the fruitcake list—Mistletoe Antiques. His heart skipped a beat when he thought of Emmy, or more accurately, last night's hug.

"I don't mind doin' these things," he said to his mother. Especially seeing Emmy again. "But you and I were supposed to spend today together."

"We've got tomorrow. And the next day." She walked over to the freezer side of her fridge and took out six frozen loaves of fruitcake and placed them on the table. "Go get your shower," Mum said, shooing him out of the kitchen. "And wear something nice."

He looked over his shoulder. "You want me to dress up?"

"Um, no." Her eyes shifted to the left. "Just be presentable."

"I'm always presentable."

"Now that you cut off all that hair, you are." She smiled and shoved him through the doorway.

Kieran was certain something was up, but he went upstairs to his old room to get ready.

She was far too eager for him to get started on the list of nonurgent errands. And Sheryl had seemed overly excited when he had arrived at the shop a few minutes ago. "I'm so happy to see you!" she practically squealed, giving him a big hug.

"You too." He embraced her.

"Where's that fruitcake?" she said, moving out of his arms.

He handed her the loaf. "This is for you? You hate fruitcake more than I do."

But Sheryl wasn't looking at him, and he could tell she wasn't paying attention to his words. Her gaze was on the back of the store. "The boys have been asking for Nana's fruitcake ever since we got back from our trip. Oh hi, Emmy!"

He turned, his pulse thumping when he saw her. Whatever Sheryl was saying didn't register as he let his gaze linger on Emmy. She was dressed in holiday colors again, wearing a hideous Christmas sweater that somehow looked good on her, jeans, and white tennis shoes. Her bangs were pulled back by gold reading glasses, a complement to her lovely green eyes. He thought he said hello to her, but he wasn't sure. She seemed to become prettier each time he saw her.

Sheryl tapped him on the shoulder. "Have you had lunch?"

"Not yet—"

"Neither has Emmy." She grinned, motioning to the door. "Why don't you two go together?"

He glanced at his sister, catching the sly glimmer in her eyes.

Then he looked at Emmy, who seemed unsure about having lunch with him. Ouch.

"You usually eat after Carina gets back," Emmy said.

"We're slow right now." Sheryl held up the loaf again. "I'll snack on this while you're gone."

"I thought that was for the boys," Kieran said, arching a brow.

"They can't eat all of it."

He almost laughed. Her kids could eat a loaf each if she'd let them, and if they'd liked fruitcake. Which they didn't. First his mother was acting strange, now his sister. He glanced at Emmy again, and just when he realized what was going on, Sheryl was shoving them out the shop.

"Have fun!" she said, shutting the door behind them.

Kieran and Emmy faced each other. He held up his hands, palms out. "She asked me to drop off the fruitcake. That's all, I promise."

"I know." She crossed her arms, hugging herself. "I'm just glad it was for the kids and not me."

He couldn't help but chuckle. "Not a fan of fruitcake?"

"No, but don't tell Maggie. I don't want to hurt her feelings."

"Mum's the word." He did a zipping gesture across his mouth. The snow had stopped about an hour ago, and none of it had stuck to the ground. It was still cold outside, about two degrees Celsius, he guessed. "Mum's had me running all over town this morning. I am feeling a little peckish."

She nodded but didn't say anything else. It was clear Emmy was growing chilled and didn't seem all that keen to be with him. He tried not to take it personally. He was the one on vacation, not her. She didn't have time for his mother and sister's matchmaking foolishness.

"I've got some vegetable soup in the Crock-Pot upstairs," she said. "You can, um, join me if you want."

Of course he wanted to, but he didn't like that she was obligated to offer him lunch. "I think I know what Sheryl's up to."

"Oh, I *know* what she's up to." Emmy half chuckled. "She's not being subtle, is she?"

"Not a'tall." He moved closer to her. "We don't have to eat togeth—"

"C'mon," she said, motioning for him to follow. She opened the door, and they headed upstairs.

When he entered the apartment, he was hit with the delicious scent of vegetable soup and a whole lot of Christmas décor. The living space was small, warm, and cozy, with a dove-gray love seat and leather recliner situated in the middle of the room around an oval wooden coffee table. A modest tree loaded with vintage ornaments was in the corner, and the dining area was separated from the kitchen by a bar with three stools in front.

"Nice place," he said, taking off his coat.

"Thanks." She entered the kitchen. "We're plumb out of castles around here."

He chuckled. "A pity, that. The Ozarks could use a few palaces among the mountains." A coatrack was near the door, and he hung his coat on it and looked around the room again. There were several pictures on the wall, mostly of a school-aged Carina. Two graduation pictures took pride of place, and he assumed one was from high school and the other university. Then he saw a collage on the opposite wall filled with candid pictures of Emmy and Carina, along with a few with Emmy's parents.

Not a single one with a man, other than Emmy's father.

Emmy set two bowls on the four-seater table in the dining room. "Do you take crackers with your soup?"

"Please."

Moments later they were seated with a package of crackers between them and glasses of ice water near the bowls. They took a moment to pray over the meal; then he picked up his spoon. "This looks great," he said.

"I don't know what I'd do without my Crock-Pot." She crumbled a few crackers into her bowl. "I use it several times a week. Just toss in some ingredients, and when I get home from work, it's done."

He noticed there were more pictures on the dining room wall. Again, of Carina. "You must be proud of her," he said, nodding toward one of the two of them grinning in front of her store, a Grand Opening banner above them.

She glanced at the pictures, then back at him. "I suppose you have some questions."

"I am curious."

"Most everyone is when they first meet us." Emmy stirred her soup. "About twelve years after high school I went to work at Beacon Middle School as a teacher's aide. It's about half an hour from Mistletoe. Carina was in foster care at the time, and it was an awful situation. When I met her, I wanted to help her. I *had* to help her."

She didn't go into any detail, but from her shadowed expression he could tell that Carina had been in a tragic situation.

"I became a foster parent and took her in. She was eleven, and I adopted her when she was twelve."

"Wow," he said. "That had to be difficult."

"It was, especially at first. It's not easy being a single parent. And Carina was a preteen, so there was a big adjustment period. I am proud of what she's overcome and the young woman she is now. I couldn't run the store without her."

"That's amazing, Emmy," he said. "Raising a daughter, running your own business. You've done well for yourself."

"So have you. You're the only person I know who owns a castle."

"Owned," he corrected. And while he had traveled many miles and seen many things, plus had a full bank account ready to be invested, he realized he had little else to show for himself. No wife, no children, no permanent connections other than his mother and sister. For years that was how he wanted his life. He had the freedom to do what he wanted—to live for himself.

He watched Emmy as she ate a spoonful of the piping hot soup filled with carrots, celery, potatoes, onions, and seasonings. A warm, restful feeling came over him, one he hadn't experienced in a long time. Sharing a simple meal with Emmy Banks, surrounded by her obvious love for her daughter—not to mention Christmas décor—he felt grounded. And it was satisfying.

She looked at him. "Is the soup okay?"

"Perfect." He dipped in his spoon, and for the rest of the meal he answered more of her questions about Ireland and the UK, her eyes wide with curiosity. When they were finished and he helped her clear the table, he asked, "Have you ever thought about travelin'?"

"Every once in a while." She turned on the faucet and put the bowls in the sink. "I've got a lot of responsibility here, though. But I have to admit . . . it would be nice to get away." She turned to him. "Maybe someday. Right now I'm working toward buying the building next door."

"Do you plan to open another business?"

"Sort of."

He listened as she told him her idea to put a café in the space. "Sounds brilliant," he said. "When will you start?"

She shrugged, her mouth tugging into a frown. "It's a pipe dream right now. I can't afford it, thanks to a bad decision."

"Well, runnin' a business isn't easy. Mistakes happen."

"This was a personal mistake." Glancing at her watch, her brows lifted. "I didn't realize what time it is. I've got to get downstairs."

"I didn't mean to keep you, lass."

She turned off the tap and dried her hands. "You didn't. I enjoyed the conversation."

"Me too." He enjoyed everything. And while he had to wonder what she meant by "a bad personal decision," it wasn't his business.

They quickly went to the front door, and he grabbed his jacket. As he opened the door for her, he happened to look up at the green sprig hanging above the doorway. "More mistletoe?"

Her cheeks flushed and she averted her gaze. "I . . . uh . . . don't have too many visitors. Actually, you've been the first one in months. I think mistletoe is pretty, that's all." She moved past him and ran down the stairs.

Kieran knew she was in a hurry to get back to the store, and she was practically flying down the staircase. He looked at the mistletoe again. Was she afraid he would try to kiss her?

It would be so easy to.

He closed the door. No worries there. She'd made it plain that she only thought of him as a friend. No, more like an acquaintance. His mother and Sheryl would have to face the reality that there was nothing between him and Emmy.

I need to face that too.

FIVE

Come visit Mistletoe Antiques." Emmy smiled and handed the two middle-aged women coupons for her shop. "Ten percent off your total purchase until Christmas Eve."

"Oh, I've been here." The shorter one, wearing white knitted earmuffs and a fuchsia leather coat, eagerly took the coupon. "You have such beautiful things." She turned to her friend. "June, we need to stop by after we're finished with the festival. You will adore this shop."

"How kind. Thank you. Come by soon for some free hot chocolate too. Merry Christmas!"

Emmy grinned as the pair walked away. She let out a relieved breath, creating a small cloud of white mist that instantly disappeared. Those were her last coupons, and now she was free to enjoy the festival while Carina manned the shop. They were never busy during Jingle Fest, and she didn't mind hanging out in the courtyard area of downtown Bird Valley, handing out coupons and wishing people a merry Christmas. Now it was late afternoon, and she was cold and tired and her feet hurt. But the business she generated today would be worth it.

She wandered down Main Street and marveled. It didn't matter how many times she'd attended this event, she was always astonished at the sheer amount of lights, sparkle, and glitter. After she got a hot cup of coffee and sat down for a bit, she would walk the entire festival, which wended its way through three streets in downtown Bird Valley.

As she approached a vendor selling coffee, tea, and hot chocolate, she saw Sheryl waving to her from the funnel cake booth a few stands down. Sheryl's husband, Ben, their three kids, and Maggie were also in tow.

Emmy wasn't surprised to see her friend here. Sheryl and her family always came to Jingle Fest, and she figured she would run into them eventually. Several times during the day she wondered if Kieran was here, too, but she hadn't seen him.

Sheryl left Ben to handle the kids and funnel cakes while she and Maggie walked over. Emmy paid for her coffee and stepped away from the booth. Small crowds of people filled the street surrounding them, walking, laughing, eating, and enjoying the day.

"How'd the big handout go?" Sheryl asked.

"I ran out of coupons, so I would say great." She sipped her coffee. *Ah, good and hot.*

"Excellent." Sheryl glanced around. "There are a ton of people here. More than last year, I think."

"I agree." Maggie looked adorable in her red-and-black plaid flannel coat, red beret, and black snow boots, even though there was no snow in the forecast. But this was southern Missouri, where the weather changed without warning, and it was good to be prepared.

Ben and the boys headed their way, and Emmy was dying to ask Sheryl where Kieran was, but she didn't dare. It was bad enough Sheryl had forced her to have lunch with him. That was embarrassing. She didn't want Kieran to think it was her idea, so she'd tried to act nonchalant about it. Then he said he was hungry, and knowing she had lunch ready to go upstairs, it didn't seem right to avoid inviting him up. Besides, there was a tiny, confused part of her that had *wanted* him to join her, even though they were simply sharing a meal and nothing else.

"Hey, Emmy." Ben handed one of three plates piled with funnel cake to Sheryl. "Did you want some? I can go back and get you one."

"Thank you," Emmy said, appreciating the gesture, "but I'm fine."

When the boys clambered for their share of the cakes, Maggie shushed them, taking the two plates from Ben. "I'll feed the rug rats," she said, gesturing to an open area where numerous picnic tables were set up. "You and Siobhan enjoy yourselves."

"Are you sure, Mom?" Sheryl asked, her brow furrowing.

"She's sure." Ben put his arm around his wife's waist and swept her away. "See you later, Emmy."

"Nana, why do you call Mom *Sha-von*?" Thomas, the youngest son, tugged on his ear. Unlike his brothers, who favored Sheryl, he had the same sandy-blond hair as his father.

"Because that's her name."

"I thought it was 'Sheryl.' And what's a rug rat, anyway?"

"A charming young boy who always listens to his elders." Maggie winked at Emmy.

Thomas shook his head. "I'm not a rug rat, then."

Maggie sighed as the older boys giggled, then arched a disapproving brow at Trevor and Toby. "None of you are. Now let's go sit down before the funnel cakes freeze."

"It's not that cold out, Nana," Toby said as they headed for the eating area.

Emmy smiled. Maggie and the three boys continued to bicker until they disappeared into the crowd. She looked around. Still no sign of Kieran.

Oh well. Lately she had gotten used to enjoying the festival on her own. Some years she spent it with Sheryl and her family, even though Emmy felt like a spare wheel. When she was a child, she and her parents had enjoyed going, but Mom and Dad hadn't been back to Mistletoe in three years. And up until Carina went to college, the two of them had gone together.

Then there was the one time she and Josh went, and he couldn't wait to leave. He didn't even want to go on a carriage ride together. It was her personal tradition, and she'd always ridden with her parents, with Carina, or by herself. Riding with Josh was going to be her first romantic ride, but he had refused to go. *"I don't like horses,"* he'd said, checking his watch. *"Are you done seeing everything? The game starts in an hour."*

She didn't like football, and he didn't like almost everything she did. But she swallowed her disappointment, and they left to watch the dumb game. It was the only year she'd ever missed her carriage ride.

Emmy blinked, taking a mental sledgehammer to the painful memory. That was a long time ago, and this was now. She was going on that carriage ride by herself, and she would enjoy every second of it. She spun around and crashed into someone, spilling coffee all over her gloves.

"Oof," Kieran said. His eyes shone with mirth as they met hers. "We gotta stop doin' this, lass."

"Sorry," she mumbled, looking at the two huge coffee stains on her mittens. "I just bought these," she lamented, then glanced at Kieran again, who appeared apologetic. "It's okay. I got them on sale." But she really loved them. Maybe she could lift the stains later. She fumbled with her cup as she tried to take off the sodden things.

He took her hand and removed one of the mittens, his fingers gliding over bare skin.

She shivered, and not from the cold. And it wasn't like he was purposely trying to touch her. But she couldn't help her response, and she watched as he took her cup so she could take off the other mitten. His expression was inscrutable, and he was staring at the contents inside the cup as if he was wondering what she was drinking.

"Decaf," she said, pointing to the booth behind them.

"What?" Then he looked at her. "Oh, right." He quickly handed her the mitten and empty cup.

"Maggie and your nephews are over there eating funnel cakes." She pointed at the eating area.

"That's why I couldn't find them," he said. "They told me they'd be by the funnel cake booth. But when I got here, I didn't see them."

"You came alone?"

"I had an errand to do for Mum's party. My sister's made good on her promise to put me to work."

Emmy nodded. Maggie's party was turning out to be a huge event, and so far it was still a secret. "I'm not sure where Sheryl and Ben are," she said, several flakes of snow floating down between her and Kieran. "Maggie set them free for a little bit."

He chuckled. "That sounds like Mum." He shoved his hands into the pockets of his wool coat.

Once again Emmy tried not to stare at him, but it was an impossible feat, just like it had been back in high school when she was crushing on him. He was handsome and smelled amazing, of course, which always helped. But she also enjoyed watching him take in the festival with unabashed wonder, as if he'd never seen such a display. It was wonderful to be around someone who was as taken with the splendor as she was.

"Have you been here before?" she asked.

"Not since I was a young lad." His gaze moved back to hers. "I don't remember it being so . . ."

"Magical?"

He grinned. "'It's magical, all right." A faint buzzing sound came from his coat pocket. He pulled out his phone and glanced at the screen. "Text from Sheryl," he said, swiping his thumb over it. "'The kids have eaten too much junk and Mom's tired, so we're going home. Enjoy the festival.'"

"They're leaving already?" Emmy frowned. "They usually stay until the fireworks at the end."

"They have fireworks in winter?"

"Just a few." She ticked off her cold fingers. "A candy cane, a Christmas tree, a snowflake, and Santa. Then everyone sings 'We Wish You a Merry Christmas.'"

"Sounds like fun." He put his phone in his pocket. "Is Carina with you?"

"She's at the store. I'm on my own today."

He tilted his head. "And now I am too. Would you mind givin' me a wee tour?"

Oh, his deep voice and light Irish accent was doing a number on her knees. Her first instinct was to say no. He had an effect on her, one she was still trying to figure out. But there wasn't any harm in showing him around the festival. It wasn't like she was going to be infatuated with him again by the time the fireworks went off.

"Sure," she said with a smile. "I'd be happy to."

Kieran *did* think Jingle Fest was magical. He thought Mistletoe had gone all out for Christmas, but it paled in comparison to the way Bird Valley had transformed its entire downtown area. The last time he'd been here was the Christmas before his father had died. Back then only one street had been decorated, and there had been only a few vendors. Nothing compared to what it was now.

Similar to the feeling he'd had eating fish and chips at the diner, nostalgia washed over him, along with muted, unexpected grief. The grief wasn't new. He'd experienced it more than once during his visit, since almost everything seemed to remind him of Dad. It didn't help that his mother kept a gallery of family pictures with his father prominently displayed all through the house. When he'd decided to visit, Kieran had reckoned since so much time had passed since Dad's death, he didn't have to worry about missing him when he returned to Mistletoe. He'd been wrong.

"Kieran?"

Emmy's sweet voice brought him out of his reverie. They had been walking along Main Street and were now at the end of it, the snow falling thicker and faster than it had moments before. "Aye, lass?"

"Are you okay?" She moved closer to him. "You got quiet all of a sudden."

He had the urge to take her hand, and not only because he wanted to hold it. Just the brief feel of her soft skin against his fingers had sent his senses into overdrive, so strong and quick that he had to distract himself with the coffee to get his bearings. But he also needed some grounding right now. "I'm fine," he said, mustering a smile.

She stopped walking and faced him. "You're missing your dad."

His eyes widened. "How did you know?"

Her expression turned soft. "I would be missing mine if I were in your shoes. Christmas is a magical season, but it can also be painful."

And just like that, he had the grounding he needed. "I think that might be part of the reason I never came back here," he murmured. "As long as I focused on chasing adventure and then renovating Castle O'Neill, I didn't have to think about Dad too much. Truth be told, he's never been far from my mind . . . and heart. Even in Ireland. But here . . ." He shook his head. "I don't know why I'm tellin' you this."

Her chilly hand slipped into his. "Because you need to."

Kieran met her gaze. Sparkling green eyes filled with understanding looked back at him. "Thanks, Emmy."

The *clip-clop* of a horse's hooves and jingling bells sounded behind them. Emmy began to pull her hand out of his, but he held on to it.

She glanced at their clasped hands. Then at him. And to his endless relief, she didn't pull away.

When he looked over his shoulder, he saw a horse and canopied carriage, gaily decorated with green and red garlands and gold bells. He turned to Emmy. "Want a carriage ride?"

Her pretty face lit up. "Absolutely."

A few minutes later they were tucked in next to each other in the carriage, but they weren't holding hands anymore. The driver, wrapped up in a thick coat and wearing an old-fashioned top hat, signaled for the horse to move. The pace was slow as the carriage meandered through the winter wonderland, and Kieran didn't mind that one bit.

Emmy rubbed her hands together, and in one move Kieran entwined his bare fingers with hers again. "We'll keep each other warm," he said. When she relaxed against him, he couldn't stop smiling.

"Do you think they planned this?" Emmy said. At his questioning look she added, "Sheryl and Maggie. It seems coincidental they would go home just as you showed up."

"The thought had entered my mind," he admitted. "Mum's been after me to find someone for years. Sheryl too."

"And Carina's been hinting for me to start dating again."

His ears perked at the word *again*. "You, um . . ." He cleared his throat. "Were you serious about someone?"

"Yes. The wrong someone." She sighed. "I have terrible taste in men. The last one was a complete jerk. So were the other two, back in college. Then there was . . ." She stiffened next to him. "Never mind. Let's just say I'm resigned to being single." Her hand moved out of his, and she stuffed it into her coat pocket.

"Me too." But he said the words with little enthusiasm. It wasn't that he was opposed to marriage. He'd just never met anyone who made him want to settle down. To share a home together. Even have children, if the good Lord was willing. Not a single lass he'd gone out with had ever caused his heart to—

The carriage rattled and lurched as it ran over a huge rut in the road, jostling him and Emmy so much he instinctively put his arm around her.

"Sorry about that!" the driver shouted. "Had to take a detour because they're getting ready for the fireworks later tonight."

Kieran looked at Emmy. "You okay?"

She nodded, and for a moment he thought she would move away. Instead, she nestled against him.

Pitter-patter. His heartbeat danced, and he tightened his arm around her. He smiled as the snow gently fell around them. As the carriage took them back to the center of town, Emmy snuggled against him.

Now this is magical.

SIX

Mom?"

Emmy felt a tap on her shoulder, and Carina's face came into view.

"You're a million miles away." She shook her head and cut into her pancakes. "I've been talking nonstop for five minutes. You probably didn't hear a word I said."

"I'm sorry." She sat back in her chair, her pancakes untouched. It was Sunday, and she and Carina usually had breakfast together at her apartment before they went to church. "What were you telling me?"

"That two of my friends saw you looking cozy with Kieran yesterday at Jingle Fest." Carina popped a bite of syrupy pancake into her mouth.

Emmy froze. "They what?"

Carina swallowed. "They saw you and Kieran taking a carriage ride." She sighed. "How romantic."

"It wasn't . . ." She couldn't even protest properly, because it would have been the biggest lie she would ever tell. Cuddling with Kieran during a winter carriage ride *was* the most romantic thing she'd ever experienced. Or at least it would have been, except for what happened later . . .

"So when's the wedding?" Carina teased, finishing off her pancakes.

Emmy grabbed her uneaten breakfast and got up from the table.

"All we did was take a ride." *And kiss during the fireworks.* She put her plate on the counter and stared at the potted succulent plant on her small window above the sink.

Ever since last evening she'd been in a delightful daze, reliving her afternoon with Kieran.

After the driver dropped them off, they'd wandered around the festival some more, sharing warm chestnuts and apple cider as they waited for the fireworks. He told her about some of the Christmas customs in Ireland, and she was particularly fond of the one where folks put a candle in the window as a guiding light to greet loved ones coming home for the holidays.

Then it was time for fireworks, but it was so crowded they couldn't find a place to stand, much less sit. Finally, they ended up in a short alleyway between two buildings. Even the alleys had been cleaned up and decorated for the festival.

"We won't be able to see the fireworks," Kieran had said as they stood by one of the brick walls draped with tiny twinkling, colored lights. "But we can hear them."

She didn't give a fiddle about fireworks right then. When they were in the carriage, she had tried so hard to keep her attraction to him at bay. And how was she supposed to do that when they were sitting so close and he was holding her hand? Then when the carriage had swayed, he'd put his arm around her, so she gave up and cuddled with him. Even then she thought he was just being polite, like when he'd taken off her mitten and held her cold hand.

But there was nothing polite about the intense way Kieran was looking at her then. She was growing warm from the inside, and as soon as the first firework went off, he leaned in close. "Remember prom night?" he said, his voice husky and low.

All she could do was nod. Her back was pressed against the wall, and he'd put one hand next to her on the brick.

"I have only one regret from that night." He angled his head toward hers.

"Wh-what's that?"

He caressed her cheek with his thumb. "That I didn't do this." He lowered his mouth to touch hers.

She'd practically launched into his arms. The Jingle Fest fireworks were almost over, but hers and Kieran's had just begun.

Carina appeared by her side with her dish. "You've got it bad."

Emmy stared at her. "Got what bad?"

"The hots for Kieran." Carina put the dish in the sink, then picked up Emmy's and started wrapping it in foil.

"The hots?" Emmy said, taking the covered plate from her and putting it in the fridge. She'd warm it up later for lunch. Or dinner. *What's Kieran doing for dinner?* She yanked back the thought. A carriage ride and a kiss—all right, several kisses—didn't mean anything. *Right?* "What is it with you and these old-fashioned words?"

"They seemed appropriate." She winked, then crossed her arms over her maroon ribbed turtleneck. "Tell me I'm wrong."

"You're . . . you're wr . . ."

She grinned. "I knew it. And I approve."

"There's nothing to approve of." Emmy leaned her hip against the counter. "Just because we kissed—"

"You *kissed*?" Carina's jaw dropped. "Chelsea and Robyn never said anything about kissing!"

Oh boy. "Carina, I know you want me to start dating. But I'm not ready. And even if I was, Kieran isn't a viable option."

Her brow furrowed. "Why not?"

"He's going back to Ireland." She brushed by her daughter, fighting to ignore the stab of pain in her heart.

"Are you sure about that?" Carina followed her to the coatrack, and they both put on their winter garb. "He doesn't seem like the type to kiss and jet away."

"How do you know?" Emmy selected a white scarf from the three different ones hanging on hooks.

"He's Sheryl's brother. She'd kill him if he did."

Emmy couldn't deny that was a possibility. And for some reason the thought that he would stay gave her a glimmer of hope that he hadn't just been toying with her emotions. When they'd parted ways after the festival, he'd told her he would see her later, then kissed her cheek. But she had noticed his awkward hesitation.

Her stomach sank. She never should have kissed him. Or ridden with him in the carriage. And while Kieran's kisses had taken her breath away, not to mention being the best ones she'd ever had, she shouldn't have given in. "We're going to be late for church," she said, opening the door.

Carina glanced up at the mistletoe over the doorway. "Maybe later you and Kieran can give it a whirl—"

"Carina!" She shoved her daughter out the door.

The O'Neills attended a different church than she and Carina did, so Emmy didn't expect to see Kieran there. After the service Carina had gone off to spend the rest of the day with Jeremy, and Emmy hoped Kieran would stop by her apartment, despite her continual mental litany that she shouldn't have given in to her impulses. By three o'clock she hadn't heard from him, not even a text.

Her shop was closed on Sundays, and normally she tried to stay away from work on her day off. But she couldn't focus on TV, and she was too agitated to relax. She went downstairs, unlocked the door, then grabbed a dust cloth and some polish and started dusting and straightening shelves. When she finished, she swept the floors and cleaned out the coffeepot and hot water carafe in the café area, even though they didn't need it. By then it was five.

She glanced at her phone, even though the sound was turned on so she could hear it. No call or text.

Her spirits sank deeper. Carina was wrong. Kieran was exactly the kind of guy to kiss and . . . what did she say? Jet away?

Emmy scowled and went behind the counter, her foot hitting a box on the floor near the cash register. It was half full of old Christmas decorations that she'd meant to take to the thrift shop and donate. The flaps were open, and she knelt to close them when she saw a single candle taper with a vintage-looking white light at the top. The candle wasn't that old, since the original ones were plug-ins and this one had a battery-operated timer on it. She'd never seen it before and figured either Carina or Sheryl had added it to the pile.

She was about to put it back in the box when she remembered what Kieran said about the Irish putting candles in the window for family and loved ones. Even though she was irked at him, she liked the tradition. Emmy turned on the candle to see if it still worked and smiled when it glowed.

She stood and went to set it in the center of the picture window. Once she had the light in position, she looked up . . . and saw Kieran standing in front of her.

The snow had stopped overnight, and by morning it was gone. Kieran had spent the entire day, including during Mass, thinking about Emmy. Yesterday had been magical in more ways than one, and he wasn't sorry that he'd kissed her. In fact, he wanted to kiss her again, right now. He'd arrived at her shop just as she was putting the candle in the window, the soft light casting her beautiful face in a lovely glow, and he recalled telling her about the Irish tradition. The timing was perfect. He started to tap on the glass, but she had looked at him first, and her expression wasn't a happy one.

He couldn't blame her. He'd battled with himself over contacting her or just pretending nothing had happened between them. He was annoyed at his indecisiveness. Kissing her hadn't been part of his plan, but he couldn't help himself. He wasn't sure what to do next either. All he knew was that he couldn't ignore her. He didn't want to. But would it be fair to start something with her, knowing he was leaving next week?

There was only one way to find out.

Kieran moved to the front door and waited for her to unlock it. His palms suddenly grew damp, and his nerves fired up.

She opened the door, her expression blank. "Hi, Kieran."

"Uh . . . hey, Emmy." He thrust his hand through his hair. "Can I come in?"

After a second's hesitation, she nodded and opened the door wider. He followed her inside, but she didn't offer him a drink, only went behind the counter as if she needed a barrier between them.

There was nothing for him to do but get to the point. "About last night . . . Emmy, I . . ."

"How long are you staying in Mistletoe?" she asked.

Her question caught him off guard. "I'll be leavin' the day after Mum's party."

She took a step back. "Then why . . ." She drew in a breath and leveled her gaze at him. "Why did you kiss me?"

"Because I wanted to," he said without pause. "Why did you kiss me?"

Her cheeks reddened, and he would have thought it was cute if the tension between them wasn't as thick as a castle wall. "Because I wanted to," she whispered, glancing away.

Kieran moved toward the counter until he was almost leaning against it. "We can make it work, Emmy. Ireland's not that far away."

She scoffed. "It's an ocean away."

"But there's plane rides, phone calls, FaceTime." He could hear the desperate tone in his voice. "You can visit me—"

"And then what?" She held up her hands. "I have a business to run. Mistletoe is my home. I can't be flying back and forth to Ireland because you don't want to be here. That's not fair."

"I'll be visitin' too."

But she was shaking her head before he finished speaking. "Maybe once. Twice." Tears sprang in her eyes. "You don't know how easy it would be for me to give in, Kieran. You were my first . . ."

His heart squeezed. "Your first what, lass?"

"My first love." She took in a shaky breath.

He reeled at the news. "I didn't know."

"Of course you didn't. I was Sheryl's friend. And for one amazing night, I was yours. Problem was, I didn't want friendship. I wanted more, like I do now. And just like back then, I can't have it. We were caught up in the festival, and nostalgia. Now it's back to reality."

"Emmy, I—"

"I've made bad decisions before because I tried to force something that wasn't there. I can't . . . I *won't* do it again." The tears began to roll down her cheeks. "Just go, Kieran. Don't make it any harder on me than it already is."

He wanted to dispute everything she said, but he couldn't. His place was in Ireland, and hers was here. Neither of them would budge on that. And it was selfish of him to start something with her that would eventually end.

Kieran opened the door and walked out into the cold night. He glanced at the candle in the window, and his heart sank in his chest.

SEVEN

That evening, a knock sounded on Kieran's door.

"Are you decent?" Mum asked from the other side.

He added the T-shirt he'd just folded into his suitcase, then opened the door. Mum walked in as he went back to packing.

"I just stopped to tell you good night . . . What are you doing?" she said, alarm in her voice.

"I've got an early flight tomorrow morning." He added his black toiletry bag to the suitcase.

"You're leaving?"

He turned and looked at her, fighting the ache in his chest. More than once as he drove home from Emmy's, he'd thought about going back to her, to try to work things out. She was giving up on them before they had a chance. But ultimately, he knew she was right. They lived in different worlds, literally. "I've got a business deal I need to tend to," he said. "I told you about that apartment complex in Dublin—"

"Rubbish! That's not till next week." She put her hands on her slim hips, and he noticed she was wearing a red bathrobe with a Santa Claus embroidered on one lapel. "What happened between you and Emmy?"

"Nothing." And that was why he was leaving. "We both know what you and Sheryl were up to."

"Kieran," she said, her tone softening. She dropped her arms and went to him. "Emmy's a wonderful woman."

"I know." The words came out against his will.

"Then why won't you give her a chance?"

He sank down on the edge of the twin bed he'd slept on his entire childhood. Even his bedroom had remained the same, down to the baseball-themed wallpaper he'd wanted when he was eight. "There's nothing between Emmy and me."

"I don't believe that." She sat next to him. "She adored you when you were in high school."

Guess I was the last to know. "That was a long time ago."

"She never married. Neither did you. You two are meant for each other."

He didn't want to hear any more of his mother's pie-in-the-sky words. "I need to finish packing."

"So you're running away, like you did before?"

Kieran's eyes snapped onto hers. "I'm not running away."

"Aren't you?" Her jaw tightened as she stood. "You ran off to Europe as soon as you could. I thought it was just a phase, that you would get your wanderlust out of your system and come back to Mistletoe. Then you went to Ireland. Even then I thought you'd eventually come home. But you never did." Tears began to mist in her eyes. "And now you're leaving again. Before my birthday. Before *Christmas.*"

"Mum . . ." he said, his throat closing. "I . . . I have to go."

"Fine." She waved her hand. "Go close your business deal or whatever. Hide in Ireland, or France, or Egypt, or wherever you decide to land. Just know this. You can't outrun grief. Or a broken heart. Trust me, I know." She hurried out of the room.

Kieran stared at the suitcase, then at the shelf on the opposite wall. His Little League trophies were there, along with a picture of the last team he played on . . . the one his dad had coached. He stared at the black-haired man standing beside the group of kids, his stomach a little paunchy and his hair more than a little thin.

But he beamed with pride as his hand rested on twelve-year-old Kieran's shoulder.

Kieran shoved the suitcase aside and sat back down on the bed, his head dropping into his hands. His mother was partially right—when he left Mistletoe, he hadn't planned to stay away very long. When his father died, the pain was so intense, he didn't think he could survive it. But he had to be strong for Mum and Sheryl, and he was able to push down the grief and get through it. And he could ignore it completely while he was abroad.

When he eventually went to Ireland, he fell in love with the country, especially when he found out that the O'Neill castle was for sale. Renovating it was a way to honor his father and ancestors. And anyway, the longer he stayed away from Mistletoe, the more disconnected he was to his hometown.

But when he came back and spent some time around his family, that feeling had somewhat changed. There was a mix of grief and joy as memories came flooding back, more good ones than bad. He realized how much time he'd missed with his nephews, and he'd loved being with them. He also appreciated the quaintness of his hometown.

And of course, there was Emmy.

Kieran rubbed his hand over his face. Emmy's rejection had stirred up so many emotions, the chief one being heartache. It didn't make any sense. He'd reconnected with her only a couple of weeks ago, but she had consumed his thoughts and feelings ever since. He could stay and try to shut out the pain, like he'd done with his grief. But he didn't know if he could do it, not really. He could avoid Mistletoe Antiques easily enough. But Emmy would be at his mother's party. Even now his chest constricted at the thought of seeing her again, knowing they couldn't be together.

He stood up and resumed packing. He was being a coward. And a jerk. But his mother and sister would forgive him eventually. And with enough distance between him and Emmy, he could get over her. Then he could carry on with his life, his new adventure . . . and leave the pain behind.

"I'm going to kill him," Sheryl said as she burst into the shop on Monday morning. She stomped to the counter, oblivious to all the customers in the store.

Emmy was a few feet away helping a young woman find a gift for her grandmother. Naturally she wanted to look at the Irish glass in the display case. Bad enough Emmy had spent last night alternating between tears and anger over Kieran. All she'd had to do was agree to a long-distance relationship, and they would be together.

But she didn't want Kieran only part of the time. She wanted all of him, always. And that was an impossibility. He'd proven as much when he left as soon as she told him to.

Sheryl slammed her insulated lunch bag on the counter. A few customers turned around and stared.

"You should probably keep it down a little," Carina said in a low voice.

Emmy's customer was engrossed in looking at every piece of glass and didn't seem to notice. But Emmy did, and she was positive she knew who Sheryl was referring to.

"Who's on your naughty list now?" Carina smirked at her own joke. Her smile faded when she saw Sheryl's face turn crimson.

"My no-good, selfish brother." She whipped off her scarf and threw it next to the lunch bag. "He has permanently taken the number-one spot."

"Ooh, this is pretty." The woman picked up an emerald glass paperweight rimmed in gold, with the country of Ireland etched in the middle. "She'll love this." She turned to Emmy. "I'll take it. "

"Great choice." Emmy's hands trembled slightly as she locked up the case and carried the paperweight to the counter. What had Kieran done to make Sheryl so angry?

"I'll be in the back," Sheryl said, giving Emmy a frustrated look. She tromped toward the café area.

Carina shrugged and went to help another customer.

It wasn't until almost five when business slowed enough that Emmy could talk to Sheryl. She pulled her friend to the side in the café. "What happened?" she asked, although she feared she already knew the answer.

"He left." Sheryl scowled. "He told Mom he got a call from his real estate agent in Dublin, and he needed to fly out ASAP for some meeting about a property he wants to buy. I still can't believe he did that. He's so full of himself."

Emmy reached for a napkin and handed it to Sheryl, who blew her nose and continued.

"Instead of postponing it, he said yes and left at 3:00 a.m. to catch the first flight out. He said he would visit after Christmas, but you know how that goes." She shook her head. "I should have known he'd bail on us. He doesn't care about family. He doesn't even know what the word means." She started to cry. "He broke Mom's heart."

The color drained from Emmy's face. "This is my fault," she whispered.

Sheryl's head popped up. "Huh?"

Emmy told her friend what happened the night before and a little about the carriage ride at Jingle Fest, leaving out the kissing and her declaration of love to Kieran. "I think he left because of me."

Sheryl shook her head, her ponytail swishing indignantly. "Don't you dare take the blame for him, Emmy. I'm sure his ego was bruised, but he didn't want to be here in the first place. You know how eager he was to get out of Mistletoe after graduation. I just thought when he finally agreed to come that maybe . . ." She collapsed in the chair and looked up at Emmy. "I'm sorry."

Frowning, Emmy sat down. "For what?"

"For pushing you two together. I knew you liked him back in school."

"Really?"

"Girl, everyone knew. Except Kieran, Mr. Obtuse." She took Emmy's hand. "I thought if he had another reason to be here, he would stay. I didn't mean for you to get hurt."

"I'm not hurt." She stared at her lap, feeling foolish that she hadn't hidden her crush like she thought she had.

"Your eyes have been puffy all day, and you have on one black sneaker and one white sneaker."

Shocked, Emmy stared at her feet. "Why didn't anyone say anything?"

"We were busy today." Sheryl sniffed. "And I doubt anyone noticed other than me, Carina, Mrs. Weatherly, Joe Quarles—"

"Okay, got it." She was sure her friend would have named half the customers who visited the store today if Emmy hadn't stopped her.

"Kieran's a knucklehead all on his own." Sheryl's eyes flashed with anger as she got up from the chair. "And we'll carry on without him. Just like we always have."

Emmy watched her friend walk away, and she sighed. Kieran was being a jerk for hurting his family, but he wasn't a terrible man. And no matter what Sheryl said, Emmy would always feel like she was partly responsible for him leaving.

For the next week, Emmy was so busy she could hardly catch her breath. Between running the store and helping Sheryl with Maggie's party, she was exhausted. After the new year she would have some downtime, thank goodness.

But her exhaustion didn't keep her from thinking about Kieran, especially when she was alone. Sheryl had calmed down over him leaving, although she was still mad at him. Maggie was more restrained, although Emmy knew her well enough to sense her underlying sadness. Neither of them had said a word about him since he left.

Sheryl had insisted on a semiformal theme for Maggie's party, so Emmy dressed in the only fancy outfit she owned—a black sequined dress with a flared skirt and off-the-shoulder long sleeves. To make the getup a little Christmassy, she added her holly berry earrings and matching necklace, along with a silver headband. She wore black tights with low-heeled, black shoes, and something rare for her—makeup. She was touching up her red lips when she got a text.

Carina: Ready to go? We're in front of the building.

Emmy grabbed her coat and scarf and went downstairs. Jeremy's SUV was parked in front of the shop, and snow covered the ground. Carefully she walked over the inch of snowflakes and climbed into the back seat. "Thanks for the ride," she said as she shut the door.

Carina whipped her head around. "You look amazing! Is that eyeshadow I see?"

Batting her eyes, Emmy said, "Sure is. And you're beautiful." She squeezed her daughter's hand.

"She sure is." Jeremy grinned at Carina and put the car in Drive. He and Carina talked quietly to each other while Emmy settled into the back seat and found her thoughts drifting to Kieran again. Eventually she would get over him. For good this time.

They arrived at the party and Sheryl immediately dashed over, then turned and faced the crowd of partygoers. "Ben took Mom to get some last-minute presents," she said to everyone in the room.

"He texted that they were five minutes away, so get to your hiding places."

Emmy helped Sheryl herd the group, which was a challenge considering over half were senior citizens and a quarter of them weren't wearing their hearing aids. By the time headlights shone in the parking lot, everyone was in their spot, including Emmy, who was crouched down next to Sheryl. She held her breath as the door opened, and Sheryl popped up and turned on the nearby light.

"Surprise!"

Kieran stood there, a huge bouquet of roses in his hand and a gift under his arm. "What the—"

"Kieran!" Sheryl hustled over to him, not an easy feat in her high heels, and grabbed her brother. "Mom will be here any minute!" She dragged him over to where she was hiding and pushed him toward Emmy. "Get. Down."

He complied as the room went dark again.

Emmy's skin tingled as Kieran shifted next to her. He didn't say anything, and it was too dark to see if he was looking in her direction. But she could sense his warmth and smell his woodsy cologne.

"When did you get back?" Sheryl whispered.

"Three hours ago," he said, the scent of cinnamon on his breath. "I had to—"

"She's here!"

The room went quiet. The door opened, and a wedge of light illuminated the door. "Ben," Maggie said. "Why is it so dark in here—"

"Surprise!"

The lights flicked on, and Maggie's face contorted in shock. For a minute Emmy thought there might be something wrong and they had scared her. But then Maggie burst into laughter as everyone started singing "Happy Birthday." She was in tears by the end of the tune, and her gaze had landed on Kieran. She walked over to him and gave him a big hug.

"You came back," she said, pulling away from him but keeping her hands on his arms.

"I told you I would, Mum." He held out the red and white roses to her. "Happy birthday."

Maggie hugged him again, and Emmy stood to the side as he was greeted by family and friends. Sheryl punched him in the arm before hugging him fiercely.

"If you ever pull another stunt like this again, you'll be sorry," she said, her voice thick.

"I won't." He gave her a serious look. "I can promise you that."

Emmy smiled, her heart almost full. Kieran was back. She didn't know for how long, although she was certain it was just for the party. Or maybe he would stay for Christmas. He wouldn't be here past the new year. That she was sure of.

The O'Neill family was swept away by the partygoers, and even though Emmy knew everyone, she felt a little on the outside. She spied Carina and Jeremy sitting close to each other at a table, their heads together and whispering.

I approve, Emmy thought.

Music started playing, and the party was underway. She slipped away and found her coat, suddenly needing some air.

After Kieran had surprised everyone—and was a little shocked himself, even though he knew it was a surprise party—he searched for Emmy. He thought he saw her standing near the front of the party area, but she wasn't there. He'd had to fight the desire to reach for her hand when they were crouching next to each other in the dark. Even though he'd been gone only a week, he'd missed her so much. Her, his family . . . and Mistletoe.

He felt a whoosh of cold air and turned around in time to see Emmy slip out the door. His package still under his arm, he followed her outside.

"Emmy!" he said, catching up to her.

She turned around, and to his delighted surprise, she smiled. He thought she was still upset with him.

"Hi," she said when he reached her.

"Hi, lass." Snow had started to fall again, and the weather had been dicey all the way from Dublin. But if he'd had to paddle his way to Mistletoe, he would have done it.

"Did anyone know you were coming?" she asked.

"I thought about telling Ben, but I wanted to surprise everyone." Her face looked different under the parking lot lights, and he realized she was wearing makeup. Tastefully done and pretty, but she was pretty without it too. "I'm glad to see you." *The understatement of the year.* He waited for her to say the same. He was disappointed when she didn't, but he also understood why.

"You made your family very happy tonight." She huddled farther into her coat.

"Good thing, since I made them plenty mad when I left."

"Is that why you came back? To make it up to them?"

"Mostly. Emmy, I messed things up. When I got the call to go to Dublin, I should have put off the trip. Mum begged me to, but all I wanted was to leave."

"To get back to Ireland," she said.

"Nay. No." He took a step toward her, relieved when she didn't move away. "I wanted to leave the pain. Not just the memories. I would have dealt with those. But I couldn't stand the fact that I'd hurt you. I couldn't face it either. But I know."

Emmy shook her head. "You sound human to me. I'm sorry I hurt you, Kieran—"

He put his finger on her lips, then removed his hand and held out the gift. "Merry Christmas."

She took it from him. "You didn't have to get me anything."

"I wanted to." He put his hands behind his back and grinned. "Open it."

She carefully removed the wrapping and lifted the lid from the box. "Mittens," she said, pulling out an almost duplicate pair of the ones she'd spilled coffee on.

He'd searched for over a week in the Dublin stores to try to find them. "They're not exactly the same—"

"They're perfect." She slipped them on. "And better. Mine were on clearance." She held her hands close to her face. "Do they go with my outfit?"

He laughed. "That they do. There's something else in the box."

She gave him a questioning look as she peered inside. "A list?" When she struggled to pick up the paper with her mittened hand, he took over and handed it to her, and she began to read it aloud. "Number one—find a house." She looked at him. "I don't understand."

"I don't mind livin' with Mum for the short term." He tried to keep his tone light, but the emotion was getting to him. "But eventually I'll need my own place here in Mistletoe."

Her eyes widened. "You're moving here?" At his nod she said, "But what about Ireland? You love it there."

"And it isn't goin' anywhere. But my home is here. I realized that as soon as I landed in Dublin, because I kept seeing things."

"Things?" she asked, confused.

"Candles." He smiled. "Single candles were everywhere. Store windows, house windows, apartment windows. Every time I saw one, all I wanted was to come back to Mistletoe."

She half smiled. "To be with your family."

"And with you, lass." He leaned toward her. "Don't tell Sheryl and Mum, but you edged them out by several kilometers."

Her smile brightened, then immediately disappeared as questions filled her eyes. "Are you sure?"

Kieran closed the space between them. "I don't know what the future holds for us, Emmy Banks. I just know I want to discover it with you. *Tá mo chroí istigh ionat.*"

"What does that mean?"

He took her hand and put it on his chest, over his beating heart. "My heart is within you."

Her eyes sparkled. "That's the most romantic thing I ever heard." She put her arms around his neck and kissed him, then whispered in his ear, "And mine is within yours."

❄

Christmas Eve

Emmy stood in front of her mirror in her bedroom, wondering if she should change her ugly Christmas sweater and put on her other ugly Christmas sweater. She glanced at her watch. Nope, there was no time—

The doorbell rang. She hurried out of her bedroom and opened the door. Kieran stood there, looking as fine as he did every day, whether he was dressed up like he had been at Maggie's party or wearing his wool coat, jeans, and a pullover. They had spent a lot of time together the last few days, mostly at Carina and Sheryl's insistence, confident they could handle the rest of the Christmas shoppers without her. Emmy had discovered Kieran's keen business sense, and together they came up with a financial plan that would help her reach her goal of opening a café—if not next door to the antique shop, then somewhere else in Mistletoe.

"Hi," she said, grinning. "I'll just grab my purse and the presents, and we'll go." They were expected at Sheryl's tonight for her annual ugly sweater Christmas Eve party.

Kieran opened his coat, revealing a hideous sweater that rivaled her own renowned collection. The Christmas tree in the center was fine, along with the tiny gifts at the bottom. But it was the green pompoms around the collar, the dancing Santas on the shoulders, and the red and green tinsel wrapped around each sleeve that got her laughing.

"What?" He flashed her a grin and turned around for full effect.

"You look like a flamenco dancer," she said, still giggling.

"Too much?"

"You're a shoo-in to win the coveted annual prize."

"Which is?"

"A twenty-year-old loaf of fruitcake that's been passed around Mistletoe at least fifty times."

"One of Mom's?"

Emmy grinned and nodded. "She's a good sport about it, though. I don't think anyone has the courage to open it, much less taste it."

Kieran laughed. "You won't find me volunteerin', that's for sure. Are you ready to go?"

"Aye," she said, imitating his accent.

He pulled her into his arms. "I'll have you speakin' like an Irish lassie in no time."

"And it won't be long before you'll be talking like a Missouri country boy again."

"Fine by me." He glanced up at the mistletoe. "Last time I was here, I really wanted to take advantage of that sprig o' green above us."

She gazed into his eyes. "What's stopping you?"

His eyes danced as he leaned in to kiss her. "Merry Christmas, lass."

And it was.

A MISTLETOE PRINCE

Pepper Basham

ONE

Partially self-imposed exile.

What had his life come to?

Prince Arran St. Clare of Skymar sighed as he drove, staring out the window at the unfamiliar passing landscape. If only he'd known his parents' plans when he'd asked them for help, he may have chosen to continue his more entertaining, but less fulfilling, role of rogue prince. But the past few months, as the mounting tabloid and newspaper headlines continued to flaunt his ungoverned lifestyle, the shame he had for his behavior had intensified.

How could he have allowed a broken heart to lead him into utter madness for nearly two years?

Especially since he'd been making better choices over the past few months, only to become, quite unexpectedly, caught up in another mistake. A mistake that led him to using royal funds for a rather scandalous party aboard a yacht. Accidentally, of course.

His body drooped from the internal wrestling match between his pride, his need for change, and his towering list of mistakes.

Images of the most recent media photos rushed to mind. Famous women and superficial relationships. Parties with less-than-ideal outcomes. A video of him landing a punch on Lord Darrick.

He winced.

If he'd known Rachelle was the daughter of the overprotective and highly popular conservative leader in Skymar, Arran wouldn't have pursued a harmless moonlit swim with her.

Punching her father had been entirely provoked. And, unfortunately, captured on video for the whole world to see.

An uncomfortable twinge tightened his chest. Words from the most recent newsprints repeated in his head.

Playboy.

Troublemaker.

Embarrassment.

All arrows finally hitting their mark.

He couldn't continue on his present course. The disappointment on his parents' faces bled clearly into his mind. Perhaps he deserved his fate: eight weeks with his little sister and her new American husband, living as a commoner and working construction in a small, backward town in North Carolina . . . *without* royal funds.

Plus, part of the agreement with his parents meant Arran would assist with some Christmas charity.

Well, at least he knew how to navigate service projects, a skill for which he particularly excelled among his siblings.

A text popped up on the screen of the car.

Ellie: Expect a feast for dinner. Luke is grilling steak.

Ellie: And watch out for bears. You're coming in late, so there's a chance one might run along your path.

Arran stopped the car in the middle of the street and stared at the message. Bears? Seriously? Bears "along your path," as if it were the most normal remark in the world. He shook his head, a new twin wave of humiliation and annoyance rising in his chest.

He didn't need the oversight of his *little* sister or her country husband to reform. Oh no! He could manage his own reformation.

After all, he was twenty-eight years old.

Plus, bears? Where on earth had his parents sent him?

The GPS glitched and then turned him down a street with brick and stone buildings lining either side of the road. Only a few shops glowed with welcome in the dusk shadows. Most looked closed for the evening.

He brought the car to a stop at the next traffic light and waited for another GPS command. Nothing. Giving the phone a quick refresh, he tried again.

The connectivity circle kept spinning.

Of course. Bears, exile, and no internet connection.

Perfect. Sounds like a regular modern fairy tale.

The interruption of a car horn brought him back to attention, a green traffic light lit above him. Arran sent a glance over his shoulder and pulled the car into a nearby parking spot to give himself time to gather his bearings.

Last time he checked the GPS, he was about twenty minutes from Ellie's house.

His attention shifted to his phone. He could text her for directions.

He groaned and pressed his head back against the headrest. Having to contact her for directions sent a double sting to his pride. For one, she was his little sister, and second, he revolted against asking for help *again*. After all, he'd be spending the next two months with her and her husband in all their happy honeymoon afterglow.

He cringed at the very idea. The last thing he wanted was to prove himself more inept than his sister or brother-in-law already thought he was.

A flicker of light to his right pulled his focus to a blinking sign in a nearby window reading "Murphy's Brew." The warm glow of welcome tugged his interest.

He glanced at the GPS.

Asking a local for directions should be simple enough, right? Less painful on the pride in this particular situation.

After a moment's hesitation, he killed the engine and unfolded from the car.

A quick drink, an easy conversation, and he'd be back on the road with directions in a quarter of an hour or less.

Simple.

He pushed open the door of the bar and found the atmosphere not too different from a Skymarian village pub. Dimly lit, the space offered a blur of activity, from billiards on one side to darts on the other. Combating aromas of perfumes and colognes mingled with the hints of savory dishes.

A responsive growl erupted from Arran's stomach, reminding him that he hadn't eaten since flying out of Skymar early that morning.

The idea of Luke's steak sounded better and better.

A burly man stood behind the counter, his full beard and flannel shirt giving off a similar vibe as the Scots in the northern mountains of home. "You look a little lost, stranger."

"A stranger, yes." Arran took a seat on an empty stool, unfurling his grin. "Lost? Not anymore. I was hoping to find a place like this one for a brief respite and a bit of direction."

"Respite?" The man's dark brow rose along with one corner of his mouth. "Sounds like you came a long way to stumble into my door." The man leaned an elbow onto the counter and studied Arran through narrowed eyes. "Tourist?"

Arran hesitated at the man's unreadable expression. Did the bartender have something against tourists? "I'm actually here to visit my sister." He unleashed a broad smile. "You may have heard of her. Princess Elliana St. Clare?"

So much for keeping to anonymity.

"Nope." The man gave a shake of his head before stretching back to stand upright. "Can't say we have much use for princesses around here." The man shared a smile with a nearby woman. "Now, if you were related to Andy Griffith or some famous sports player, that'd be different."

The smile slid from Arran's face, a sudden ... discomfort squeezing in his chest. Even when he preferred anonymity at times, someone *always* recognized him. They had his entire life.

Prince Arran. Fourth child of King Aleksander and Queen Gabriella of Skymar. Fun-loving, formerly contentious, playboy royal. On the arm of the rich and famous.

Who else was he?

He stumbled around in his head for a response to this new epiphany. Did he even know anymore?

"My ... my sister married a local. Luke Edgewood?"

The man's gaze darted to Arran. "Luke Edgewood?"

Arran's body tensed. "Yes?"

"You're *Ellie's* brother?" With a raised brow and a tip back on his heels, the man surveyed Arran anew, as if measuring him. "The fancy fella who'll be working with Luke for the next few months?"

"Y ... yes." He drew out the word even more slowly than before. *Fancy* fellow?

"Well, why didn't you say so from the start? Luke told us we ought to set you right if we saw you."

Set him right? What could that mean? Especially from a brother-in-law? "Actually, I was hoping to get directions to Luke's house, if you could ... set me right with those."

"Sure thing." The man raised a brow, a mischievous twinkle lighting his pale eyes. "But first, we're gonna give you a Mount Airy welcome."

Arran had no time to ponder further because the man called to the room. "Hey, y'all!" The voices hushed, faces turned toward the bar.

"This here is Ellie Edgewood's brother, and he's in need of a warm Mount Airy welcome."

An eruption of voices rose in response, as men and women alike raised their glasses in salute.

"First things first, Ellie's brother." The man leaned back against the bar. "Let's introduce those royal tastebuds of yours to the best brew this mountain's got to give. That is, if you think you're man enough to handle it."

The glint in the bartender's eye inspired a rise of caution in Arran's stomach, but he shrugged it off. Though he'd rarely taken whiskey over the past month in an attempt to start cleaning up his life, Arran knew how to hold it.

And what better way to show the locals he meant to enjoy their comradery? "My home is known for some of the best brew around. You'll have to work hard to impress me."

"Oh, not to worry, Ellie's brother." The glint deepened in the man's eyes. "We're more than ready to meet the challenge. In fact, this stuff may knock you right off that royal seat of yours."

"Sure."

A single word propelled Charlotte Edgewood from her comfortable, introverted role as behind-the-scenes support person into the lead coordinator for The Mistletoe Wish program.

And as the word slipped from her lips, she shuddered in shock.

She was *not* a leader. How was she supposed to manage something as large as the annual Christmas fundraiser?

"I can't thank you enough." Lori Paxton sent an unadulterated look of appreciation as she placed a protective palm over her extended abdomen. Her gaze traveled down Charlie and back up. "And I know it's not your usual choice, but I'm sure you'll . . . figure out how to manage everything. And the Christmas Gala too."

Charlie's face went cold as she cast a look down at her work-worn jeans and faded T-shirt.

The Christmas Gala?

She gave her ball cap a tug, just to look a little less like the tomboy she was, and a powdering of dust hit the floor. She bit back a whimper.

I can't do this.

Did she even own a pair of heels? And she'd never worn an evening gown.

"With the babies due any day, there's no way I can participate, let alone coordinate."

Charlie forced her lips into a smile.

Hopefully.

"But . . . but do you think maybe Diane would be the better option? I mean, she's been more involved at the party and hosting level than me."

Was that Charlie's own voice? All wobbly and breathless?

What had compelled her to volunteer in the first place? She was a *carpenter*! Not a presenter!

Her gaze dropped to Lori's middle, and her shoulders drooped. However, *someone* needed to help. But Charlie was the worst qualified *someone* for the job.

"Diane is tending to her mama after her surgery, remember?"

Hope withered to match the dust from Charlie's hat. "Of course." She drew in a breath, praying for courage.

Maybe she needed to do this.

This could be her chance to prove to everyone, including herself, that she could step beyond her fears and the mold she'd resigned herself to. That there was a brave woman living underneath her faded jeans and six-year-old work boots.

"I'm happy to do it," she finally said.

Which wasn't a lie. Completely. Charlie had assisted in the Christmas fundraiser for years. She knew the schedule, the people, and how it worked.

Unfortunately, her smile must not have registered the appropriate holiday cheer.

"You'll have support from our usual volunteers." Lori rushed ahead. "Besides, isn't that prince coming to help?"

That prince?

Charlie's smile tensed at the reminder of her cousin Luke's brother-in-law assisting in their little mountain service project. A rebel prince, from what she'd heard. She quelled an eye roll. How could *he* possibly help?

"Doesn't that sound like the strangest thing to say?" Lori laughed. "A prince coming to our rescue."

A memory rushed to Charlie's mind: her eight-year-old self in full princess costume, dancing around the living room while watching copious amounts of princess-themed movies. Real-life disappointments had certainly redefined those childhood dreams. Besides, the last thing she needed was to babysit a maverick monarch while navigating such a daunting leadership role.

"I don't really expect him to help," Charlie offered. "There's a good chance working for Luke will be enough to keep him busy."

"It's a wonder he's offered to come at all." Lori chuckled. "A prince! Building houses! In our little town?"

It didn't make sense to Charlie either.

After Lori shared a few more suggestions, Charlie gathered her bag, scooped up the fundraiser's files, and took the stairs down to the street. The lamps lining Main Street attempted to compete with some of the few shops still open after 7:00 p.m. on a weekday.

Charlie's gaze landed on the little steeple rising above the other buildings at the end of town, and she sent a prayer heavenward. Surely God would help her through this. Even if it involved a hairstylist and—she swallowed the lump in her throat—possibly wearing . . . heels.

The sound of laughter pulled Charlie's attention next door to Murphy's Brew, one of the most popular nighttime spots in Mount Airy. Light blazed from the bar's windows, teasing passersby in for warmth, fellowship, and some of the best cheese pretzels on the planet.

She shook her head at the idea of Caine Murphy and the pride he took in his potent home brew, then made her way to her truck.

She'd just started the ignition when her phone buzzed to life.

Luke: Have you happened to see a prince in town?

Air burst from Charlie's crooked lips as she reread the note. *Interesting intro to a conversation.*

Charlie: I gave up that pursuit in grade school. Why do you need a prince, anyway? Don't you already have a princess living at your house?

Luke: My princess happens to have lost a brother. He was supposed to be here a couple hours ago.

Charlie's bottom lip dropped, and she sent another look down quiet Main Street. *How on earth could anybody get lost in Mount Airy, of all places?*

Charlie: Clearly, my skills at locating princes are pretty rusty. Does he resemble your wife? Blond hair, blue eyes, practically perfect in every way?

Luke: No one looks as good as my wife.

Charlie's grin stretched. Give the man a wife, and suddenly there's an influx of romantic talk.

Charlie: So, I'm looking for a slightly less perfect, male version of your wife?

A photo popped up on the screen to reveal a man who resembled Captain America a little too much for Charlie's peace of mind. Styled blond hair, pale blue eyes, perfect smile.

In a tux.

Have mercy!

She cleared her throat.

Luke: Before you fall in love with him, know that one of his ears is shorter than the other.

Charlie belted out a laugh before she typed out a reply.

Charlie: I've outgrown my infatuation with princes, so I think he's safe from me.

Luke: Well, since you're not going to marry him, at least shine some of that good heart in his direction. I think he could use it.

Charlie: Sounds like he could use some direction in the geographical sense, too, if he's lost in Mount Airy.

Luke: Clearly, looks don't equal smarts. Except in my case.

Charlie shook her head with a sigh. Rescue a troublemaking prince? That's exactly how she wanted to spend her evening.

Her gaze caught sight of her shadowed reflection in her rearview mirror. Large gray eyes stared back at her, highlighted by the glow of the streetlamps.

Her daddy had always said she looked like her mama, but thankfully, he'd never held that against Charlie. He'd rarely spoken about the woman who married him, bore him a daughter, and then disappeared when Charlie was nine.

Without one look or note back.

In fact, last Charlie heard, her mama still had a few years left of her prison sentence for armed robbery.

Charlie pulled off her hat, and strands of her ash-brown hair fell around her pale face. Maybe the hair and face shape resembled her mom's, but the vulnerable eyes staring back didn't at all. One of the last memories of her mama flashed through her mind, the woman's expression tightened into a customary frown.

"I had hoped you'd be blond like my mama."

"Why don't you have the fine bone structure of some of the other girls?"

A dozen other phrases echoed from the past with a rush of condemnation.

"Your eyes are too large."

"Your nose is too small."

Charlie closed her mind to the memories, returning her cap and starting the truck.

Raised with boys.

Works with boys.

How on earth was she going to learn to dress and act like a lady?

She shifted the truck into gear and drove twenty minutes to the nearby town of Ransom to her somewhat-restored brick Victorian. Her dad had purchased it with a plan to renovate and sell it, but he'd only partially completed things before unexpectedly dying in a construction accident two years ago. Her heart twinged at the memory, as it always did.

Though her daddy had been no Prince Charming, he'd done his best to love her enough for two parents. She closed her eyes and leaned her head back against the seat. What she wouldn't give for one of his hugs right now.

She blinked away the sting in her eyes and stared back at the massive house. She really ought to sell the place, but the idea of getting rid of it somehow felt like losing another piece of him.

The fancy sconces her daddy had placed on either side of the front door shone into the night as if they were a private "welcome home," so she nodded toward them in acknowledgment and stepped from the truck.

As soon as Charlie's feet hit the drive, she froze.

A low growl reverberated nearby, sending a chill from the base of her spine to the crown of her head. She took a slow turn and looked down the quiet street populated with old houses and flickering streetlamps.

Another growl.

A bear? Her face cooled. Wolf?

She pressed her back against the truck.

The growl came again.

Her head jerked in the direction of the sound. Whatever it was waited at the back of her truck.

She cast a glance to her front door. Should she make a run for it?

The growl sounded again, but this time it ended with a high-pitched whistle.

A whistle?

And now that she thought about it, the growls sounded rather rhythmic.

She moved a few steps toward the sound, another "growl" turning into a . . . hum?

What in the world?

Flipping on the flashlight on her phone, Charlie peered over the bed of her truck and nearly dropped her phone at the sight. Lying on his back, mouth open and hair erratic, slept Prince Captain America.

TWO

How had Prince Captain America found his way into the back of her truck?

No scenario in her mind gave an answer.

Charlie peered closer, and a full whiff of his breath hit her in the face. She coughed and drew back.

Drunk?

Captain America was *drunk*?

Her brain glitched on the idea, but then she looked up into the starry sky.

"When I prayed for a prince as a little girl, Lord, this is not what I had in mind."

It was much easier to appreciate God's sense of humor in other people's lives.

She leaned her hip against the truck and pulled her phone close. First day in America, and the man couldn't even make it to his sister's house without a mishap? Prince Lit certainly didn't need to get involved with *her* fundraiser!

Charlie: So . . . I found the prince.

Luke: Um . . . that was really weird to see in print.

Luke: Where did you find him?

Charlie: In the back of my truck.

Luke: In the back of your truck? I'm trying to think of reasons, but none of them are good. What did you do to him?

Charlie: I didn't do anything to him! When I pulled into my house, I found him in the truck bed. Drunk asleep.

Luke: Just so you know, magic kisses don't work on drunk princes.

Charlie: Not to worry. I prefer my men sober and sensible before I sweep them off their feet.

Luke: Glad to know his royal good looks haven't disarmed your logic.

Luke: And I'm sorry, Charlie. We'd thought he was making steps in the right direction, but it sounds like he's going to need a little mountain TLC to get on the straight and narrow.

Charlie: Prince Valiant doesn't stand a chance with a brother-in-law like you.

Luke: I was made for this moment.

Charlie: Since it's starting to rain, I'm going to try to get him inside.

Luke: Ellie and I will be there in about thirty minutes.

Charlie: See you then.

Charlie stared down at the unconscious man. Of course the only type of prince she'd ever meet was a rogue one. She lowered the tailgate. Further proof of the ridiculousness of those childhood fairy tales.

She tugged at the prince's foot, distracted for a second by the fact he wore tennis shoes.

She wasn't sure what she'd expected, but . . . tennis shoes? She huffed and tugged again. Luke's wife, Ellie, was a princess, and she was *almost* normal, so why wouldn't Ellie's brother wear tennis shoes?

At another tug, the man groaned.

The rain intensified, followed by a nice roar of thunder.

Perfect.

With a very unladylike growl, proving all the more how unqualified she was for this whole Mistletoe Wish coordinator business, Charlie grabbed the prince's feet and pulled until she'd moved his body to the edge of the truck bed.

A few more tugs brought him to where his legs dangled over the tailgate.

Good. Progress.

She fisted his jacket in both hands and raised him to a sitting position. With great lack of ceremony, his head drooped against her shoulder, and his cool, damp hair pressed into her neck and jaw.

How had her life come to this?

Beneath the scent of alcohol, the warm, spicy fragrance of cardamom filled her airway. Heat flew into her face.

Not fair. At all.

She pushed back from him, steadying him by his shoulders—his strong, muscular shoulders.

The warmth in her cheeks sparked to sizzling.

It was a good thing he was nearly comatose right now.

Another roll of thunder sounded, and Charlie sent a longing look to her front porch. There was no way she and Prince Drools-A-Lot Charming would make it to the front door if he didn't help a little. She gave his shoulders a little shake.

"Hey . . ." Oh dear, what was his name again? Adam? "Wake up!"

His head bobbled like a rag doll. Another round of thunder grumbled its warning.

"I *could* just leave you here." She raised her voice, giving him a stronger shake. "And you could . . . get struck by lightning."

A strangled sound erupted from him.

Was that a laugh?

Well, at least it proved a good sign he might be waking.

The sound gurgled again. Louder.

And if she'd had her wits about her, she'd have dodged out of the way. But her brain didn't respond fast enough. She blamed the cologne.

Because the sound grew in volume, and in one very foul swoop, the prince upchucked all down the front of her shirt. She squeezed her eyes closed and whimpered out a laugh.

Yep. The perfect twisted fairy tale.

"I'm . . . I'm . . . sorry." He hiccupped, slowly opening one eye as his head weaved. "I . . . I've never gotten s-sick on someone before."

Even in her stupor, she had to admit the accent sounded nice.

Blast those stinking costume dramas.

"Listen, Prince." Yes, it was stupid to call him *prince*, but right now intelligence seemed to have left the vicinity on both sides of the conversation. "I need you to put your arm around my shoulders and walk with me to my house."

He looked down at her from his perch on the tailgate, his eyes squinting. "You're a woman?"

"Smart and handsome, I see."

He attempted a grin, maybe, but his facial expression moved with about as much speed and accuracy as his words.

Another shock of thunder rallied him a little, and he shifted until he stood, sort of. Charlie slipped her arm beneath his, wrapping it around his back, and they trudged toward the front door. As Charlie was one of the shortest people in her family, the prince towered over her.

"I'm usually better at this," he slurred.

"What? Walking?"

A snort erupted from him. "Nooo." He drew out the word, his breath hitting her face with such force, she coughed. "Holding my . . . my drink." He gave his head a shake. "But I . . . I've not been drinking much lately, you see? Trying to m-make better choices."

They started up the steps.

"You're doing a stellar job."

He snorted a laugh again and then paused, rubbing his nose. "I don't mean to be rude, but I think you need to change your perfume."

"I think my current perfume has more to do with the gift you left down the front of my shirt." She pulled him up another step.

Two more to go.

"That wasn't very nice of me." He groaned, staring down at her shirt. "I do want to be nice, you know."

Oh Lord, please don't let him be one of those emotional drunks. After her day, the last thing she needed was an intoxicated prince weeping on her vomit-covered shirt.

"One more step, Your Majesty, and we'll be out of this rain."

"Actually, *Majesty* is reserved for my parents." He paused and turned toward her. "*Highness* is for rank like mine."

"Highness? Pretty appropriate for the moment, don't you think?"

His grin quirked again, and he narrowed his eyes at her, slowly taking the final step. "You are a very nice person," he murmured as his face dropped against her head. "My parents would like you."

It was her turn to snort as they shuffled to the front door. His parents? Yeah, she proved the very model of a royal daughter-in-law. Perfume and all.

Charlie propped the prince against the wall beside the front door as she dug out her keys from her pocket. Within another few seconds, they hobbled inside, only to have her drop her keys upon entry.

Lord, help me.

Charlie loosened her hold on Prince Pukey to flip on the light, but the man tipped forward. She pivoted to catch him, only to have him straighten so quickly, his head slammed directly into her nose.

She stumbled back, losing her hold on him, her vision blurring as she reached for her face. He merely groaned and slid down into a sitting position on the floor.

Her nose shot a warning throb from her forehead to her lips. Blood was coming.

"Your keys, my lady." The prince raised Charlie's keys to her view, his grin crooked. If Charlie's nose hadn't been stinging, she'd have laughed.

"Are you alright?"

The prince started an unsteady rise, so Charlie rushed forward, redirecting him to the couch. He refused to budge, his brows rising as his gaze dropped to her nose.

"Did . . . did I"—he gestured toward her face with the keys, his eyes close enough for her to get a clear view of how incredibly blue they were—"hurt you?"

The agony in his voice, in those piercing eyes, distracted her from her pain for a moment.

A flicker of lucidness steadied his attention. "Forgive me."

The raw words rasped out of him as if they came from some deep place inside that broad chest of his.

Something like the faintest flutter of hummingbird wings flittered alive in her stomach.

And then his focus grew in intensity, and he started falling forward. If she hadn't guided him safely to her couch, more blood may have spilled in her living room than the stream coming from her nostrils.

She ran to the kitchen and gathered a handful of paper towels. Smashing them to her face, she returned to the living room to the sound of . . . snoring.

Again.

She leaned against the doorframe with the towels against her nose, a chuckle tickling the back of her throat.

At eight, she'd dreamed of a fairy-tale prince coming to sweep her off her feet. But nearly twenty years later, she stared at a drunk, snoring, *actual* prince who'd just busted her nose after puking on her.

It was a good thing she'd outgrown that pesky childhood fantasy, because one thing was certain. This prince was *not* for her.

Where on earth was he?

Arran's eyes refused to open, even as the sound of footsteps neared.

And how had he found himself wherever *here* was?

He groaned. Thoughts refused to congeal.

"You definitely know how to make a first impression, brother-dear."

Brother-dear? The voice bled into recognition. Ellie?

"And I'm afraid you made a bit of a mess of things on your first night."

A strange scratching sound erupted to his right, followed by light flooding into the dark recesses of his sluggish thinking.

The action immediately incited a headache. Or reminded Arran of the headache he already had. Because, somewhere in his foggy memory, he felt certain he'd had a headache for a long time.

Arran pushed open one eye to find his sister staring down at him. "Not the best way to start turning over a new leaf."

His chest seized at her words, but he couldn't quite piece together the reason why. "What happened?"

"We can discuss it once you get up and dressed." She sat down on the bed, her gaze more compassionate than he deserved. "Then, after you're cleaned and sobered up, I'll drive you to the worksite."

The words hit him in quick succession, and his brain attempted to catch up.

"Luke loaned you some work clothes for roofing a house, but you're going to need to purchase your own if you want some that fit."

Words. Arran knew he understood them, but none of them made sense. Work clothes? Roofing?

He pushed himself up to a sitting position, and the pain in his head exploded into an agonizing pulse. Wincing, he pressed his palms against his forehead, trying to recall what stupid thing he'd done to get himself into this degree of misery. The sinking recollection began dawning through the fog. A small-town street. Murphy's Bar?

"I'm not certain what is different about the native nectar of the Blue Ridge," he growled. "But I only had two servings of Murphy's special brew and barely remember what happened next."

"How on earth did you find your way into his pub?"

"GPS stopped working, so I sought out directions." He attempted to sit up straighter. "And it was the only place that seemed open."

"From what Luke says, Murphy takes pride in making his homemade whiskey as strong as possible." Ellie sighed. "You had no idea how hard it was going to hit you."

"And on an empty stomach, no less." He groaned, blinking both eyes open. Last night? Arran's head throbbed from the effort to pull up syrupy thoughts. A woman? Gray eyes. Had she been real? Arran pressed his palms into his aching eyeballs. "Last night wasn't supposed to happen like that."

Ellie didn't respond.

"Despite the current representation, this has *not* been my routine for the past month." He pushed a hand through his hair, but even that seemed to hurt his head. "I had already begun to make changes to my life. Dropped those toxic friends, started to show up to family and royal events." He raised his gaze to hers. "I even went to one of Gran's horse shows as her plus-one."

"And caused all of her geriatric friends to swoon at your charm, no doubt." Ellie placed her hand over his on the bed. "Like old times. Before Angelica."

He closed his eyes, in part due to the pain, in part to avoid Ellie's knowing look. "I lost my way, El, but I don't mean to stay there." He met her gaze. "I don't *want* to stay there anymore."

"Which is why you're here." Her brows hovered northward to add emphasis. "Of your *own* accord."

"With some heavy prodding from our parents."

"But still of your own accord, which shows where your heart truly is." She searched his face, the gentleness in her expression dousing some of his self-loathing. There was barely a year of difference between them, and surprisingly, he was the elder of the two. But over the past two years, she'd superseded him in wisdom and solid life choices. "You know I understand how hard it is to rise from bad choices, but here you are."

"Here I am, for my fresh start."

And he'd bungled it masterfully so far.

An image of the silver-eyed woman emerged in his mind again, and this time he was standing in front of her, looking down into her heart-shaped face.

"What . . . exactly happened last night?"

Ellie's nose wrinkled with her frown, digging a deeper trench for his unease. "Do you remember anything?"

He closed his eyes, and a few images filtered through. The first one . . .

Arran shot a look at his sister. "Did I get sick on a woman?"

"You did." Ellie squinted. "All over the front of her."

His stomach knotted as another foggy memory emerged. "And . . . and I hit her in the face?" His eyes wilted closed again, the pain in his chest now rivaling the one in his head. "I've never hit a woman."

"You didn't *mean* to."

The story of his life. He didn't *mean* to mess up, and yet he did. He didn't *mean* to look like an idiot. But here he was.

"Is she alright?"

"She's fine, I believe. Her name is Charlotte. She's Luke's cousin."

His shoulder slumped beneath the weight of his ongoing stupidity. "Then I'll see her again so I can apologize properly."

"Arran." Ellie leaned forward and squeezed his arm. "You're going to be alright. I know you are." She drew in a long breath. "Apart from our parents, I know you better than anyone else in our family. You love hard, so you hurt deeply, but you're choosing to change. Father and Mother have seen it. So have others. Getting away from the past and unhealthy distractions as you try to move forward is a good idea. Working with your hands and your heart is too, whilst you attempt to remember who you *really* are."

The scene in the bar rushed back to mind. If he wasn't Arran St. Clare, Prince of Bredon and the Western Isles, who was he?

And was it possible to find out in this obscure little town in the Blue Ridge Mountains?

The idea worked through him like a splinter, almost emerging from the skin but not quite. The ache in his chest grew. If he looked too closely at his own heart, he wasn't too certain he'd like what was left without a crown.

THREE

What exactly is 'roofing a house'?" Arran asked from the passenger seat of Ellie's car.

Arran's head still ached, but his heart ached worse. The idea of failing so expertly within the first hour of his planned reformation, wounding an innocent woman, and sorting out how to crawl out of this monstrous hole of his own creation loomed so large, it felt impossible.

What he needed was a little time. Reflection. A few days to work out a plan.

Not . . . whatever it was that sent him careening up a mountainside for some "project" of his brother-in-law's.

"Am I putting an actual roof on a house?" he asked.

"The shingles." Ellie pinched her lips tight in a failed effort to tame her smile. "The top of the roof has to be replaced."

He accepted this information with a nod. "Manual labor, I can do."

"Your *ability* has never been in question. You've proven it years before this situation with Angelica." The tenderness in Ellie's voice drew his attention back to her. "The goal is to get your head and your heart in the right place, to match whatever future you choose. Royal or not."

Her declaration, spoken in a gentle way, hollowed out his chest even more, nailing the earlier epiphany into painful clarity. He'd never considered any other life.

"Here we are."

The car rolled to a stop in front of a large house made of white stone and windows, all poised in a clearing overlooking the treetops. Layers of mountains spread on all sides, revealing threaded colors of red, orange, and yellow overtaking the evergreen. The world in full autumn glory.

It was magnificent.

And reminded him of home.

"At least you'll have a nice view while you work." Ellie tossed him a grin as she exited the car, and Arran followed. "Maybe it will inspire a proper perspective too."

"You used to be funnier." His brows rose in challenge, but she laughed.

"And you used to be more laid-back."

Arran opened his mouth to respond, but a noise from above caught his attention.

"Just in time."

Arran followed Ellie's gaze and cupped his hand over his eyes to shade the sun. Luke Edgewood, green ball cap on his head, stared down at them from the housetop.

"We just finished removing the shingles and are ready to start the *real* work." The man's grin broadened. "But don't worry. I always start off *real* easy for the pampered folks."

The tip of Luke's grin disappeared into his close-shaved brown beard at the challenge, which bristled every competitive bone in Arran's body.

So this is how his new brother-in-law wanted to work.

Arran pulled his borrowed cap out of his back pocket and crammed it down on his head. "Point me in the proper direction, and I'll happily show you what I can do."

"I like the sound of that." Luke gestured with his chin. "The ladder's on the side of the house."

Arran bid Ellie goodbye, found his way around the side of the house, and with more of a struggle than anticipated, climbed the wobbly ladder.

The view took on an even more spectacular appearance without trees blocking the horizon, but it also highlighted how exposed their position was.

And high.

A welcome cool breeze wafted over the tops of the trees, bringing the scent of pine . . . and a little waver to Arran's stance. He pressed his feet into the roof to attempt to ground himself. Which sounded ridiculous when on a roof.

"Good to see you, Arran." Luke walked toward him as if simply stepping across pavement instead of a slanted rooftop. "We can certainly use another hand up here."

"Seems that's what I'm here to do."

Luke rested his palms on his hips and studied Arran from cap to boots. "Well, you look the part." One of his dark brows rose. "I reckon the right attitude will take a little longer."

The wink he added at the end somehow doused the edge of Arran's discomfort. "The work is that rigorous, is it?"

A measuring look, which somehow made Arran stand a bit taller, crossed Luke's face and his grin widened. "You may walk funny for a few days, but I have high hopes you're gonna be just fine." Luke held Arran's gaze long enough to hint that the man's words meant something a little deeper than not plunging to his death, and Arran embraced his current situation with a bit more hope than a moment before.

Could this man take him at face value? Even knowing his past as Luke did?

Luke's honest confidence somehow transferred over to Arran. Perhaps his brother-in-law wasn't such a bad sort after all.

"That's Dave." Luke waved toward a burly man nearby, his

ginger hair and beard in contrast to Luke's darker features. "If I'm not around, he can answer your questions, but don't expect a conversation. He's not much for talking."

Dave nodded and turned back to his work.

Luke started across the roof, presumably for Arran to follow . . . with much less confident steps. "He's taking over the business while I'm in Skymar with Ellie next year."

At one point, as Arran unknowingly veered too close to the edge of the house, Luke grabbed him by the arm and tugged him away.

"Careful there." He patted Arran's shoulder. "I promised Ellie I'd take good care of you, so you'd better watch your step." He chuckled and led the way at a slower pace. "The rest of the team is working on another project south of town, so it's gonna be the three of us until Charlie joins us after lunch."

The three of them? For an entire roof? Arran's gaze trailed the length of the space. Was that normal?

Another breeze drew his attention to the kaleidoscope of autumn color.

"Not a bad view for a workday, is it?"

Arran pulled his gaze from the horizon. "Not at all."

"As long as that pretty view doesn't pull you too close to the edge." Luke waved toward Dave again as the man moved over the roofline, hammer in hand, body bent as if searching for something. "Since we already stripped the roof, we have to search for loose nails, roof damage"—he raised a finger with each item—"or rot that may need repairing before placing on the new roof."

Arran didn't fully comprehend all the word choices but got the basic meaning.

At least he hoped, because the last thing he wanted to do was prove more imbecilic than his actions had already shown.

He stifled a groan.

Brilliantly imbecilic. He ought to write a book: *How to Make Ten Imbecilic Choices Within Three Hours in a New Country.*

Luke pulled a hammer from the tool belt around his waist. "Ever swung a hammer?"

"A few times."

"Welp, this is a great way to get warmed up." He gestured with the hammer toward the massive roof. "Just go along this side. If you see any nails sticking out, you'll either drive 'em back in so they're flush with the roof or pull them out if they're loose." He pressed the hammer into Arran's outstretched hand and reached into the front pocket of his tool belt. "Here are some nails if you have to replace any."

Maybe Arran overestimated his skill set. Walking on a roof poised atop a mountain, attempting to locate loose nails without falling to his death as the breeze gave a mocking ruffle to his hair, tempted fate.

"Make sense?"

"Aye." Arran scanned the space, keeping his gaze from Luke's in case the man could mind-read fear. "I believe so."

"Good." Luke gave a curt nod. "It's not the steepest roof, but why don't you stay near the midline of the house, for starters?"

Arran dipped his head, and Luke walked off to work with some sort of large black sheets of . . . paper?

Four hours later, Arran's body ached, sweat rolled over every part of his skin, and his vocabulary had expanded with new words like *tar paper*, *drip edges*, and *flashing*. Despite his love for more strenuous sports like mountain climbing, they'd failed to sufficiently prepare him for the rigor of holding one's balance on a roof while simultaneously attempting not to tear the tar paper or knock a fellow worker to his death.

Roofing also increased Arran's prayer life by volumes.

As Arran sat for a moment, finishing off a bottled water, Luke joined him, his own water in hand. "You might want to take your time getting out of bed in the morning. Your thighs aren't going to be happy with you."

Who needed to wait for the morning? Arran's body already ached from neck to ankles. Even his ears hurt.

"I'd take an ibuprofen or a few Tylenols tonight too." Luke raised his water to his lips. "It'll help for tomorrow. Besides, you'll need to be ambulatory by Thursday, at least."

"Thursday?" A sudden dread doused his newfound sense of comradery.

"Shucks, I thought Ellie would've told you." He took another drink of water, in no hurry to abate Arran's curiosity, it seemed. "It's the first fundraiser for The Mistletoe Wish, the charity you've been roped into as part of your time here."

Ah yes! One of the stipulations of his penance.

1. Earn an income.
2. Become involved in a charity.
3. Discover who he was and what he wanted (his own personal addition).

The first two were already in the works.

The daunting third? Well, time would tell, but as he looked out over the horizon, he embraced the desire to prove to his sister, brother-in-law, and the poor woman he'd accosted last night that he was a better man than his first impression.

Luke stood and Arran pushed through his sore muscles and followed. "What about this fundraiser, and . . ." Arran's grin twitched, seeking some levity to counterbalance the sudden desire to wince at the pain shooting up his legs. "Did you say 'mistletoe'?"

"Don't get any ideas, Romeo." Luke raised a brow. "The word

mistletoe was chosen because of what it stands for, not for the smooching it inspires."

"Stands for?"

"The idea comes from our Appalachian-Scottish heritage. You see, because mistletoe can withstand harsh winters, it was revered as a symbol of resilience, protection, and love. Which fits what we hope to instill in the children served by the charity." He walked over to the edge of the roof and dropped his bottle over the side and into a rubbish pile they'd been collecting throughout the day. "But Charlie will be able to tell you more about it. She's the reluctant coordinator this year."

Oh, so this Charlie was a woman?

And resilience, protection, and love? Worthy aspirations. Heroic, even.

"So, a Christmas charity?"

"Sure is. The towns of Mount Airy and Ransom get involved. Thursday is just the beginning of a set of fundraisers. You're helping set up the booth at the Ransom Fall Festival. It always happens the weekend of the carnival."

A festival and a carnival? Arran's muscles rejoiced in unison. He could manage those.

"Booths run up and down Main Street, with the carnival set up just at the edge of the town. With all the tourists and visitors, it's a great time to raise money for The Wish."

"I've always enjoyed a good carnival."

"Don't get too comfortable." Luke tossed a look over his shoulder as he moved across the roof. "I imagine Charlie will have plenty of work for you to do."

Luke's gaze caught on something below. "Speaking of . . . she just pulled up." Luke started moving toward the back of the house without further explanation. "Good time to ask her more about it, if you want."

A festival certainly added a bit of silver lining to near-death experiences on a roof.

Arran followed Luke and Dave down the ladder, his movements much slower than four hours ago. They rounded the front of the house to find a woman with her back to them, pulling a few boxes of pizza from a little red truck.

Why did the truck look strangely familiar?

"Sorry I'm late, boys."

The woman turned, and heat fled every part of Arran's body.

The ball cap over brown hair.

The unusual silver eyes.

The heart-shaped face and little chin.

He'd seen her before. Though he didn't recall the white bandage across her nose.

"Oh no, Charlie." Luke rushed forward, tugging the pizza boxes from her arms. "Did the doc say it was broken?"

Arran pulled his attention from the woman's striking eyes, his brain piecing together where she fit into his sketchy recollection. *Broken?*

The memory rushed to the front of his mind with full force.

He'd slammed his head into her nose, hadn't he? His stomach seized as he replayed the incident in his mind with bone-aching clarity.

Charlie was . . . Charlotte. Luke's cousin.

"Only a hairline fracture." She turned back to the truck.

"No!" The word erupted from Arran in a shocked breath. He stepped forward as she spun around, a carton of canned drinks in her hands. "Was that because of me?"

Her averted glance proved the truth he feared.

"I'm so sorry." His throat closed around a groan, and he took the carton from her. "Please forgive me."

Something flickered in her gaze before she shrugged off his apology. "I know it was an accident, okay? Let's move on."

"But if I hadn't behaved like a cretin in the first place, this never would have happened."

She studied him, a curious crook to her grin. "I'll be fine." She dismissed him with a glance. "You boys hungry?"

What must she think of him? *An utter failure and rake, is what.* And her response only secured his decision.

He'd prove to them all who he truly was: a man worthy of his position as a royal, a worker humble enough to learn a new skill and faithful enough to keep working, and—his gaze fastened on the woman—someone who knew how to treat a lady.

Despite first impressions.

It was the least he could do.

"Doc thought I ought to keep my feet on the ground for a few days, Luke." She laid out a few plates on a makeshift table of "saw-horses," as Luke called them. "Said my nose needs a bit more healing before I add heights to it."

"Take as much time as you need."

"I'll keep working on orders from home, then." Charlotte—Charlie—took a can from the drink container and opened it with a *click*. "Which reminds me, Arnold down at the quarry said he can deliver your stone to the Foxes' place at the beginning of next week."

"Good." Luke nodded, turning his attention to Arran. "That will be our next project. Laying stone for a patio and chimney. Tough work, but real pretty." He took a can and handed it to Arran. "By the time we finish with you, Arran, you might even trade in that crown for some overalls and a hammer."

"Or go running back to the castle as quickly as you can," Charlie muttered, tossing a slice of pizza on a paper plate and handing it to him, her slender brows high. "Is paper alright for you, Your Highness?"

Another memory from last night lanced through him. "I'd rather you call me Arran, my lady." His charm bounced right off her glare. "I am truly sorry about last night, Charlotte. I hope I can make a better impression in the future."

She gestured toward her face with her drink, one brow arched. "As long as your next impression doesn't leave a mark."

He winced and Luke burst out laughing. "You two better learn how to get along because you're going to be spending *a lot* of time together, especially with The Wish."

Charlotte folded her arms across her chest, making her lack of faith in him fully known.

"Now, Charlie, Arran's got a whole host of experiences with navigating social functions and speaking in front of folks." Luke sent him a reassuring look. "And he's here to prove he's fit to help serve those kids and families too."

Charlotte's raised brow told Arran three things:

1. Charlotte Edgewood wasn't too keen on his help.
2. He had a long way to go to change her mind about him.
3. Silver eyes were fascinating.

FOUR

How was Charlie going to work with Prince Nosebreaker for eight weeks?

Eight weeks!

What on earth could a pampered royal understand about these hurting kids? And she didn't need any more "impressions" from him to know The Mistletoe Wish didn't need *his* brand of help.

"I don't know if The Wish is the right fit for someone of Prince Arran's caliber."

Luke's head locked into a tilt as he stared at Charlie. "I thought you needed all the help you could—"

"Volunteering is for folks who are used to working with people in more"—she waved her drink can as if to find the word—"humble and broken situations. Which means the spotlight isn't on the volunteers." Her gaze flashed to Arran. "It's on the kids."

Prince Delinquent's golden brows took an upswing. "I realize I've not given you much reason to trust me or my abilities, but I can assure you there will be no repeat of last night."

She stared back into those blue eyes, searching for any hint of insincerity.

"Charlie, Ellie recommended him because she thinks he'd be a great help. He has experience with fundraisers on the scale of an entire country, so first impressions may not be all they're cracked up to be in this case. Besides, you know how Murphy is with new folks."

She shot Luke a powerless glare. First of all, why did he have to invoke Ellie's name? Charlie adored Ellie and desperately needed the woman's help to reform her wardrobe and public speaking abilities and . . . well, all of her.

Low blow from the cousin.

Number two? Second chances were Charlie's ultimate kryptonite. Her favorite movie and book trope.

She sent the prince another look and then released a sigh, his work-worn clothes and dusty brow softening her ire.

"Fine," she announced as heat rose into her face. "I can certainly use the help."

Arran stepped closer. "Again, I apologize for . . ." His attention moved to her nose. "Everything. And I am determined to make all future impressions much better than the first. Hopefully I can prove I am not who you think I am."

The intensity in his stare proved more uncomfortable than the ache in her nose.

And suddenly, she wasn't too sure she wanted him to disprove her initial belief. Because perhaps his determination for a second chance might leave a more lasting impression than any nose-breaking episode.

As soon as she could manage, she left the worksite and went home. Mostly because she didn't like the way the Snoring Sovereign kept looking at her. As if he truly was sorry for last night *and* . . . that he saw her in ways she didn't fully understand.

But Charlie also wanted to review notes with someone for her first supervised fundraiser.

She hated to admit it, but she *did* need another reliable person on her team . . . assuming the Royal Rascal could be reliable.

Would he really be able to prove those first impressions false?

She shook the question from her mind and revisited her own need for improvements. How was she ever going to refine herself enough to present as a well-spoken, composed lady?

Then a good old-fashioned Appalachian idea popped to mind. *What about a trade?*

Her grin tipped in sync with the growing epiphany. If she agreed to help Ellie's brother succeed at this royal reformation experiment, then perhaps Ellie would give Charlie the makeover she needed.

December offered a perfect goal point, with the Gala speech as her finale.

She pushed through the front door of her house, fixed some tea, and then settled down at her desk to review the volunteer and equipment list for the fall festival. She'd barely made it through a few files when her phone buzzed to life. Ellie's name popped up on the screen.

Charlie raised the phone to her ear and barely got out the words, "Hey, Ellie."

"Arran broke your nose!"

Charlie relaxed back in her desk chair. "It's fine. Really."

"At first I thought Arran's somber mood was due to working with Luke." The sadness in Ellie's voice paused Charlie's sarcasm a little, and the image of him asking for forgiveness came back to mind. "But then he couldn't stop mentioning his horror in hurting you and secondary remorse in behaving like a complete idiot."

Charlie's lips twitched. Okay, maybe the sarcasm could never be completely subdued. She was an Edgewood, after all.

"It's not like I haven't been hit in the nose before. I work in construction with a bunch of men."

"You need to know, Charlotte, Arran is a good guy." Ellie sighed. "I know women usually excel at being the most impacted by heartbreak, but Arran's path of self-destruction could very well win an award. It's only been in the last few months that we've seen glimpses of the man he used to be before . . . Angelica."

Angelica? Heartbreak? Her chest twinged a teensy bit in response. But Charlie decided ignorance proved the safer choice.

"And, of course, everything is distorted or exaggerated when the media becomes involved."

The very idea of the media following her around sent a shudder through her body, and her ire toward the prince eased a little more. In the grand scheme of things, Arran's initial impression truly was a small thing. Especially with the knowledge of Murphy's pride and the potency of his home-brewed whiskey.

Another chink in her frustration collapsed. Forgiveness was one of the most beautiful themes of the Bible and a comforting truth she'd revisited throughout her life. Her father exemplified his choice to forgive in the way he'd prayed for and spoken about Mom, despite all she'd done, encouraging Charlie to forgive as well.

She sighed. Everyone needed the opportunity for a second chance. Even rogue princes with perfect hair and teeth and crazy-blue eyes.

"But truly," Ellie continued, "once you see him when he's not suffering from poor judgment and an inflated sense of self-importance, you may find him quite endearing."

Charlie's tight-lipped hold on her grin started to loosen at "poor judgment" and completely disappeared at "inflated sense of self-importance." The idea of finding the guy who'd vomited on her "endearing" had her losing all control of her laugh. "Endearing? Hmm . . . I'm not sure I see that on the horizon."

"Well, at least you still have your sense of humor." Charlie thought she heard a slight smile that warmed Ellie's words. "And I truly believe working with the charity will not only highlight his strengths but prove good for his heart. He's always loved and excelled at service."

Service?

The Snoring Sovereign loves service?

Charlie barely stifled her eye roll. *Sure.*

Charlie shook away the thought and launched into her newly

concocted plan. "You want Arran to highlight his best qualities, right?"

"Yes."

"And I need someone to teach me how to present myself well: hair, clothes, dancing, public speaking . . ."

"Am I hearing you want a makeover? Oh, this is delightful!" The lilt in Ellie's voice sparked a twinge of hope and fear. "With your eyes and that hair . . ."

"But nothing extreme. Just to help me become more polished. Tips, really." Charlie's face grew hot. "Simple. Classy."

"Of course." Ellie sounded much too excited. "So, basically, you'll help Arran with a reputation and heart makeover, of sorts, while Arran and I assist you in a makeover at the superficial level."

Wait. *Arran?*

"It's a perfect exchange," Ellie continued. "When I'm gone for business, he'll be here to help you. And you can provide some added motivation for Arran's reformation."

Charlie's stomach dropped. "What do you mean?"

"He is determined to prove to you that a pint and pub are not the sum of who he is."

Charlie's grin twitched again, the entire situation almost un-believable. A mutual makeover, of sorts, between a prince and a carpenter?

Crazy stuff. Sounded like a reality TV show idea.

"So, you'll agree to it?"

"You have a deal." The smile in Ellie's voice was undeniable.

"Perfect, because I could really use some public speaking help soon. My first presentation is at the end of the month, at a county-wide in-service for all the faculty of the schools. I'm trying to en-courage community involvement in The Wish. Plus, teachers and social workers can offer more names of folks we can serve."

"I'll email you a list of ideas. Some staples for your wardrobe and fashion tips. And we could meet next week, perhaps, to talk about dancing and presentation?"

Charlie's stomach vaulted at the idea of revisiting the long-forgotten waters of . . . girliness. "Sounds great."

They hung up, and Charlie leaned back in her chair.

Maybe she'd never learned how to be a "lady" since she was raised by a mountain-man single dad and inclined to hang out with "the boys." But deep inside she wondered if her tomboyishness had something to do with the fact that if she put forth effort to look attractive or poised, and failed . . . then she was only proving Mama right.

That Charlie wasn't enough.

And proving her mama right was the last thing she ever wanted to do.

FIVE

There's a good chance Luke Edgewood enlisted in Operation: Reform Arran to instill torture.

Or at least that's what Arran's muscles had been screaming each morning he woke to begin yet another workday. Though the hard work and comradery of his brother-in-law provided a twin sense of pride and . . . surprising friendship. Plus, he'd enjoyed observing Luke and Ellie together in the privacy of their home, their mutual affection and complementary relationship plain for all to see. They teased each other, shared the work, and enjoyed simply spending time together, with Luke supporting Ellie's interior design skills and diplomatic responsibilities and Ellie encouraging Luke's business.

A real team. A friendship. With all the added benefits of romance.

Arran drew in a deep breath. He'd always wanted a romance like that. Genuine, thoughtful, and lovely romantic friendship. A ridiculous thing to voice aloud, but tucked between his ears the thought settled over him with renewed welcome.

Angelica, with all her pretense and selfishness, could never have given him a home with such authenticity and joy. And that's what he knew he wanted now, a home filled with the same connection and joy he saw with Luke and Ellie, the same he'd witnessed in his parents. A shame it took him so many mistakes and two years of heartache to sort it out.

The walk down Main Street in Ransom helped stretch out his muscles and introduced him to an even more storybook-like setting than Mount Airy. A well-organized conglomeration of manicured buildings sat along a principal street lined with lampposts and a few trees—a lovely way to intermingle nature among brick and stone, with the blue-toned mountains on the horizon.

As Arran neared the city center, an assemblage of aromas, from buttery popcorn to nuts roasted with brown sugar and cinnamon, ushered him into the fray of voices and laughter and children's giggles.

He checked his watch. The fair and carnival didn't begin for another two hours, yet hundreds of people already weaved among the booths lining the street. With Luke's directions in hand, Arran followed the pavement to an old brick church with a steeple towering into the blue sky. A green tented booth stretched along the front of the churchyard, myriad potted flowers taking up one side of the grass beside the tent, each tied with a ribbon.

Were those potted plants donated by a garden center for The Wish? Luke mentioned donations for the charity came all year long—hand crafts, small furniture items, quilts, and even flowers.

The power of a community coming together truly held its own magic.

He rounded the edge of the booth to find Charlotte behind a central table wearing a T-shirt, jeans, and a ball cap and sorting through a box.

"Are all those flowers donations?"

Charlotte's gaze came up, the white bandage across the bridge of her nose a poignant reminder of his stupidity.

"Isn't it remarkable?" Her lips curved into a cautious smile. "And this year we've gotten the most donations ever." Those silver eyes brightened with her statement. "I think we'll be able to serve at least a dozen more kids if we can sell all this."

"I'm glad I'm here to help, then."

"Sure."

But her voice lacked conviction as she looked away. He wasn't sure why—maybe it was the broken nose and his complete idiocy, but once again, the desire to prove to her he wasn't the sum of their first meeting pushed him into action.

"What would you have me do?"

Charlotte studied him for a moment before stepping around the table toward him, her long ponytail swishing behind her. "I could use help organizing and pricing the furniture there." She gestured toward the group of motley chairs and small tables, even a decorated bookshelf or two. "I've marked down everything on this itemized list." She offered him a clipboard. "And made the price tags. But I've not had a chance to sort them."

"I can do that." He took the clipboard.

"Thanks." Her brow creased as she studied him again. "And a local farmer, Jack James, is donating some fresh pumpkins that we'll need to set up for sale too." A flicker of light returned to her eyes. "Big ones."

"Excellent."

Was that playful little spark a glimpse at the real Charlotte? Each time he'd met her before during the construction work, she'd remained somewhat distant, but that spark of excitement hinted at something more.

A charming playfulness.

"We only have about two hours before everything begins." She waved toward the items. "So you'd better stop dillydallying and get to work."

"Dillydallying?" He paused in his turn, tentatively stepping into a little teasing. "You mean to enjoy bossing me around a little bit, don't you?"

"Oh no." She shook her head, her lips twisting into a crooked grin. "I plan to enjoy it a *whole* lot."

His eyes narrowed ever so slightly, and then, with a sweeping bow and his gaze never leaving hers, he said, "It is my honor to serve, my lady."

A rush of lovely pink brushed her cheeks, and the sight made him pause. It had been a while since he'd seen a woman sincerely and sweetly blush. The picture stuck in his mind.

She was lovely.

"Very funny." She shook her head and backed away. "Now get to work before I think you're afraid of it."

They worked over an hour, sorting and organizing and pricing, before Jack James and his pumpkins arrived. Enormous. Arran had never seen such pumpkins.

"Told you." Charlotte walked up beside him as he stared at the massive offerings in the back of Jack's truck.

"You could build a village inside of those."

"Not quite." She coughed out a laugh. "But imagine the pies you could make."

"How many, do you reckon?"

She stared down at the pumpkin Arran had just pulled into his arms. "Three or four, maybe?"

"Three or four pumpkin pies." He sighed and turned toward the booth. "I love pies."

She came up beside him, a smaller pumpkin in her arms, but still larger than he'd expected her to carry. Of course, she worked with Luke, so she must be strong. "Have you ever bobbed for apples or played the 'Shoot the Ducks' game at the fair, Your Highness?"

He frowned at the honorific. It didn't fit here. Or her.

"I can't say I even know what you're talking about, Charlotte."

"Of course." She rolled her eyes. "You're a prince."

"And a foreigner," he added, lowering his pumpkin to a designated spot and walking back to the truck.

"What about a hayride? Or a big, loud, sometimes dangerous Thanksgiving dinner?" Even as she spoke, her smile grew wider, and something akin to a glow spread through his chest like internal sunshine.

Strange. And . . . unnerving.

"Am I supposed to *want* to experience the latter option?"

"You haven't fully had an Appalachian American experience without one." She shot him a look. "I have another question."

He settled another pumpkin in place. "Alright."

"Did you decide to call me Charlotte just to irritate me?"

He studied her, his grin twitching for release. "*Does* it irritate you?"

"Not irritate, exactly." Her brows creased as she looked up at him. "It's just that everyone calls me Charlie."

"Charlotte is a lovely name, and"—he studied her, the defined and feminine curve of her chin, the slender slope of her nose, and those steely gray eyes—"it suits you better than Charlie, to my mind."

Her nose wrinkled with her frown. "Your sister said the same thing."

"We have a particular fondness for the name. There are quite a few impressive Charlottes in our family history. You'd fit in with them, I think."

One of her brows rose. "Would I?"

"Oh yes." He picked up another pumpkin, pinching back his smile. "Strong, bighearted."

"Well, that sounds nice."

"A bit stubborn."

"Hey," she warned.

He peered over his shoulder, watching her lips war with a smile as she caught up with him. "But am I wrong?"

She shrugged. "*Determined* sounds better."

"Ah yes." He nodded. "You're right. Then I feel certain you are the *very* determined sort."

She raised her chin, stepping back. "And what sort are you?"

He sighed. "I'm afraid you've already come to your own conclusions on that score."

She placed her pumpkin down next to his and then studied him with hands on her hips. "Well, I'm all for you proving me wrong."

And with a little tip of her head, she turned toward the booth.

His grin grew as he followed her retreating form all the way into the booth, her declaration fueling his determination all the more.

"Miss Charlie!"

A boy rushed forward, copper-colored hair bouncing atop his head with his frantic pace. He pushed passed Arran into the booth. "It's the worst ever." His young voice rose with dramatic flair, his large blue eyes equally desperate. "We're ruined."

"What on earth is wrong, Jay?" Charlie didn't respond with the same desperation. "You're loud enough to wake the dead."

"But it's just awful. Patton is sick, and Lou Duncan's got a broken leg." His bottom lip quivered. "And my booth is supposed to open in fifteen minutes. *Fifteen*."

"Is there something I can do to help?" Arran stepped forward, drawing the boy's attention toward him for the first time.

Jay grimaced, unimpressed, and turned back to Charlotte. "You reckon there's somebody who can take the spot until Danny shows up? He's gonna be here in an hour, but that's a whole hour of losing prime customers. We make a lot of money the first night." He released a sigh so large it shook his whole body. "This ain't never happened in all my living days!"

Which only looked to be about eleven or twelve years.

"I can't leave this booth, Jay." Charlotte turned to Arran. "Could you stand in, just for the hour? It would certainly be a valiant thing to do to rescue one of the"—she made air quotes—"'best money-making booths of the festival.'"

Valiant rescue? That sounded like a worthy way to improve her opinion of him. "Of course."

"Jay, this is Prince Arran." She shook her head as if she hadn't planned to refer to him, title and all. "What exactly did you need help with?"

"Well, I reckon he'll do." The boy gave Arran a thorough perusal, lips at an uncertain smirk. "Doesn't take a whole lot of thinking anyhow. Just gotta sit real still."

Sit still?

Charlotte's brow creased with a confusion similar to what Arran felt. "I feel certain he can meet that expectation."

Her confidence was underwhelming.

"Alright, Prince." He waved his hand for Arran to follow and used the word more like a first name than a title. "You're so big, you'll be an *easy* target."

"Target?" Arran shot a look at Charlotte, whose eyes grew wide.

"Yeah." Jay ushered Arran forward. "For the pie-throwing contest."

Pie throwing?

A laugh erupted behind him, but when he turned, Charlotte wore a look of utter innocence. She offered a helpless shrug and waved toward the boy.

"Perfect, Jay." Charlotte's grin spread as slow and dangerous as the Cheshire cat's. "Arran is the man for you. He loves pies."

SIX

Two hours.

Charlie hadn't seen Arran in two hours.

What on earth had Jay done to the poor man?

As soon as her cousin Penelope relieved Charlie from her post, she rushed up the street, passing several vendors in search of the prince.

Fading daylight had ignited the glowing lampposts lining Main Street, but they failed to provide any sign of Arran. Then a loud shout erupted from the large crowd up ahead, slowing Charlie's approach.

Her gaze lifted to the sign above the crowd: "Pie Throwing." And scrawled in hasty handwriting beneath those words were: "Pie a Prince."

Air burst from her lungs.

What? She squeezed through the crowd to the front.

And her jaw dropped.

And, maybe, the teeniest bit of pity welled up at the sight.

Two chairs sat a few feet apart. One held sixteen-year-old Danny, who regularly participated in the pie-throwing booth. Next to him sat Arran, much worse for the wear than Danny. White cream splattered his neck down to his knees, with vanilla pudding studding his torso in varying-sized blobs.

His blond hair curled up on one side, sticky and stiff, while the other side dripped flat.

Charlie stopped just in time to watch a pie land directly in the center of Arran's chest with an unsatisfying *thud*. The crowd exploded as the remainder of the pie slid down to the man's stomach and fell over onto his lap.

Her bottom lip dropped. *Oh, good heavens!*

Her attention flew to the mischievous little ginger at the table, taking cash from folks in line with a smile to compete with the best swindler.

Eleven-year-old boys could be incredibly sneaky when they put their minds to it. But though Jay tended toward the rascally side of normal, did he have the power to convince Prince Arran of pie pummeling?

As soon as the little boy's blue eyes met Charlie's, his grin spread from one dimple to the other. "You won't believe it, Miss Charlie. It's only the first night, and we've already raked in over a hundred dollars!"

His announcement paused her inquiry. Over a hundred dollars? In less than two hours? How was that even possible?

Her attention flitted back to Arran. Thankfully, this time the pie only landed on his knee, but the crowd shouted with no less enthusiasm.

"Come on, lad!" Arran shouted to the teenager who'd thrown the pie, his accent curling. "Can't you do better than that? My knee?"

Charlie's comment to Jay died on her tongue. Arran was egging on the throwers?

The teen stiffened and rushed back to the table, purchasing another pie.

"See?" Jay said, pointing in Arran's direction. "He's been like that from almost the start. Once he realized it brought in more folks."

"How did you lot best Britain with aim like that?" Arran called back to the crowd, resulting in a mixture of laughter and outcry. "My granny's got a better arm than the likes of you!"

Charlie was still trying to formulate words in her head. What on earth was happening?

"*He* came up with the idea, Charlie. I promise. Things were going swell before Danny showed up, but once Danny arrived, Arran said we ought to have a *real* competition."

She blinked from Arran back to Danny. "Competition?"

"You know how the cost is two dollars for a regular throw. Well, Arran suggested we say it's five dollars to Pie a Prince, and then the extra proceeds can go to The Mistletoe Wish."

That strategy certainly didn't fit the Pukey Prince from a few nights ago.

"And he just keeps getting folks riled up enough to come back for more."

Charlie stared at the prince in question, trying to get her brain to reconcile her assessment of him with this entire scene. "Well, I think it's time to give the poor man a break, Jay. He's been at it long enough."

"Yeah, okay." Jay looked down longingly at the tin box of money and sighed before returning his attention to Charlie. "I don't think he's a real prince, anyway. Real princes don't do pie-throwing contests."

Evidently this one does.

She blinked through the thought a few more times.

How could Arran mess with her "prince" assumptions on both ends of the fairy tale? Sloshed Sovereign and Pie Prince? She didn't know of one fairy tale with that combination. Flynn Rider from *Tangled* probably got the closest.

"You throw like a girl, mate. Can't you do any better?"

She caught her laugh with her palm. Who was this guy?

At that moment, Arran's gaze found hers and the grin froze on his face.

One of his brows arched.

She steadied her expression, her own brow mirroring his as she stepped forward. "'Throw like a girl'?" Charlie called above the crowd. "Are you disrespecting women, Your Highness?" The crowd quieted at her words. "Not a very noble trait for a prince."

His grin fell for only a second before it resurfaced with a glint in his eyes. "Do you plan to prove me wrong, Miss Edgewood?"

An "Oooh!" came from a few folks nearby, encouraging the challenge.

"Oh yeah." She pinched her lips tight against a laugh. She liked this version of Prince Nosebreaker. "I sure am."

She reached for a pie on the table, but Arran shook his head. "No cheating, Charlotte."

The use of her name brought a rush of warmth to her cheeks.

He needled her with a teasing look. "It's five dollars to Pie a Prince." His brows rose in challenge. "Even for you."

A few in the crowd laughed in response.

Charlie almost joined them. Without breaking eye contact, she reached into her back pocket, pulled out a bill, and slapped it down on the table in front of Jay.

"That's a ten, Charlie," came Jay's response.

She nodded, picking up two of the pies. "It sure is."

Without one hitch, Arran leaned back in the chair and folded his arms across his chest, waiting with a much-too-relaxed air for her liking. Very princely.

"Go for his face, Charlie!" came a call from the crowd.

"The hair! Get him on the hair, then it'll drip down his face!" cried another.

Man, these folks were ruthless.

Her gaze never left Arran's as she drew up to the throw line.

"Okay, y'all!" Charlie called back to the crowd. "How many of you will give an extra dollar if I hit him on the chin?"

Hands flew up.

"A dollar?" Arran shook his head as if unimpressed. "For this chin? It's worth much more than that."

She snorted out her laugh.

"What about the nose?" Charlie said back to the crowd.

"Two dollars!" someone called.

"Cheap." Arran scoffed, gesturing toward his face. "This is a royal nose."

She nearly lost the battle with her grin yet again. "Who's in for two dollars each if I get him on the nose and put this Mouthy Monarch in his place?"

Arran's golden brows shot high at her moniker, but the crowd's approval roared.

"Let's not make this personal, Charlotte." His warm voice steeped over the night air, sending another temperature hike to her cheeks. "Mouthy Monarch?"

"What about Royal Rogue?" She drew the first pie back.

"I think what you meant to say was Sexy Sovereign."

The comment shook her from her focus, and the pie didn't even make it to his shoe. Disappointment echoed from the crowd, despite a few chuckles. In fact, Charlie had even laughed at *that* title.

Sexy? With his hair in all directions and melting cream dotting various spots of his blue shirt?

Her attention fixed on his strong shoulders and chest.

Okay, well, maybe *sexy* would work, but she wasn't about to admit it.

"How about Prince Nosebreaker?"

And, with his mouth wide in response, she released the other pie. It flew through the air and landed with a *plop* directly on Arran's face.

Applause and laughter exploded around them, and within a few minutes, Arran was released from his position as target practice.

As she approached him, her smile almost dissolved into another laugh. He wore an impenetrable grin, which failed to match the rest of his pummeled self.

With great ceremony, he took his finger, wiped it alongside his face, and then licked the cream off. "I told you I like pie." He shrugged a shoulder. "And it worked out well, didn't it?"

"For The Wish, yes." Her gaze skimmed down his front and back up as she tugged a towel off her shoulder. "For you? Not so much."

"I have a pretty good track record of grand gestures to support charities. Well, in previous years. The past two haven't been my best, but before then, I was often chosen to bring attention to things like this." He gave his brows a playful wiggle. "And I don't mind being ridiculous."

"Clearly." She took the towel, wiped it across his chin, then held it out to him for more cleanup.

"But this was good. It reminded me of those times." His smile softened. He took the proffered towel and searched her face. "So, are we even now?"

Even? What?

"You got to hit me in the nose too."

A large drop of cream took that opportunity to slide off his forehead and land on the end of his nose.

She looked heavenward, as if in thought. His request, his desire to make things right, somehow hitting her in the chest. With a deep breath, she glanced back at him. "Yeah, I think we're even."

"Good." He pushed the towel across his face and into his hair.

"Eating that amount of humble pie should definitely earn some compassion points."

Arran's lips crooked. "We can be friends, then?" He offered his hand.

A friendship with a prince? She studied him a second and then sighed. "Sure." She took his hand, ignoring the tightening in her stomach while giving a nonchalant shrug. "Who doesn't want a royal friend to brag about now and again? Very make-believe."

"As you are painfully aware, I am not the fairy-tale sort." He stood up to his full height, tipping up his chin in regal fashion. "But I have every hope of restoring my fairy-tale potential."

She rolled her eyes playfully as she turned and started walking toward the street. "Watch out, you're in the mountains. We're not impressed with princes here." She looked over at him as he fell in step with her. "But folks who will suffer humiliation for a good cause? Well, those kinds of heroes are worth having around."

"Good. I'll aim for that one, then." His expression softened with a gentler smile and he looked ahead. "So, tell me a little more about this Mistletoe Wish."

Friends?

With a prince?

The idea sounded as preposterous as this list of items Ellie had sent her to purchase.

Teardrop earrings. Mary Jane pumps. Peplum-waist blouse.

Not to mention the makeup. Or undergarments.

A balconette? Her cheeks heated at the idea. What even was that?

And how on earth would a bra make a difference in Charlie's presentation abilities?

Charlie stood in front of the largest department store in Ransom a few days later, fighting the desire to run back home and burrow deep into her baggy sweaters and worn-out jeans. The elegant crimson gown on display in the store window mocked her plight.

Impossible.

"You'd look fantastic in that gown."

Charlie spun around to find Arran beside her staring at the window display.

"What?"

"The color and style are stunning for someone with your eyes and figure." He looked over at her as if he'd just said something as flippant as *the sky is blue*. "Breathtaking, even. Are you considering it?"

She blinked over at him, trying to find her voice. "No, I'm not *considering* it." She waved toward the window. "Do you see the size of that skirt? I'd need mice, a pumpkin, and a fairy godmother to justify wearing something like that. And I can't even imagine walking in it."

He looked at her, then back at the gown. "I believe your fear may be magnifying the dress in your mind. If you tried it on, you—"

"Nope. I'm not here to purchase a ball gown for a party at the castle, Your Highness." She gave her head a strong shake. "Besides, I've got enough to do already. I'm trying to sort out this list your sister sent me for my"—she made air quotes—"'becoming a lady' makeover. I think she made up the names for some of these things."

His lips lifted ever so slightly, and he sent a look down her body.

She'd never been so aware of the frayed edges of her baggy sweater and the tightness of her leggings in her life. Ugh. And was she wearing tennis shoes with mismatching shoelaces? Heaven, help her!

"Ah yes. Ellie mentioned something about that while she prepared my own list." He held up a small piece of paper.

"*Your* list?" Charlie slid a step closer, trying to peer at his paper. Weren't his makeover items more like *stay on the straight and narrow* and *work hard*? Because there was nothing wrong with his style. His pale blue polo and fitted jeans proved his list and hers were surely very different.

"I need work clothes. Your cousin has kindly allowed me to

borrow some of his for my first week on the job, but I've been tasked with purchasing some of my own today."

She blew out a long stream of air. "Oh, my list is *so* much harder than yours."

"Is it?"

"Are you kidding?" She snatched his paper from his hand and pointed to a few items. "Yes, see? You just need jeans, flannel shirts, warm socks, boots, and gloves." She turned her paper toward him. "I have things like shoes with names and types of hair clips and ... wrap dresses."

His grin spread so wide, his cheek dimpled just a teensy bit and almost distracted her from her meltdown.

"What in the world is a wrap dress? Sounds like a present."

He leaned in close and wiggled his brows. "It may be, to the right guy."

She offered him a solid glare, despite the volcanic heat rushing to her face and an overwhelming need to laugh. "You just spew charm, don't you?"

"I could spew worse, of which you've been victim."

Charlie's laugh burst out, followed by a horrifyingly impressive snort.

Arran's golden brows shot skyward, his lips breaking into a wicked grin.

"See? This is why I need a makeover. I can't snort-laugh in front of the mayor of Ransom!"

"You're having a makeover because of your snort-laugh?" The glint in his eyes was not helping her sense of mortification. "It really wasn't that bad, Charlotte. My mum has an excellent snort-laugh, and she's queen."

"A snort-laugh is the least of my worries." Charlie sighed. "I'm not ready to present to donors and school boards and the bigwigs of the county. And I certainly can't show up like this." She sent a look down her super casual and not-at-all-classy outfit. "I mean, I'm glad Daddy taught me how to work hard and love people well, but not having a mom . . ." She cringed, looking up at him as if he'd understand. "I just feel like there were things I should have . . . things I ought to . . ."

"Working hard and loving people well are much more admirable qualities than which shoes to wear and when not to snort-laugh." His gentle expression tightened the precarious friendship she'd reluctantly accepted from him. He drew in a breath and gestured toward the front doors of the store. "What if we help each other out? After all, it's what friends do, right?"

"You'll help me with *fashion*?" She tilted her head in challenge.

"I'm fairly good with knowing what looks nice on ladies."

She rolled her gaze to the black awning overhead. Sexy Sovereign, indeed. "Oh, I bet you are."

"Not in the way you're thinking." He shifted back into her line of vision, the pucker of his frown triggering her guilt. "It's part of the world in which I live, where we pay attention to things like style and poise and appearances. *That* is what I mean." His deep blue gaze searched hers. "I've made a grand disaster of the last two years of my life, and I'm in the process of my own makeover. It's not an easy plight, trying to dig oneself out of the ruin of one's own making."

The regret in his voice, the hurt in his eyes, nudged her a step forward. "I'm sorry, Arran." Her smile quivered wide. "If the guy you used to be is like the one I've been getting to know over the past few days, then I think you're definitely moving in the right direction. And if Ellie, Luke, and your parents believe in you, then you have a wealth of good support. I mean, to get on Luke's good list speaks volumes."

"I think his kindness is more related to his love for my sister."

"Maybe a little, but not enough for him to take the extra time and consideration he has with you. To teach you? To offer you encouragement? He sees something good in you too."

His gaze searched her face—for what, she didn't know—and the look sent her heartbeat into a little faster rhythm. "Well, perhaps I can show off a bit of my goodness right now, then?" He offered his arm. "What do you say we face the daunting department store together?"

❈

It had taken a half hour to convince Charlotte to accept his help and another to convince her to model some of the clothing he'd encouraged her to try. At first she'd flat-out refused, turning every shade of red in the color wheel. But then, as he listened to her fears and offered gentle suggestions, she'd agreed.

The awareness of her growing trust in him, of her faith in his opinions and presence, heightened his interest in helping her even more, just as a friend ought to. And the idea of building her confidence and courage? It held a little "hero" in it.

"You were right! This suit really does look like something Princess Kate would wear," Charlotte called from inside the dressing room. "Oh my goodness. I didn't realize I could dress like Princess Kate."

Arran lowered his mobile and stared at the closed door. Her little bits of pleased exclamations and communications added more fun to the entire experience. She was utterly delightful.

"Are you going to let me see this one?"

Silence followed.

She'd refused to leave the dressing room for all the others.

"You're not allowed to laugh. The only thing you're allowed to do is say, 'Yes, Charlie, you *do* look like Princess Kate.' Is that understood?"

He sat to attention, suppressing a grin. "I promise."

The changing room door creaked open, and Charlotte stepped out in the well-fitted navy suit. It was the first time Arran had seen her soft brown hair flowing down around her shoulders.

She wobbled a tad in the navy heels and bit down on her bottom lip as she took a few unsure steps toward him.

He stood slowly, his grin refusing to remain subdued. "Charlotte, you look . . ." He almost said *beautiful* but then remembered his promise. "Like Princess Kate."

A fire lit her gray eyes, and she folded her arms across her chest, staring up at him from her spot a foot below. "Okay, seriously?"

"Seriously?" He gave her ensemble another assessing look. "It is an excellent look for you. Very flattering. But what do *you* think?"

"I like it." Her grin crinkled her nose, and she leaned forward. "A lot."

The glint of pleasure in those silver eyes held him in place for a moment. He rocked back a step. "As you should. And it will be *suit*able for many different types of meetings." He winked. "I even think it makes you look taller."

She rolled her eyes with a chuckle. "For a prince, you're strangely normal sometimes." She gestured back toward the dressing room. "I only have a few more items, and then we can find those boots you need at Weber's Footwear down the street."

He returned to his chair. "I'm in no hurry, Charlotte."

"I have these wrap dresses to try on, and then I'm done." She studied him again before stepping back into the changing room. "I wish the right clothes could fix stage fright as easily as they change my appearance," she said from inside the room. "I stumble all over myself."

"Part of presenting well has to do with practice, but the other part is caring about what you're saying. What sorts of presentations are you supposed to give?"

"Three. One at a regional school employees' meeting, one at a fundraiser, and the other is"—she whimpered—"at the Mistletoe Gala, where I have to speak in front of important people who have contributed to the charity."

"It sounds like the perfect training ground."

A snort erupted from behind the door. "Are you always this blindly optimistic?"

"Only when I'm working with smart people who just need a little encouragement."

"Ah, and the charm rises to the challenge yet again." Her soft chuckle made it through the door and brought a smile to his face.

"So, if you've helped with The Wish for so many years, what about it keeps you volunteering? Why does it matter so much to you?"

Silence greeted his question before she answered.

"I've never really thought about why, except to help. I started volunteering when I was sixteen because one of my favorite teachers told me they needed help. And when I experienced the joy of bringing Christmas gifts to these children . . . well, I just never stopped volunteering."

"I think you have the beginnings of a speech right there."

"Really?" The door flew open, and she stepped out in a dark blue wrap dress, complete with simple yet fitting heels.

Definitely a *gift* for his eyes.

She walked forward, completely unaware of his appreciation for how the dress hugged her lovely frame. "I can talk about things like that?"

The blue of the dress deepened the fascinating silver blue of her eyes, and Arran struggled to recall her question. "Um . . . yes, of course." He stepped closer. "Also, I definitely believe you should purchase this dress."

"Thanks." Her smile softened as she stared up at him, another swell of pink deepening her cheeks. "I haven't been much of a dress girl in a long time, but this . . . well, this is nice."

Her declaration, paired with a few snippets of information he'd learned from Ellie and Luke, gnawed at the back of his mind. He couldn't help feeling as if there was more to *her* story.

She moved back to the dressing room, but Arran continued the conversation.

"Did you mention before that the criterion for children to qualify for The Mistletoe Wish was to be part of a single-parent home? And that many of the children you work with have a parent who is incarcerated or deceased?"

"Or . . . just left." Silence followed. "It's important that these kids don't feel forgotten. That they know people still see them—*really* see them—even when it might look like they're doing just fine."

He mulled over her words. Hadn't Charlotte mentioned her own mother leaving? Arran's chest constricted.

Had she been one of those children who felt forgotten? Unseen?

Could her nondescript clothing and ball cap be a response to her past?

Arran paused on the thought. Maybe Charlotte had been like one of the kids he'd met in a school for which he was patron. The young girl attempted to hide herself behind her hair or baggy clothes because she'd been hiding something much more painful for a long time—a physical expression of a deeper hurt.

"Well, you have a speech half written, especially if experience has anything to do with it." Something in Arran's heart bent at this new revelation. Did this lovely, tenderhearted, and strong woman realize she was worthy of being seen?

"I know you didn't come all the way over here to help me sort out my life, Arran." Charlotte emerged from the dressing room in her leggings and sweater, the glow in her smile the loveliest thing she'd worn all afternoon. "But thank you for being willing."

He grinned at the irony.

Perhaps, in the process of showing Charlotte who she truly was, he'd work a little of his own magic in rediscovering the man he used to be.

"It's my pleasure, Charlotte." He met her smile with one of his own. "After all, what are friends for?"

SEVEN

How could Charlie feel simultaneously glad to be working alongside Prince Smolder *and* mortified?

After all, he'd helped her shop yesterday. Even waited outside the dressing room to comment on her choices.

Ugh.

Surely he had a thousand better experiences in his royal life than something as simple and . . . *ridiculous* as that!

But he'd never given off any sense of wishing to be anywhere else. In fact, the way he looked at her a few times, well . . . she wondered if he wasn't even enjoying himself. Which seemed even more ridiculous, because any man of her acquaintance would rather take a fork to the eye than go clothes shopping with a female.

Or even shopping at all.

It was probably because of the clothes. Her cousin Penelope always said men responded to the way women wore clothes. But surely a prince was used to much prettier clothes on much prettier ladies than . . . well, *her*.

Then they'd gone to Weber's, found Arran some boots, and walked through Ransom Community Park eating hotdogs and talking about their childhoods.

Like friends.

Friends!

And now here she was, laying stone on a patio, surrounded by mountains, and having another "friendly" conversation with Prince Arran of Skymar.

Much like they'd had for the past three days.

The more time she spent with him, the more he kept proving her first impressions wrong. To beat it all, he kept doing "princely" things like holding doors open for her, gently putting a palm to her back when crossing uneven terrain, and walking on the curbside of the road. He even brought coffee to her one morning.

Of course, Luke did similar things for Ellie.

And occasionally Dave offered to go get her a coffee.

But the guys usually treated her the same as the rest of the team, which meant like one of them. Not Arran. Even when she was wearing her sweatshirt and mortar-stained jeans, he somehow made her feel very feminine.

It was instantaneously unnerving and comforting. And . . . attractive.

She shook her head and carefully situated the next stone Arran handed her into the mortar on the patio.

"This work is hard, but"—Arran gestured toward the half-finished patio of multicolored fieldstone—"what a result!"

"I've always loved stone." She slid the trowel over the "mud" to clear off the excess from the stone. "It has a natural beauty to it."

"Then you'd love Skymar." He lowered himself to her level, offering another stone. "Stone buildings, streets, and fences aplenty."

She created a hole large enough so the slightest suction could settle the stone in place. "Does our world look bland to you, then?"

"Not at all. I've found the atmosphere and people . . ." He paused and tipped his head toward her. His mussed hair and hint of stubble on his jaw forced the phrase "Sexy Sovereign" back to mind. She diverted her attention back to the stone as he continued.

"I've found it all a welcome and needed reminder of what matters most in life. I think you know enough about me now to realize that in my past, I'd become stuck in a self-destructive way of thinking to douse my pain. And in the end . . . well . . ." His shoulders sagged and he looked off into the distance. "It brought me here."

The longing, the regret in his voice, pulled at her heart, so she offered a lighter turn. "Well, I know Luke and Ellie are glad to have you." She raised a teasing brow. "Not to mention a few . . . um . . . churchgoers?" Her snicker, snort and all, shook free as she referenced Luke's humorous recounting of Arran getting mobbed by mothers at the local church looking for a date—or a husband—for their daughters.

"Heaven help me." He groaned. "You've heard?"

"You're fresh meat."

"What?" His smile widened.

"Single male from a good family?" She slid her gaze up and down him, followed by a low whistle. "Fodder to all southern mamas in search of the perfect man for their daughters."

He rocked back on his feet, his frown deepening. "After the service there were so many of them, most with high-pitched voices and overpowering perfume."

A belting laugh burst out and she tried to cover it, but instead she plopped some mortar on her face along with the movement. "Ack! Look at me, so ladylike." She sighed and rolled her eyes.

He crooked his lips and tugged a handkerchief from his pocket, offering it to her. "My grandmother used to say that what makes a lady is on the inside, Charlotte." The way his voice warmed her name almost distracted her every time he said it. "We only need to show on the outside what you already have on the inside."

She took the proffered handkerchief. "And what is that?"

"You're kind. And your kindness is a big part of who you are. Anyone can see that by the way you interact with others. And you're smart, resourceful." He waved a hand toward her. "A hard worker."

"In carpentry."

"Carpentry doesn't make you any less a lady." His expression gentled. "It is something you *do*, but not who you *are*. And this weekend you certainly showed off your ability to dress the part of a lady, should you wish it."

A flush of heat rushed with power-drill speed into her cheeks. "Being poised and coherent during a speech might be a nice addition."

He tilted his head, studying her with those striking blue eyes of his. "I want to discuss The Wish and your speeches sometime. When could you meet this week?"

Her thoughts still clung to the way he'd complimented her and then completely validated her job and personality at the same time, so it took her a few seconds to catch up with his request. "Right. We need to do that." She blinked back to awareness. "Saturday?"

"Perfect. Text me details?"

"I . . . I don't think I have your number."

"Ah, right." He reached into his back pocket and pulled out his phone. "Do you mind putting in *your* number?"

She stared at him. Prince Arran was asking for her phone number.

A wonderful flood of delicious warmth tingled up her body. Attraction?

No sirree.

Besides, he wasn't asking for her number in a romantic way.

At all!

He wanted her number as a colleague. That's it. Maybe even as a friend.

And that was good. Fine!

"Sure. Yes." She wiped her fingers on the handkerchief and then took his phone, quickly adding her number.

"And it's fine if I text you mine?" He took back the phone.

"It would make the communication happen a lot easier if you did." *Good*. Her sarcasm had come to the defense.

"A sense of humor can suit a lady too." He winked as she offered him the handkerchief, carefully tugging it away.

"Hey, are you two over here holding hands or working?"

Charlie looked up to see Luke approaching, a rascally expression on his face. Heat invaded her cheeks all over again. *Family!*

"I think the protocol is to exchange mobile numbers first, and then the hand-holding can commence," Arran replied, nonplussed. And then . . . he shot her one of those lopsided grins. "Step one is complete."

"Gross." Despite Luke's exaggerated grimace, the twinkle in his dark eyes only intensified Charlie's mortification.

"The only hand-holding he's needed was the initial stonework placement." She smiled in mock sweetness. "Otherwise, his hands have been too busy for holding."

Luke rolled his eyes, as if he didn't believe a word of it, before looking down at his watch. "Aren't you and Ellie meeting this afternoon?"

Charlie froze. "Oh, right. Dancing talk." She pushed to a stand and dusted her hands on her jeans. Praise God for small means of escape. "I lost track of time."

"Lost?" Luke heaved a heavy sigh. "That's the whole reason I came over here, really. You looked so lost in Arran's eyes, I figured I'd better come rescue you before I had to send a search party."

Her glare bounced off his smirk.

"You're merciless, Luke." Arran chuckled, warm and much too entertained. "Charlotte is too levelheaded to set her sights on a rogue prince."

Her level head and his crooked smile were not playing fair, actually.

"Riiiight." Luke drew out the word, then shifted his attention between the two of them before gesturing back the way he'd come. "I'll clean up my tools back at the rock wall and then come take over Charlie's spot here with you."

With another humor-filled look in Charlie's direction, Luke moved back across the floor, careful of his steps on the wooden planks they'd marked for safe passage over the stones.

"I'll see you tomorrow." She offered Arran a side wave and made to step back when he caught her by the arm.

"You never told me how to avoid the southern mothers at church."

Her grin resurfaced, her sarcasm rising above the effect of his nearness on her internal temperature. "I'm afraid there are only two remedies."

His brow tipped in question.

"Death." She squinted her nose with her frown. "Or . . . not being single."

❆

Charlie walked by her laptop for the fifth time, stopping in front of it to stare at the search screen. After a humiliating dance lesson with Ellie, her curiosity had gotten the better of her, and she not-so-subtly asked for more details about why Arran came to Mount Airy.

She'd caught a few hints in discussions, but the details stung with renewed clarity.

A woman.

The woman Arran dated for two years before everything ended on the night he proposed. Then it became clear she'd only used her connection with Arran to advance her career in film.

And his heart had been so broken, his trust so crushed, he'd attempted to drown his hurt in all the wrong ways. Pulling away from his family, engaging in superficial relationships, and ignoring his responsibilities.

Only in the past few months, the family noticed a turn in the right direction. Real healing, and at Arran's initiation.

So the man she'd laid rock with and even—cringe—shopped with was the real Arran St. Clare, and he'd finally been released from the curse of heartache to transform from a rogue back to a prince.

Hmm . . . very fairy-tale-like, if she thought about it.

Ugh. She shook her head.

Steer clear of fairy-tale thinking.

Dangerous.

NOT real.

She stared back at her computer, tapping her fingers against her chin.

No. She didn't need to Google Arran.

Seriously, why would she indulge in something so silly? With a shrug to her inner voice, she slid down into the chair and typed in "Arran St. Clare."

Dozens of links popped up, the first listing his full name: *Arran Diederik St. Clare, Prince of Bredon and the Western Isles.* She blinked. Somehow, the title made his "prince-ness" a little more real.

What would dating a prince be like, anyway? Ellie mentioned how careful she'd been when dating Luke, sharing how, though the choice of a spouse was personal for a royal, it also had some bearing on the monarchy.

So, when Arran chose to propose to his ex-girlfriend, he'd weighed those options.

And she'd not chosen him back, but instead had used his affection for selfish gain. Her heart ached at the very idea.

Arran's photo on the screen stared back at her, in full crooked-grin charm. Very princely.

Seriously, what little girl at some point in her life didn't secretly wish to marry a prince? It seemed pretty common.

She narrowed her search terms, looking for who he was before his heartbreak.

Videos and photos showed Arran serving alongside his family, his smile quick to respond. Often, he was one of the first of the royals to move toward the kids, kneeling down to talk with them, bringing out their laughter. He cut ribbons, played sports, served in the Skymarian military, worked alongside people within the community, and gave speeches.

Good speeches.

And then . . . a post popped up about his split from Angelica, which led to another post and another. His entire demeanor changed. No longer did he approach people but rather stayed in the shadows. He appeared aloof; his joy vanished.

And then there were photos of him at wild parties. Headlines of the Rogue Prince followed ones of his ex-girlfriend enjoying the glamorous life of Elstree, Tanalyn, and even Hollywood.

Charlie paused a video of Arran looking at her from the screen. A wounded Arran stared back at her.

A man hiding his pain behind fake happiness. A plastic smile. Nothing like the man who'd helped her with shopping or building.

She pressed a palm to her chest, rubbing at a sudden ache.

The wounds she carried through her childhood had soaked into the person she'd become. Self-doubt plagued her choices, as her mother's condemning words loomed in the back of her mind. Even though she knew the truth, sometimes memory crowded out the truth . . .

And then she let insecurities win.

She looked down at her baggy sweatshirt and pants, a contrast to the new looks Ellie and Arran had introduced.

Sure, sweatshirts weren't inherently bad. In fact, she liked them.

But had she also used them to "hide" herself? To keep from disappointing a possible suitor? To prevent failing? Was she afraid that if someone saw her as a viable dating option, he'd reject her because she wasn't enough?

She flinched as a thought came to mind. Like her mother had.

Her gaze rose to meet the Arran on the screen. She understood heartbreak. Fear. "Pretending" in order to ease the pain.

This news about him hit her. Instead of raising all the red flags in her mind, it did the opposite. It touched all the bruised, lonely places in her heart from one walking-wounded to another.

Sure, his life was light-years different from hers, but maybe he wasn't so different at the heart level. Perhaps he needed to know how beautiful a faithful and reformed heart truly was.

That he was seen too.

EIGHT

I thought we could work in the dining room." Arran followed Charlotte through the front door of her house. "We'll have more space to go through everything."

Her ball cap was pleasantly absent, and her hair fell in a long braid over her shoulder. Plus, she wore the fitted green sweater he'd picked out for her in the shop, along with a pair of her new jeans and new calf-high boots.

His grin tipped. Maybe she was starting to like this makeover a little bit.

Arran tugged off his jacket as they entered the dining room, papers scattered across an antique table. "What is all this?"

"Contacts, finances." She sighed down into a chair. "A list of kids' names from the past."

He took a chair across from her, surveying the mess. "Is anything digital?"

Her eyes withered closed and she leaned forward, elbows on the table. "The previous organizer believed in the old-fashioned way of filing."

Ah, a definite way to assist. He leaned forward, elbows on the table, to match her pose. "Well, tell me what we have here and what the schedule is, and then we can sort out how to manage it all. Create a spreadsheet, if necessary."

"Wait a minute." Her grin flickered. "I didn't know royals used spreadsheets. Is that one of the courses you take in prince school?"

"Oh yes." He curbed his smile into a thoughtful grimace, chin tipped. "Along with how to maintain unwavering posture, appropriate throat clearing..."

"How to style the perfect wave to your hair." She gestured toward him.

"Most assuredly. Every prince in the movies has a perfect wave."

At this Charlotte snort-laughed, and a warmth bloomed in his chest at the sound. "And, of course, various ways to fight dragons."

His gaze caught hers. "And rescue damsels in distress."

Her smile flared wide. "Well, then I can't imagine you *not* being prepared to help with The Wish. You are fully qualified, especially for the rescue part."

They spent the next half hour sorting the tangled information into manageable data. In the process, the sweet scent of apples kept distracting him.

Charlotte's scent. And it suited her. Sweet with a little tang.

"So your first presentation is at the school meeting next week?" Arran asked.

"Followed by the fundraiser at the Ashby Theater," Charlotte added. "Which is a big deal, because it's the first time in years that the Ashby's offered to have a jam session."

"Jam session?" Arran replayed the phrase in his head. "That sounds violent."

Charlotte's grin resurfaced. "It's when folks get together to play bluegrass music. And in this case, *Christmas* bluegrass."

"Bluegrass?"

Her eyes lit. "Oh, you definitely need an introduction to bluegrass."

"With an activity known as a 'jam session' and music referred to as 'bluegrass,' I'm simultaneously intrigued and terrified."

Her lips quivered toward another smile. "Well, there *is* food involved too. And dancing, of course."

"And you dance?"

A rush of pink deepened her cheeks, and he stared for longer than he'd intended. "*That* kind of dancing, yes. Not"—she waved at him and looked back at the papers—"*your* kind of dancing."

A blush suited her.

Very well.

So did laughing.

In fact, the soft, feminine look of her in that cozy sweater and long braid matched the woman he was beginning to understand better with each passing day. What a marvelous combination for such a strong, skilled woman to possess a gentle beauty she didn't even seem to know she had.

"I'm less concerned about dancing and more about my presentation skills, or lack thereof."

He relaxed back in the chair and studied her. "When I first started public speaking, my grandfather told me to remember three points. Of course, there were additional things like volume and rate of speech, as well as eye contact with some in the crowd. But in writing the speech, he boiled the necessities down to three."

Charlotte rested her chin on the heel of her palm, waiting.

"Firstly." He held up one finger. "Gratitude or welcome. So, simply welcoming those who are listening or thanking them for their time."

"That doesn't seem so hard."

"Right." He grinned. "A natural thing to do when you're thankful for the opportunity, yes?"

She nodded, and he continued by raising two fingers. "Acknowledge the story."

"The story?"

"This part is the heart of your speech. Taking the history or the passion of what you're discussing and passing it on to your listeners. This is where you can give a brief history of why The Wish was created and, perhaps, the reason you believe it's worthwhile."

"Yeah, I've been thinking about that." She studied him, her brows pinching a little, before she steadied her gaze in his. "I . . . I was one of those children."

Even though he'd suspected as much, the declaration constricted his chest.

"At first I didn't think my mom's absence impacted me so much because she had slowly been disappearing from my life for months before she finally left. But then as those weeks turned into years, this lingering ache began to grow." She looked down at the papers, her hand moving to squeeze her braid, almost as if the action brought comfort. "I had this weird sort of wrestling match going on inside of me, between wanting to hide because of my own shame and to escape people's pity, or to just let people see how lost I was."

"*Your* shame?"

Her gaze rose. "I know it's not true, but there was this lingering feeling that I was the reason she left. That I wasn't good enough for her to stay, to choose me over her drugs."

"Charlotte," he whispered. And without a second thought, he covered her hand on the table.

"But then again, I didn't want to be forgotten. I didn't want people to assume my life was like everyone else's, and that there wasn't this giant mom-sized hole taking up permanent residence in my soul."

A glossy sheen filled those silver eyes. He slid from his chair and moved to the one nearest her, taking her wrist into his hand as she turned to him. She didn't seem to notice his touch, lost in her hurt.

"And finally," she said with a sniff, "I chose the easiest of the two options."

"Hiding?"

She nodded. "But when I turned sixteen, someone nominated *me* for The Mistletoe Wish. At first the idea of being one of 'those kids' horrified me." Her lips curved into a sad smile as she shook her head. "But the woman who brought me my Christmas gifts—her name was

Grace Mitchell. She's kind of a legendary matriarch here in Ransom." Charlotte chuckled even as a tear slid down her cheek. "One of the gifts she chose for me was a painting of an old castle on top of some cliff with a sunset in the background. A little girl with her long hair flowing in the breeze, waiting at the door of the castle, with a massive lion standing beside her." Her grin grew. "Ma Mitchell had known me since birth, so my reputation of dressing up as a princess and searching for castles still followed me into my teens, I'm afraid."

His grin responded to hers, the way she tried to find humor even in the middle of sharing this heartbreaking story. "I imagine you were the sort of princess who fought dragons."

A light lit her eyes. "It's the only type of princess worth being."

"Indeed, it is. Because in real life, there are still a great many dragons to face."

Her eyes watery, she smiled before she drew in a breath. "One of the best parts of the painting were the words written on a little gold placard at the bottom: '*Have courage, dear heart.*'" Charlotte shook her head. "I think that's what she wanted me to know most. Maybe she'd seen how I'd lost my courage and confidence over the years and wanted to remind me I still had them." She shrugged a shoulder. "And I had my dreams." She paused for a moment before she sighed. "That painting didn't immediately change anything, but it told me that someone saw my pain and believed there was more to me than just 'the little girl whose mom left.' That there was hope."

A solemn silence followed her words. She drew in a shivering breath before releasing a small chuckle. "Um, sorry, I don't think you wanted all of that, did you? But, well . . ." She shrugged. "You asked."

"I'm glad you told me." His thumb trailed the inside of her wrist before he released his hold, the feel of her skin sending awareness through him. "It sounds as though you have a great deal of wisdom and passion to bring to your speech."

Her face broke into a grin, and he somehow felt the movement in his pulse. "I think being pushed into this role propelled something to the front of my mind that I'd hidden in the back. Truths I hadn't considered for a while, maybe ever."

"You've expressed two important things every thoughtful human wants." He studied her face. "To be seen and loved for who we really are."

"Seen and loved enough to stay," she whispered, barely loud enough for him to hear. The declaration shook through him as if she'd spoken it directly to his soul. *Enough to stay.*

He leaned back in his seat a little, the intensity of her words shaking him. A cry his heart knew all too well.

"Your father instilled some excellent qualities in you, Charlotte." Arran waved toward her, attempting to distract himself from the unexpected connection her wounds held with his. "And I'm certain, with your intelligence, you can master public speaking."

She looked away, another rush of pink rising into her cheeks as she cleared her throat. "So, if number two is to acknowledge the story, what's number three?"

Deflection? Perhaps she recognized the connection too?

He held up three fingers. "Purpose of the speech. Oftentimes, this is where you encourage people to join the story. So, for example, after your riveting and heartfelt acknowledgment of the story—"

A burst of air erupted from her in a silent laugh.

"You'll either *invite* others to join you or *thank* them for joining you, depending on the purpose of the speech."

"That makes sense."

"But, Charlotte." He nudged her hand again. "Putting elements of *your* story into your speech would make it more meaningful." Her gaze caught in his. "I'm *certain* you have the courage."

She searched his face, as if his words mattered to her. "Are you?"

"You've continued your friendship with me despite my appalling first impression and poor carpentry skills."

His response not only brought out her smile but encouraged the proper turn of the conversation in a lighter direction.

"Well, I do have a weakness for the perfect hair wave." She offered a one-shoulder shrug. "And it's good to know that sometimes the prince needs a rescue now and again."

"*This* prince needs rescuing on a regular basis and is humble enough to admit it." He tapped the table. "So I'm certainly not fit for the fairy tales."

"I don't know." She shoved a file toward him. "Maybe the best stories are when two people rescue each other a little bit. No girl wants to constantly live in damsel-in-distress mode. Not only would it be exhausting, but also a little humiliating."

He rather liked that definition of a relationship.

They shifted through a few other papers before Arran broke the silence. "Do you still have the painting?"

Her brows rose, the question taking a moment to register, and then she frowned. "No. When Dad and I moved into this Victorian, somewhere in the middle of all the packing and purging, the painting disappeared." She raised a palm. "But I did buy a necklace with '*Courage, dear heart*' written on it, as a type of replacement."

"A good reminder?"

"Yeah." Her gaze met his. "That being seen in all my brokenness isn't so bad after all."

He couldn't look away. A flicker of something . . . vulnerable, almost like a question, waited in her expression. The look pulled at a point in his chest, drawing him forward in a way he hadn't felt in a long time. "That's a very good reminder for any story, even a fairy tale."

NINE

Charlie saw Arran standing on the porch of Luke and Ellie's sprawling log house, his blue button-up and jeans proving he'd probably just gotten home from church too. Her pulse gave an appreciative upswing at the sight of him. Of course, that morning in church she'd been called to appreciate God's creation, so . . .

Good job on that one, God. Stellar, even.

And then he smiled as he walked toward her truck, and the "Hallelujah Chorus" rushed to mind, unbidden.

She looked down at her purse to gather her emotions. Just because he'd improved exponentially upon further acquaintance didn't mean she needed to get all googly-eyed over some prince who was headed back to his country in a little over a month.

A prince!

Silly really.

Ridiculous.

But something had changed in their friendship after their meeting at her house.

A tender understanding.

After what she'd discovered about him from Ellie's comments and her online search, maybe he understood her struggles a little more than she could have imagined. How surreal not only to have casual and not-so-casual conversations with a prince but to connect with him at such a very real heart level. In those conversations . . . well, he hadn't seemed so much like a prince as much as just a regular guy. Struggling, searching, hoping like a normal person.

Except he smelled like cardamom, had a distractingly lovely accent, and looked like a blonder Chris Evans.

Which was not her usual "guy group" of sweaty carpenters who tended to speak in partial sentences using sports references.

Her grin tipped. *Well, not all of them. Just the majority.*

He opened her truck door, and that blue gaze trailed down her and back, appreciation lighting his eyes.

Hallelujah! Hallelujah!

He offered his hand. "The brown skirt and blue wrap blouse, Miss Edgewood?"

"Too much?" She cringed. "It is, isn't it?"

"Not at all." One corner of his mouth rose as his gaze took another sweep of her. "Certainly a gift for all who saw you this morning, I'd imagine, but . . ." His gaze moved back to hers. "You look lovely in a ball cap and jeans. The real question is, what do *you* think?"

He said this nonchalantly, as if the phrase "you look lovely in a ball cap and jeans" didn't just pause her brain from all ability to respond for five seconds. "Seriously? This"—she waved to the outfit—"compared to my ball cap?"

"I do prefer seeing your hair, because it's beautiful, and you certainly don't hurt my feelings by showing off your figure." His lips quirked, an added glimmer in his eyes, which lit a responsive fire on her face. "But hopefully, we've become good enough friends that I already know you're beautiful in all the ways that matter most. This is only an added bonus if *you* like it, because then you'll wear it with confidence. And that's what other professionals will see."

Ah, professionals. He wasn't *attracted* to her.

The realization doused all the previous heat from her cheeks. Not that she should be surprised, of course. It was very practical of her to keep her thoughts in the professional-friendship realm too. Very practical.

"I'm getting used to it." She released his hand as her feet hit the ground. "I mean, it's not bad."

"No." He shook his head, the soft tone in his voice drawing her attention back to his face. He stared at her a moment longer and then drew in a breath. "Not at all."

Okay, so . . . maybe he felt a *little* attraction? That was good. She didn't need any more from him than a little, because the idea of "a little" was already causing her relatively functioning brain to shut down.

And reforming all her previous misconceptions about princes and romance.

Or maybe not *reforming* so much as *reminding*?

She cleared her throat and looked toward the house. "But I don't understand how clothes can cause such a stir at church. It's not like half the people haven't known me my whole life."

He raised a teasing brow. "You were attacked by the southern mothers, were you?"

"I'm duly chastised for responding so sarcastically to your previous introduction to them."

He studied her face in the same way he'd done at her house the other night: carefully, intensely, as if he read all her current fuzzy thoughts. "Well, I'm glad to know your wardrobe updates caught their attention enough to realize you are worth seeing." He leaned close, his gaze soft. "Though they should have noticed all along, in my opinion. But none of us are without our own particular blindness at times, are we? And sometimes it may take a shock to get our attention to see properly."

She slowed her pace. His subtle reference to his own behavior reignited her connection to him. Well, it was safe to say the last few weeks had certainly shocked her attention in his direction. And she couldn't seem to *stop* paying attention to him or seeking out his company.

But it was an interest doomed to failure.

She was *not* princess material. She'd just started wearing heels, for heaven's sake! Weren't princesses born in heels? But there was something *way* too attractive about a repentant man who treated a woman like a . . . lady.

Case in point: Instead of both trying to fit up the porch stairs, he gestured for her to take them first. She sighed. Her dad had been a good man. Kind. Strong. Gentle in his own way, but a mountain man who wasn't prone to holding doors and caring much for frills or lace.

And the few guys she'd dated over the past years hadn't really shown those qualities either.

Arran's care and consideration felt . . . nice.

She stood up a little straighter, turning back to him as he crested the steps. "So . . . I finished my speech last night."

"And you've brought it with you?" His smile held only encouragement.

"Well, you'd mentioned maybe going over it before I present tomorrow."

He grinned as he reached around her for the front door. "Of course, you can practice in front of Ellie, Luke, and me."

All heat left her face. "Arran, I . . . I . . ."

"Wouldn't you prefer a familiar audience on whom to work out any difficulties rather than an unfamiliar one?"

She searched his face, squeezing the strap of her purse until her fingers pinched.

"You're going to do better than you think. Today *and* tomorrow." He placed a gentle palm to her arm, his words soft. "I'm sure of it."

"And if you're wrong?" She forced more confidence into her voice than she felt.

He squinted upward in thought, but his lips seemed to wrestle with a smile before he looked back down at her. "You can throw more pies at me."

Her shoulders shook with a sudden laugh. "Deal."

Arran slid into a seat in the front row within the large auditorium of the school, the venue more expansive than he'd expected. Nothing too intimidating for an experienced presenter, but for her? Well, he wished he'd thought of giving her a few more tips.

The fact that she'd invited him to join her for her first big presentation encouraged his protectiveness.

As if she not only wanted him there but even garnered a little confidence from his presence. The idea somehow fortified a bit of his own confidence that he hadn't failed beyond hope in regaining her trust.

Plus she'd worn her navy suit.

And she hadn't wobbled one bit in those heels either.

Something about knowing her insecurities and watching her push beyond them increased his pride in her and his protective instinct all the more. If he could be one cog in the larger workings to help her see her own worth, then he'd certainly take this entire North Carolinian sabbatical as a win.

But it had already been much more. Heart-changing more.

He tapped his finger against his lips, his smile growing.

After the head of the school board welcomed everyone and reviewed a few housekeeping items for their continuing education day, he introduced Charlotte and ushered her forward.

She walked to the lectern, shoulders a little bent, her lips pinched in a frown.

Arran folded his hands on his lap, squeezing his fingers together. *Smile, Charlotte. You've got this.*

She took to the lectern and stared out into the crowd, her face much paler than her usual complexion.

"Good morning."

Her volume barely dented the vast space. Those eyes shot a frantic search through the crowd and finally found him, her gaze locking to his.

He pushed up a reassuring smile and gestured for her to move closer to the microphone.

With a slight nod and the tiniest smile, she complied.

"Thank you for the opportunity to speak to you today." She halted and swallowed, but her volume came with more authority. "Have any of you ever wanted to make someone's wish come true? Especially a child's? My name is Charlie Edgewood, and this year I am the coordinator for The Mistletoe Wish." She cleared her throat a little too close to the microphone, and her eyes widened in horror, her gaze finding his again.

He gently shook his head, hopefully communicating it was no big deal.

"I appreciate the opportunity today to help you learn how . . ."

She paused, her smile dying on her face as her attention roved the crowd. The pause grew longer.

Oh no! She was freezing up.

He released a cough, gaining her attention, and with a subtle move of his hand, he raised two fingers.

Point two. The story.

Her gaze dropped to his fingers, and then the most beautiful smile dawned on her face. She rested her palms on the lectern, which adjusted her posture to a more confident stance, and drew in a deep breath. "I know the value of The Mistletoe Wish because I was one of those children who desperately needed a wish to come true."

And on she went, glancing at him occasionally. With each shared smile, her body relaxed even more, her presentation stronger. She ended by inviting teachers, social workers, and administrators to contact her if they knew of any families within their schools who could benefit from The Mistletoe Wish, and even introduced Arran as her assistant.

A moniker he'd never held before, but undoubtedly one of his proudest.

Applause followed her as she exited the stage. He met her at the side door of the school, her pace almost at a run.

As soon as they made it outside, she turned to him. "Did I ruin it?"

"What?" He caught her in a stumble, placing a hand on her arm. "Of course not. You were great."

"I froze." Her brow puckered with her frown. "I looked out into the dark crowd and my mind went blank. If you hadn't—"

"But you brought it back together and ended splendidly." He gave her arm a little squeeze. "So next time, at the Ashby, you'll feel more comfortable."

"And I'll just envision you in the front row holding up two fingers." Her frown gave way to a smile. "Actually, that might help a lot. It's a good distraction."

He leaned in and gave his brows a shake. "I'm a distraction, am I?"

She narrowed her eyes, fully recovered from her discomfort. "Not enough to distract me from finding food right now. I'm starving."

"Sometimes we rescue the princess from dragons, and other

times from hunger." He offered his arm. "Let's find you some food so that I won't have to compete with your stomach."

When she slid her arm through his, Arran realized two things:

1. His heart wasn't broken anymore, because he fancied Charlotte Edgewood.
2. And it was an impossible romance.

Why would she ever fall for a very imperfect prince?

TEN

"Well, I must say you handled your second presentation like a pro."

As Arran walked Charlotte to her truck, the wind blew the scents of popcorn from the theater behind them and pines that lined the edges of town—a warm, wintry combination, if he thought about it. Stars twinkled in the early November night, blinking high above the streetlamps as the sound of Christmas music filtered from the Ashby's open doors.

Partial anonymity and small-town life had settled over Arran like a warm blanket, and he tucked into it a little more each day. Especially after these past few weeks with Charlotte.

It was a strange sort of thing, to feel unsettled yet energized by a woman. Over the past year, Arran had moved through relationships like a carousel ride, from one woman to another without a future in mind. But now he knew his heart had never been made for temporary.

He wanted forever.

Home.

"Thanks." She released a sigh as if she'd been holding it in the entire evening. "I had to look at you for moral support only twice this time."

"As happy as I was to provide assistance, I consider your rescue of *me* tonight much more impressive than my menial assistance to you."

She squeezed close to his side, her arm linked through his. "It's a truth universally acknowledged that eighty percent of women, regardless of age, want to dance with a prince." She tipped her gaze skyward as if in thought. "Maybe ninety percent."

"And a few were hoping for more than a dance, from the way their hands—"

"Okay, we don't need to relive the antics of Arlene Green." Charlotte shook her head, her hair spun up in a beautiful array of curls. "No one needs that mental image any longer than necessary."

"Or tactile experience." He shuddered, encouraging another chuckle from her. "So what is next on our list of duties?"

"Look at you," she cooed, a smile lighting her stormy eyes. "Embracing our little fundraiser with such enthusiasm."

"Being here has been a sobering lesson, but also a welcome reminder that life isn't made up of people who only want to use me for my status or connections." He looked down at her, her apple scent slipping into his pulse with welcome familiarity. "And I needed the reminder of how much I enjoy service and community. Shunning the two in my hurt proved a self-inflicting wound."

"Service is a beautiful way to spend a life."

He studied her again. "But not a life for everyone."

"Because it requires sacrifice. And sacrifice, by definition, is hard, or at the very least uncomfortable." She gestured with her head back behind them. "Like learning to speak in public."

His grin flashed wide. "But then there's the reward of discovering you have an innate talent for it, and . . ." He tipped his head closer to those fascinating eyes. "The right heart."

She looked away. "I suppose some of the scariest things in life are the most rewarding?"

"Indeed. But then, we know where to look to face those fears." He placed his palm over her hand. "Take courage, dear heart."

She nodded, faced forward, and continued walking toward her truck, which was not too far in the distance now. "In answer to your question, before I derailed the conversation." She sent him an adorable wink. "Our next item of business is to make home visits to our list of children and then go shopping for them."

"Excellent." His steps took on an added bounce. "I've always loved purchasing gifts. It's as close to being Father Christmas as I've ever come, except once, when I played the part for a charity back home."

Her lips pinched. "You don't strike me as the Father Christmas sort."

"Not jolly enough?"

Her gaze slid down him. "Yeah, that's it."

He couldn't help the crook to his lips then. Maybe she didn't mind reformed princes so much after all? He tugged her a little closer.

In the Ashby, as he'd danced with Charlotte, a new awareness dawned: the way she relied on and even welcomed his support, sought out his company, even the way the sweet blush slipping over her cheeks matched the hue of her lips. He hadn't wanted a serious relationship in a long time, his heart too sore and broken to try. But Charlotte tempted him out of his self-imposed exile. He wanted to be with her. To be a hero for her.

"We don't make such a bad team, do we?"

"Not at all." Her response arose in breathless form. "Even if it's not an expected team."

But sometimes the best things came quite unexpectedly, didn't they?

"And, despite your protests, you proved an excellent dancer."

"I grew up doing that kind of dancing." She gave her head a shake. "Not *your* kind of dancing. And I am *nothing* compared to you on the dance floor." Her grin resurfaced. "From the way you were moving to those bluegrass Christmas songs, I'd say you're closing in on becoming a proper hillbilly."

"I feel certain a proper hillbilly would dance those jigs with much more assurance than me."

"Just using the word *jig* in a sentence is a step in the hillbilly direction." She grinned over at him, stopping beside her truck. "Though I hope you don't go full hillbilly, *ever*."

"Afraid of the power I would wield on the dance floor?"

Her laugh bubbled out across the night air. "Well, there *is* that." She chuckled, holding his gaze for a moment before looking away. "But it's more about your"—she frowned and waved toward him— "gentle manliness that's . . . nice."

His brows rose." My gentle manliness?"

That silver gaze flicked back to his, a shy tilt to those lovely lashes. Heavens, the look invited him forward.

"Um . . . well . . ." She shifted a step away, her back almost making contact with her truck. "It's just that you don't treat me like a coworker or tomboy." Her brows drew together. "You treat me like . . . a lady."

He studied her, the way the collar of her black coat caressed her smooth jaw, the way her hair swept in waves around her face, the way her shoulders pulsed with her quickening breaths. He slipped a step closer. "You *are* a lady." His words barely pushed through his throat. "A beautiful lady."

Her gaze flashed to his. "You think I'm beautiful?"

How could she doubt? He turned to face her, drawing a pace nearer, desperate to convince her. "I've always thought you were beautiful."

She swallowed, the faintest hitch in her breath teasing him closer, that quicksilver gaze dropping to his lips long enough for him to notice.

"Charlotte." His palm came up to rest on the truck to one side of her shoulder. "You are one of the most genuinely beautiful women I've ever met, from the heart out."

Her hand rested against his chest, fingers slipping beneath the lapel of his coat, encouraging him to breach the distance. His breath hitched as he halved the space between them, those pink lips promising him that kissing would be dangerous to his heart.

Wonderfully dangerous.

Her eyelids flickered closed, her breath warming his chin.

And, of course, a hero embraced the danger head-on—his grin tipped—or in this case, lips on.

"Whoa there, Prince. Are you . . . leaning?"

Arran jerked to a stop as Luke's laugh took on extra volume.

"You did *not* just use a reference to a rom-com, did you?" came Ellie's chuckled question. "Not *my* husband."

"It's one of the disgusting consequences of being around girls my whole life," came Luke's humored reply. "Don't get used to it, Princess."

Charlotte kept her attention fastened on Arran, almost as if she waited for him to decide on the next move. Those eyes wouldn't release him from their hold.

"I still see leaning in progress," came Luke's voice, nearer.

Arran lowered his head, inches from her. "Should we give your impish cousin the satisfaction of ruining this moment, Miss Edgewood?"

Her breath caught, her attention dropping to his mouth and igniting all sorts of curiosities. With a slight twist to her lips, she raised her gaze back to his. "Not a chance."

She shot him a wink, tightened her hold on his lapel, and drew him the short distance to her lips.

Have mercy! He wanted to keep her!

The kiss lasted only a moment.

Much too brief.

But enough of a taste to leave him wanting much more than a kiss.

He wanted her heart too.

✳

Just a kiss.

That was all it had been.

And a little kiss too.

Charlie stifled a frown as she and Arran left another house after visiting a family on the Wish List. He hadn't mentioned the little lip-on-lip moment, so she'd refrained as well. Of course, with the teasing Luke employed the rest of the evening—and a few days later—maybe Arran wanted to forget all about it.

Or maybe he already had. After all, they'd kissed to spite Luke.

Hadn't they?

Heat rose up her neck at the tangible recollection of his mouth against hers and the way his palm slid up her back, surrounding her in his comforting strength and his warm and wonderful cardamom scent. The cursory moment only awakened her aspirations for another opportunity. If one small kiss left her quivering from the lips down, what would more thorough practice do?

Her cheeks flamed and she walked toward her truck, lost in a wonderful memory.

Maintain your composure, Charlie. It was just a kiss.

Nothing serious.

Just a kiss? When was a kiss ever *just* a kiss?

Her mind revolted against falling for the prince. But his teasing humor drew her in, and his kindness completely unraveled every logical argument to steer clear.

Why on earth did they have to work together on something with "mistletoe" in the title? It just made things worse!

She caught him looking at her as they moved to the truck, his smile big enough to snag at her pulse. He had a fabulous grin. Very Captain America–like.

Ack! Stop it, Charlie! You are becoming a lady. And drooling is definitely not ladylike.

No wonder his online history had a string of women in his wake.

Her body instantly cooled. Like her? Was she just another to fall under his charming spell as he traveled through whatever healing process he was on?

Her eyes wilted closed. Of course! As good-intentioned as he may be, why on earth would he think twice about her beyond a kiss or two? He was returning to his life *as a prince*! Not taking up a goat farm in North Carolina. No matter how many jigs he danced.

Charlie took those crazy fairy-tale thoughts back in hand. *So, Charlie, no more kissing the prince.*

"There's only one more family on our list." A dimple flickered at the corner of his mouth, and the sight somehow sparked another heat wave through her body.

Clearly, good sense was no match for a prince's kiss. She inwardly groaned.

Oh, why did she have to like him *that* way? If he'd stayed inebriated and nauseous, it would have been much easier not to like him.

"And who would that be?"

He looked down at his phone. "The Kevin Lindsey family?"

"Hmm . . . they live way back in the mountains. It might be something I should do on my own."

His expression asked an unvoiced question.

"Kevin is a good man, but he's a deep mountain man. Suspicious. Gruff." She put the truck in gear. "His wife has been in prison for two years now because of drugs. And he's trying to do the best he can with their children, but his house . . . well, it's backwoods. Primitive." She sighed. "I don't even know if they have running water."

Arran didn't respond immediately, forcing Charlie to send him a glance from her periphery.

"Do you suppose I've never seen poverty?"

His voice held no blame, but she felt guilty nonetheless. "Maybe not this kind."

She felt him studying her before he answered. "I am guilty of making wrong assumptions about Luke and his world when Ellie became engaged to him, so I imagine there are some misconceptions about my world too." He paused. "The royal life isn't always what people think or see on social media. Our responsibilities as servant leaders send us into some of the most vulnerable populations of our country. Several communities within my oversight of Bredon and the Western Isles are a few of the poorest in Skymar." His voice softened. "My father has been a good example of such tangible and person-driven leadership."

She turned up a road that would soon shift from pavement to gravel. "I can't imagine the weight of serving an entire country."

"You have the same heart of service, though."

His gentle encouragement pulled her gaze back to his.

There was no doubt Arran's life and hers had massive differences, but something about being the same at heart? Well, maybe the variances in their worlds weren't so great after all.

Not where things mattered most.

Besides, if Ellie had proven Charlie's ideas about a princess wrong, why wouldn't Arran prove her ideas about princes as incorrect too?

The road rose sharply ahead of them, large trenches from rainwater causing the truck to continue up the loose gravel at an angle. Forest hemmed them in on either side, narrowing their view and the road even more.

"This is impressive," Arran murmured.

"If you call this impressive, then I'm about ready to knock your socks off." She slowed in preparation, as the next curve in the road would give them a view of the house. "This is family land. Kevin inherited it from his grandfather, so no matter how much people try to convince him to move down closer to the road, he's determined to stay."

The small wooden house, complete with a sagging front porch, came into view. It was nestled against the mountainside, and chickens ran loose in the yard. As the truck approached, four hounds ran toward them, howling into the air.

Charlie killed the engine and turned to Arran. "Maybe you should wait here until they know who's visiting."

He tilted his head but didn't respond.

"In the mountains, folks are highly suspicious of strangers, and Kevin will know me. He respected my dad. Dad helped Kevin put a new roof on his house a few years back."

And with that, she hopped from the truck, pulled her coat close around her, and marched toward the house, dodging the dogs and chickens as she went.

Perhaps Arran's previous experiences hadn't fully prepared him for the poverty of Appalachia. The small ramshackle house looked fragile, with trees crowding in on all sides. Despite the early afternoon time, the thickness of the forest gave the day a later feel, evoking shadows within the layers of trees. Arran kept his focus on Charlotte as she dodged the dogs to make her way forward, her loose hair swishing against the back of her new coat. He grinned. She'd even worn some ankle boots with her jeans to dress them up a bit, he guessed. She absorbed Ellie's tips like the intelligent woman she was.

Charlotte had barely crested the porch steps when the front door of the house opened and the silhouette of a man filled the threshold.

Was he holding a rifle in his hand?

After a brief exchange, Charlotte turned to Arran with a smile and waved him forward.

Despite the apparent fragility of the outside of the house, Arran stepped into a surprisingly cozy room. Warm too. Very warm. A woodstove at one corner of the house proved the culprit. Dim lights glowed into a log-hewn walled living room, complete with a couch, chairs, a small television, and a worn rug in the center. A small bookshelf sat nearby, cluttered with books of various heights and levels of wear.

A movement from the couch pulled Arran's attention to two little girls, both with blonde hair, freckled faces, and big brown eyes staring back at him.

"Kevin, this is my friend, Arran St. Clare."

The man, about the same height and build as Arran, studied him for a moment. Arran offered his hand, and with a slight hesitation, the man took it.

"Kevin Lindsey."

"A pleasure to meet you, sir."

The man's brows crashed together. "You ain't from these parts."

"No, but I'm visiting family. My sister married Luke Edgewood—"

"You're kin to Luke." The man's expression cleared, and he gave a single nod as if that were enough. Mr. Lindsey turned and gestured toward the chairs. "The girls is waiting for you."

"Thank you, Kevin." Charlotte smiled at him and led the way to the couch, nudging Arran toward the older of the two girls, though neither looked over seven.

"That's Ginny," Charlotte whispered before sitting beside the younger girl.

"And I'm Mary," offered the elder, her wide eyes watching him closely as he took a seat near her.

"Hello, Mary. My name is Arran."

Her eyes grew wider. "Are you sure that's your true name, or are you joshin' me?"

"Very true." He pulled out his notebook and pen. "Is Mary your true name?"

"Nope. America is my whole name, but nobody calls me that 'cause it's a mouthful."

Arran grinned. "Well, I think both are fine names."

They chatted a little about Mary's school and friends, before Arran inquired after some of Mary's favorite things. The color in the little girl's face deepened, and she looked away. "Uncle Roe says my fancies is silly."

"But if we're going to find the perfect Christmas presents for you, we have to know what you like." Arran leaned forward, lowering his voice. "Even the silly ones. Though I'd reckon it's not as silly as you think."

Mary studied him, as if weighing his trustworthiness. Coming to some conclusion, she leaned forward, matching her volume to his. "If you can, I'd like a purdy dress."

"A pretty dress?"

She nodded. "Like a princess. And some nice shoes to go with it too." She looked over her shoulder. "And I know y'all don't get presents for the grown 'uns, but Daddy could do with some new work boots."

Arran's throat tightened at the tenderness of Mary's request. "I think we can do that."

Her grin spread to pinch into her cheeks. "You'll wrap 'em in a box and everything?"

"I will, and I'll even list you as the gift giver." He winked. "What do you say?"

Her shoulders squeezed with her silent giggle. "That's real good."

"Now, about this princess dress." Arran sobered his expression and raised his pen to the paper to communicate the importance of his question. "Do you have a certain color you'd like? Any ribbons for your hair? Or a crown?"

"A crown?" Her little mouth dropped open. "You reckon you could find one like Aurora has?"

"Aurora?" Was that one of her friends?

"From *Sleeping Beauty*," Charlotte whispered to him, humor dancing in her eyes.

Sleeping Beauty? He raked his mind for a match. Was that the old cartoon Ellie used to watch, with the terrifying woman who wore black horns?

"She's got a gold crown and a pink dress," Mary clarified, before her smile spread wide again. "And she dances with Prince Phillip. He has a horse named Samson."

Ah yes. And is there a dance in the forest? Arran's brain reached back for a foggy memory.

Mary tipped her head and studied him again. "You look a heap of a lot like him now, as I think 'bout it."

"Like the horse?"

Charlotte snorted to his left, but Arran maintained his attention on the little girl, who burst out laughing. "No, you don't look nothin' like a horse. You look like Prince Phillip!"

"You think so?"

"You even got the pretty wave in your hair too."

Arran bit back a laugh. "An excellent trait of princes, I hear."

"What I wouldn't give to see a *real* prince, like Prince Phillip." Mary's nose wrinkled with her frown. "But Daddy says Santa don't go granting wishes like that. And besides, Daddy says we ain't got no use for princes back here in the mountains."

Charlotte's struggle with her grin gave way to a cough, which sounded suspiciously like a laugh.

"I asked for a prince for Christmas last year, and Miss Charlie said that's what she'd wished for when she was my age. But she had to find a new wish since Santa ain't bent on stealing perfectly fine princes from other people's houses and dropping them in the mountains."

With this, Charlotte's smile disappeared altogether, but Arran's took on an entirely new power.

One of Charlotte's childhood Christmas wishes had been for a prince?

Well, that little bit of information certainly deserved further investigation.

Perhaps—his smile stretched so wide, it pinched into his cheeks—Santa had been listening all along.

"I don't know about that. Perhaps there's a prince or two who need a good visit to the mountains in search of the perfect princess?"

Charlotte sent him a look, and he merely raised his brows in response.

She quickly turned back to Ginny.

"Naw, that can't be so, Mr. Arran. Who'd go hiding a perfectly good princess back here in the mountains?"

"You never know, Mary." Arran leaned close, watching Mary's grin widen. "From my storybook reading, some of the best princesses are found in the most unlikely places."

"Stop with the grin."

Charlie refused to look at Arran as they drove down the mountain from the Lindseys' house, her cheeks already on fire from Mary's unintended revelation.

"Is my princely grin too much for you?"

"Arran." She pulled the truck to a stop, hoping her voice held more conviction than the laugh tickling her throat. "I'm not against making a prince walk the rest of the way home."

"This little bit of knowledge is rather rewarding, though, Charlotte." One of his brows rose in unison with the corner of his smile as he tapped a finger to his lips. "May even prove Santa is still quite adept at his job, though a few years delayed."

"Oh, hush!" She made to punch him in the shoulder, but he caught her hand, all humor leaving his face.

"We could start with a date."

"A date?" Her bottom lip dropped. "What are you talking about?"

"You know, two people spending time together in a romantic sort of way, with the hope of spending more time together."

A tingling sensation rushed through her body. "You and me?"

"That would be *my* preference."

Her previous doubts resurfaced, and she sighed, slowly tugging her hand from his. "Arran, you're leaving in less than a month. What could we possibly gain from becoming more than friends?"

"I've been told I'm a fairly good kisser."

Her attention dropped to his lips, and then . . . heat soared back into her face with volcanic fervor. "I have no doubt about that, but what about *after* the kissing?" She sighed. "The little girl who wished for the prince wanted the happily-ever-after, too, not just the kisses."

Those blue eyes captured hers in the silence, his look so intense her breath caught in her chest.

"What if the prince wants the same thing?"

The low, gentle question hit her like an explosion. Every insecurity within her rose to battle against the sliver of hope rallying to believe, to trust in the impossible.

He couldn't be serious. Not with her.

No matter what sorts of shoes she wore.

The truth still remained: she was a country girl with a broken past and a wounded heart, and he was an actual prince from a far-away land.

"I'm not princess material." She looked away, her vision fogging a little. "And my heart isn't strong enough to take the chance that I'll fall in love with you, and then you'll realize I'm not the girl you want for ever after."

He began to speak, but she raised her palm. "Please, let's just enjoy this sweet and safe friendship we have until you head back home. Could we do that?"

His gaze searched her face in the silence. Part of her wanted him to argue away her doubts and the other part of her was afraid he'd try. Finally, he lowered his chin in assent.

"Aye, Charlotte," came his soft reply. "If you haven't the confidence to trust me with your heart, then I'll happily treasure your friendship."

ELEVEN

The confidence to trust me with your heart.

The statement rolled around inside Charlie's head for the rest of the week.

Trust Arran? How could she trust him when she'd seen his trail of lady friends and knew his recent history?

Plus, he was a prince! Who was she kidding?

But her heart also knew the man from the headlines wasn't the same one she'd gotten to know over the past weeks. Ellie's own professions confirmed it: the Arran from the past had resurfaced, healed and stronger than the one before.

And he was the Arran who'd been slowly weaving his way into Charlie's life and pulse and daydreams.

But her heart?

She pressed a fist to her chest, as if the motion might stop this tug toward him, toward the impossible. It was all well and good for a little girl to imagine happily-ever-after, but real life proved the painful truth:

Some daydreams belonged just there . . . in her dreams.

Because they could never fit reality.

Besides, Arran hadn't broached the subject of dating again. Not when they'd gone shopping for some of the children's presents. Not when they'd met at her house to discuss the Gala, not even when he'd walked her to her truck after another dinner at Luke and Ellie's house.

Well, he hadn't asked her in words, anyway.

But those eyes. Something in them reached across the distance and beckoned her to change her mind. To give him a chance. To believe in those stinking fairy tales again.

Why would God listen in on silly things like the Santa wishes of an eight-year-old little girl who desperately wanted to be rescued from her heartbreak by a prince? She frowned. And she'd wished it again at nine. And ten. And maybe once more, very secretly, at thirteen.

She pulled up to Granny and Papa Edgewood's house, parking beside the other vehicles crammed all over the yard. Her attention moved heavenward, the warmth of the afternoon sunlight resting on her face like a little touch from her heavenly Father.

God cared for her. She'd wrestled through the knowledge years ago. But in his love, would he—*could* he?—offer her a dream that not only seemed impractical but completely impossible?

Her attention shifted to the Christmas wreath donning Granny Edgewood's front door.

Christmas.

The story of the impossible happening.

Her vision blurred a little.

Because of love.

Her chest squeezed, and she leaned her head against the steering wheel, digging her forehead into her knuckles.

But that couldn't mean the miracle would extend to Arran, could it?

She pinched her eyes more tightly. And what if she failed? Proved she couldn't fit into whatever life he lived? Or even disappointed him to the point he rejected her?

Her stomach roiled with the struggle.

Was she brave . . . or insane enough . . . to fall in love with a prince?

Her truck door flew open.

"It's about time you showed up," Luke said, looking down at her with a ready twinkle in his eyes. "Folks have been waiting for your mashed potatoes for a good fifteen minutes."

"Thanksgiving lunch doesn't start for another half hour!" she shot back, exaggerating her frown at him.

"There's already a line." He marched around the truck and opened the passenger door, pulling out the massive pot, still warm from the stove. "And nobody wants to be the last for these." He raised the pot higher in the air in reference.

With an eye roll for his benefit, she followed him to the house.

"Besides, I thought I ought to give you some important news." The twitch of Luke's lips reflected his continued teasing, so Charlie didn't feel obligated to respond. "You don't have to worry about any of the ladies at church stealing Arran anymore."

"I have not been worried about the ladies at church—"

"They've stopped following him around because they heard the rumors."

"The rumors?" She slowed her pace, staring so hard at the back of his head that he finally made a slow turn toward her. "What rumors?"

His dark brows swung high in faux innocence. "That he's a taken man."

"Taken?" She edged a step toward him, a knot forming in her throat. "By who?"

Luke sent her a pointed look and resumed his walk.

"Me?" The word squeaked out as she rushed up the front porch steps behind him. She quickly lowered her voice. "You can't mean *me*? We've definitely not been on any dates!"

He paused in front of the door and looked down at her. "Folks are just calling it like they see it."

"Like they see it?" she asked, and then resumed the squeaking.

He breathed out a huge sigh, as if this were the most annoying thing he'd ever done in his whole life. "The googly eyes are pretty obvious, Charlie."

"I am not sending him googly—"

"And the way you laugh when you're with him."

Her mouth dropped wide, but she rallied her wits. "You make me laugh, too, but I don't have sights to marry *you*."

"I make you laugh like you're in pain." He pinned her with a look. "*He* makes you laugh like you like him. It's different."

"I'm not having this conversation with you." She gave her head a hearty shake and moved toward the door. "He's a *prince*."

And that should end the argument.

"Wimp," came Luke's low challenge.

She pivoted toward him, hands on her hips. "Wimp?"

"You're objecting to a future with a good guy because he's a prince?" He shrugged one of those massive shoulders of his. "The poor guy can't help it, Charlie."

"I'm not objecting to *him*. I'm objecting to *me* being *with* him."

He relaxed back against the porch wall, pot in hand, and stared down at her. "Why?"

She paused, cutting her gaze up to her cousin. "Luke."

"Seriously, why? If he's looking for someone who's smart and kind and hardworking with a sassy sense of humor, then you're a great choice."

She gestured toward the door. "He's a *prince!*"

"And he's a man looking for the right woman."

"Maybe. But I could never be like the dozens of posh women he's dated in the past." The admission squeezed through her throat.

"I can assure you he's smartened up since then, and he isn't looking for a repeat of his past."

"I'm no princess, Luke." Why did the admission hurt so much?

"Okay, so now we get to it." Luke released a long breath. "I understand, Charlie. If anyone in this entire family gets it, it's me. I argued the whole thing in my head too. *Not fit to be married to a royal. Don't want to be a part of the royal life. No way Ellie would ever really want someone like me at her side.*"

Statements she'd been making to herself since the date offer in the truck on the mountain.

"But here's the truth of it," he continued. "Prince or pauper, the right woman for the right man will make all the hard-to-figure-out stuff work." He stepped closer, the corner of his mouth tugged up. "My life isn't going to look like I'd planned. It's going to be better. Harder, but better, because Ellie is worth the risk." He searched her face. "And so are you."

She was quiet for a moment, afraid to embrace the hope he peddled. "But you . . . you already knew how to do royal things like dance and wear nice clothes."

His exaggerated eye roll wasn't comforting. "You're *learning* how to dance and wear nice clothes, and you have the smarts to figure out the rest. But you already have what you need most for any man." He tipped closer. "Your heart."

The bridge of her nose tingled, and she swallowed the rising lump in her throat. "What if I'm not enough?"

His entire expression softened. "What if you're much *more* than enough?"

Her bottom lip quivered, so she bit it.

"Charlie." He looked down at her with such brotherly tenderness that the tingling in her nose spread to her eyes . . . and inspired leaking. "Just because your mama had a broken perspective about you doesn't mean Arran does. In fact, I'd say you've done a whole lot to get his perspective on the right track, which only proves he's smarter than he looks."

A weak laugh limped out of her mouth.

"Only you can decide whether whatever is going on between you two is worth all the hard stuff. But you are just as equipped to handle their crazy lives as I am." His grin twitched. "Now doesn't that make you feel better?"

"Loads." She shook her head and stared at the wreath on the front door.

The impossible?

"Why does Granny always decorate for Christmas the week of Thanksgiving?" Charlie rubbed at her nose, the topic change giving her swelling emotions a small reprieve. "Give Thanksgiving a chance!"

"Why do you ask questions as if they matter to Granny?"

"You're right." She reached for the door handle. "What was I thinking?"

"Just so you know, Arran is loving all the Edgewood insanity, which may prove he's not so smart." Luke gestured with his chin toward the door. "I thought our family would overwhelm his princely sensitivities, but he's jumped right in to play American football with the guys in the backyard. Even took on Uncle Tate in an arm-wrestling competition."

Charlie paused her forward motion. "Who won?"

"Uncle Tate." Luke leaned close with a wink. "But Arran let him. Anybody who can do stonework like him is going to beat an eighty-three-year-old couch potato."

Charlie laughed and entered the bedlam, a dozen women welcoming her with grand gestures and "Where have you been?" Children dashed here and there, laughter bubbled from various Christmas-decorated corners, while a couple of men shouted at the football game on the television in the den.

This was her family.

The least crazy side.

She'd just finished setting up the drink table when the back door opened, spilling a dozen men and kids into the house. Definitely the group playing football, from the looks of their clothes.

And then Arran walked in behind her cousin Jake, and all those mental gymnastics she'd been practicing about how they shouldn't be together died in her head.

His hair was a mess, he had dirt stains down one side of his body, and the grin he wore gave him an odd mixture of guy-next-door and Prince Charming. He made some sort of comment to Jake, which had Jake laughing, then Arran looked up . . . and his gaze found hers.

Her heart flip-flopped and, maybe, she smiled. Maybe. Whatever. Her expression, if it reflected her current feelings, may have looked a little like Luke when he'd picked up her mashed potatoes from the truck.

Evidently Arran read nonverbal communication pretty well, because he crossed the room to her as if she'd verbally called him forward.

Calm down, Charlie. Breathe.

She met him halfway, dodging a few people and pieces of furniture along the way.

"It looks like the ground won the game." She folded her arms across her chest and leaned against the doorframe separating the den from the massive family room. Her gaze made a pointed review of his current ruffled state.

"It's nothing to rugby." He leaned in and wiggled his brows, catching her breath with his sudden nearness. "And I made two touchdowns."

"Impressive." She picked a piece of dirt off his shoulder and flicked it at him. "Your talent knows no bounds."

He narrowed his eyes, his lips tipping into a smirk. "You haven't really investigated my best talents, but I'm not averse if you'd like to rethink the date option." Her hesitation drew him nearer, all humor fleeing his expression. He searched her face. "I may surprise you."

He already had. Over and over again.

"Woo-hoo, y'all! We got a couple in the hot spot."

Charlie blinked out of her Arran-filled daze and turned toward her aunt Pru, who was gesturing for folks to gather round.

Why was everyone staring at them?

"Oh, Charlie! It's like the perfect movie moment," came her cousin Penelope's squeal.

What on earth?

"Well, you might as well get on with it so the rest of us can start eating," said Papa Edgewood, his grumpy words defying the mischievous twinkle in his eyes.

Charlie followed her papa's gaze to the clump of greenery poised on the doorframe above her.

Her stomach dropped.

Mistletoe.

Calls of encouragement rang out from the crowd like the wild clan they were. She looked over at Arran to apologize, but his raised brow seemed to offer the same encouragement as the rowdy bunch calling for a kiss.

Blast Granny and her early Christmas decorating.

"Don't be yella, Arran!" someone called.

Laughs erupted around them, inciting whole new levels of scorching to Charlie's cheeks.

"What do you say, Charlotte?" Arran's voice scooped low to cradle her name before he gestured with his gaze upward. "For tradition's sake?"

Again, her face must have said things her brain didn't even know yet, because Arran slid a palm around her waist, tugging her a teensy bit closer. Her breath trembled at his touch, from his nearness.

And, if she was being honest, from a whole lot of anticipation.

With only a pause to look into her eyes, he captured her mouth with his.

The confident touch, soft yet in control, blurred the rising calls of her crazy family. His hand slid up her back, bracing her, his lips offering a longer and gentler caress than the brief time before.

Her palm instinctively rose to his cheek, a hint of stubble tickling her skin. She embraced the safe feel of his arms around her, the easy confidence in his kiss, the intimate trail of his lips skating over hers only to press in for a bolder taste.

Have mercy! A prince's kiss was all she'd imagined and so much more.

He drew back, his gaze searching hers as the sounds around them exploded with a mixture of "Gross!" from a couple of little boys, "It's about time!" from someone who sounded suspiciously like Luke, and "Now, let's eat!" from Papa.

With a careful touch to her arm, Arran guided her away from the hungry crowd, out the back door of the house. It was a good thing his brain was in working order because she left hers under the mistletoe.

"I know this"—he waved between them—"is complicated."

She blinked up at him, gathering whatever wits still remained in close proximity. "You think?"

Two words. Somewhat clearly spoken. She was rather proud of herself after being kissed into a brain blur.

"Do you think we could try to figure this out together? No strings?" His palms slid down her arms, inciting another desire for her to step closer. "Just . . . discover if what is happening between the two of us could prove worth the sorting?"

The warmth in her eyes puddled just a little. "No strings?"

He gave his head a small shake. "Unless you find you want them. I fear my heart is already entangled."

Her jaw slacked a tiny bit.

Could this be . . . real?

She pushed the fear of all the what-ifs away and focused on his face. The hope in his expression, the tenderness in his voice, pushed her heart forward a baby step. "The Christmas parade and tree lighting in downtown Ransom is on Saturday. That would make a really nice first date."

His expression gentled into the sweetest smile. "Sounds perfect."

She'd worn red.

Beneath a long black coat, the red turtleneck peeked out, adding color to Charlotte's face and drawing attention to her lips—an unneeded, though not unwelcome, reminder of her kiss.

Arran had doubted the readiness of his heart to ever love again, but as he and Charlotte walked along the quaint downtown of Ransom, Christmas decorations donning lampposts and storefronts, he welcomed the possibility.

The hope.

Yet this time something deeper wrapped 'round the feelings. Was it a better understanding of himself? An awareness that Charlotte's personality and compassion fit his life better than Angelica ever could?

He'd taken two years to work up the courage to ask Angelica to marry him. Agonized over it, as if he'd somehow known, deep in his heart, she'd never been the right one for him.

And here, within weeks of meeting Charlotte, he was ready to dive into forever.

Working so closely with her over the past few weeks, both in the day job and with The Wish, only secured his desire even more.

So fast. So certain.

Perhaps a second love afforded unique clarity a first love could not.

Clarity . . . and courage?

"Just wait until it gets dark enough for all the lights to come on," Charlotte said, staring at a bookshop's decorated front. "It's absolutely magical."

Her upturned face, the way she'd worn her hair down and loose, the warmth of her arm in his . . .

"I have no doubt."

Her attention caught in his, and her cheeks darkened. "You'd better tone down the sweetness, Your Highness. I might get used to it."

"Shouldn't you like getting used to it?" He looked ahead, squeezing her arm closer to his side, breathing in the chilly December air.

"I don't know." She glanced up at him, her smile uncertain. "I haven't had a great deal of experience with it."

"Perhaps I can take the next few weeks to help you acclimate. You may find you like it so well, you won't be able to do without."

She slowed her pace to a stop. "You're highly confident in your skills, are you?"

"More hopeful than confident, I think."

Her smile bloomed, and she resumed the walk, shaking her head. "I don't see how you and I—"

"Instead of rushing ahead into all the impossibilities of it, what if we just enjoy each other's company? We can sort out all the particulars as we go."

"Alright." She drew in a breath. "I'll just enjoy being on the arm of a . . . prince." She laughed. "It's surreal."

"Well, I would prefer if you liked the man a bit more than the title."

She paused again, turning to face him, her expression sobering.

"The title is too intimidating to think about, so I'll just stick with liking the man."

They walked a little farther, afternoon light fading into dusk with each step. One by one, white lights blinked awake. Twisted around lampposts, lining storefront windows, strung along awnings. All leading in starlit wonder to the center of the town, where an enormous decorated but darkened tree stood.

"Do they have small-town decorations like this in Skymar?"

He scanned the setting. "Similar, yes, though this display has more charm than most I've seen back home."

"You probably don't celebrate in small towns." Her comment held humor and curiosity.

"The country estate house near Crieff affords my family more of the small-town charm, but Christmas is usually most regally celebrated at my parents' main residence of Carlstern Castle. It's the location of the Annual Christmas Banquet in which our family, extended and all, dine together in grand fare. Then we walk out onto the balcony of the castle as the royal decorations in the courtyard are lit and the Christmas Banquet begins."

"It sounds exhausting."

"It *is* exhausting." He laughed. "But it's also very special. Thankfully, the banquet is an intimate affair of only fifty or so people."

"Yep. That sounds about as 'intimate'"—she made air quotes—"an affair as our family get-togethers, except with less football and more table manners."

"I'll not deny it is a grand experience." He turned her way. "And, as it happens, my father's birthday celebration is usually that week as well. But Mother contacted Ellie and I last night with the news that Father's celebration has been moved up to next weekend. On Father's actual birthday my sister-in-law's third child is being induced early, as a result of some minor complications."

"Oh." Charlotte's brow creased. "Then you'll miss the Gala."

Breath pushed from his lungs like a blow. "Charlotte, I didn't even realize." He squeezed his eyes closed and groaned. "Well, then I can just celebrate with my father later in the month—"

"No! You are *not* going to miss the king's birthday just because of this small-town gala." She frowned and tugged their linked arms forward.

"Charlotte." He paused their forward motion, searching her face, which had become more endearing with each passing day. "I will not have you thinking I take you or my commitments lightly. Perhaps six months ago, but not now and not with you." Arran shrugged. "Father has enough family to surround him that day, anyway. What is one less prince?"

"I think it would do his heart good to see how well his youngest is doing, Arran." She smiled up at him, her large eyes reflecting such admiration despite his declaration that he leaned over and tasted those lips of hers.

"You are simply marvelous, Charlotte Edgewood."

She gave her head a little shake and laughed. "This . . . this is just crazy, Arran. Guys don't talk to me the way you talk to me."

"Then they've not been the right guys."

Her gaze found his again, searching. "Maybe." Her lips pulled into a smirk as her eyes narrowed. "Or maybe you're just trying to make up for leaving me all on my own at the Gala."

"Oh, I'm staying." His arms slipped around her waist. "I can't have you thinking I'm a fair-weather prince."

Her laugh warmed the air between them. "I think you're proving much more than that." She sobered. "But I'm serious: go be with your family. It's the right thing to do. I . . . I'll be okay." She sighed. "Though I may video-call you during my speech so I can draw from your courage."

"You have courage enough, darling. You only want confidence, but I am certain you will shine because you speak from your heart."

He squeezed her close. "Though I assure you I'll take any excuse for a video call."

They walked up to the large tree in the center of town where dozens of people were gathered, most in winter hats, children on their dads' shoulders, young couples sipping warm beverages and cuddling close.

The mayor stood on a stand placed in front of the tree and proceeded to greet everyone, thanking them for coming to the fifty-second annual Christmas tree lighting in Ransom.

Charlotte pressed in close to his side. Her small frame fit so nicely there. Perfect, actually.

With encouragement from the mayor, the crowd began the countdown at ten.

Children jumped to chant the numbers, their eyes lit with anticipation.

Three . . . Two . . . One!

From bottom to top, the tree blazed alight, ending with an explosion of illumination from the massive star. The crowd erupted in celebration. Charlotte leaned her head against his chest with a sigh, and the feeling settled into his heart with certainty.

For the first time in a very long time, he made a Christmas wish.

That Charlotte Edgewood would believe in fairy tales again.

And that he would be her happily-ever-after.

TWELVE

It had taken the entire Saturday.

But what an amazing Saturday.

Charlie relaxed in the driver seat of her truck as she and Arran began the trip to the Lindseys' cabin, their final toy delivery stop. They'd spent a lot of time together over the past weeks, both in carpentry work as well as after hours. Her grin spread at the growing list of memories: lovely dates—from evening walks to cozy movie nights to candlelit dinners; wrapping all the gifts for the children; hanging out with her family. Arran even took special care to refine some of her dance moves.

Her whole body warmed at the thought.

Plus, dresses and heels were becoming a lot more common in her wardrobe, especially when they brought some admiration from her date.

Each passing moment made this crazy fairy tale more of a possible reality.

"I think you'd really enjoy Skymar," he said as they turned up the long narrow road toward the Lindseys'. "Not only is it beautiful, but people there value family and the simplicity of life, just like they do in the Blue Ridge."

She'd seen a few of Ellie's photos of Skymar and even conducted a bit of research on the country herself. The landscape reminded her of movies set in England and Scotland. Breathtaking green hills and seas framed by craggy cliffs. Fields of sheep and jagged stone ruins rising into a cerulean sky.

All of it as seemingly unreal as dating a prince.

"It looks amazing." She sent him a grin. "But I doubt that if I showed up over there, we'd hang out the same way as we do here."

"Well, I'd likely not be doing stonework." He tagged a wink onto the end of the teasing statement. "However, I am fortunate to live, if I choose, a little less in the spotlight than my elder siblings, so there's a very good chance for typical dates, as well as some that aren't so typical."

"Like royal balls and meeting heads of state and . . ." She drew in a shaky breath. "Presenting in front of hundreds of people."

"Perhaps." He chuckled. "But those don't necessarily have to be tedious, especially if you're with the right people."

Her gaze rose to his. "Meaning you, of course."

"Of course. And all the protocol for events like those can be learned. You've already proven you're a fast learner." He leaned in closer, his voice dropping low. "Though I wouldn't mind taking an extended amount of time to give you another dance lesson or two."

She stifled a sigh and kept her face forward. The way his body moved with hers, palm steady against her back, face so close. If she was supposed to give thanks in all things, God had certainly gotten a litany of praise after those lessons. "Sounds like a nice plan to me."

"If you were interested in a little trip to Skymar, I'd happily make the arrangements." All teasing left his voice. "Because I'm interested in pursuing something very long-term with you, Charlotte."

She pulled the truck to a stop in front of the Lindseys' house and turned to him. "Arran, I love the thought of it. I do. But I'm . . . I'm not sure I can ever fit into your world."

He drew in a deep breath and grabbed one of her hands. "I

didn't think I could ever fit into yours until I tried. And I know you're brave enough to try to do the same."

Howls from the incoming dogs broke into their conversation. She pulled her hand free and offered an apologetic smile. Dating him on her home turf was one thing. Traveling to his world was another.

"Let's talk about it later, okay?" And with that, she exited the truck.

He narrowed his eyes, his expression filled with teasing suspicion, but he didn't move as she started gathering some of the gifts.

"Are you coming?" she asked.

"Yes, of course." He hesitated, then waved her forward. "But you go on ahead. There's a certain gift I need to collect before I enter."

"Alright." She drew out the word, studying him for a moment, but he gave no clue to his delay. "I'll see you inside."

She closed the truck door and walked toward the house, sending one look over her shoulder before she entered. What on earth was he doing?

With another shake of her head, she entered the cabin, its toasty warmth a clear sign of the woodstove's work. Ginny and Mary welcomed her in with dimpled smiles and giggles. Their dad sent his usual nod of appreciation and a quiet "Thank you."

"My friend Arran should be bringing the rest of the gifts, Kevin," Charlie said, just as a knock came on the door.

The first hint to something being... different was when Ginny froze as she opened her gift to stare over Charlie's shoulder. The second hint came when Mary scrambled to her feet, her little hands covering her mouth as her eyes widened into giant brown saucers. With a sudden tremor in her stomach, Charlie turned to look back toward the door.

Standing on the threshold, in a full Prince Phillip costume, was Arran St. Clare. A red cape, Nerf sword, and massive shield completed his ensemble, and his wide grin proved the most attractive cherry on top.

Charlie failed to usher up one word in response.

Everyone else seemed to struggle with the same reaction, because the room went completely silent.

"I come bearing gifts, Princess Mary." He tipped his head without one ounce of apparent awkwardness. From behind the shield, he drew two gift bags.

"You . . . you *are* Prince Phillip." Mary giggled. She ran forward to take the bags, staring up at him with the same sort of awe weaving its way through Charlie. "I knew you were. I knew it!"

Arran shot Charlie a wink, which inspired a smile that matched the one that both girls wore. To make Mary and Ginny even more thrilled, once they had changed into their princess dresses, Arran danced around the living room with them and even drew Charlie into a little twirl.

Kevin stood in the background, arms crossed, watching, but the small smile on his face spoke volumes. A big, quiet mountain man, but a man who loved his little girls.

After a little more fanfare, Charlie gave Kevin a fruit basket, new boots, and a Visa gift card, then reiterated that the Gala was for all families, and that a few of Kevin's friends would be joining with their own children.

Then she turned to the girls. "You could even wear your dresses to the Gala."

The girls lifted hopeful eyes to their father, who stepped forward, his head already shaking. "Now, girls, a fancy dinner ain't no place for the likes of us."

"Why not, Daddy?" came Mary's cry before she twirled again. "I'm fit as a fiddle for a fancy dinner." She turned to her sister. "So is Ginny."

Charlie's stomach dropped as she realized the problem. Kevin wore work-worn jeans and a long-sleeve T-shirt during his daily grind at the stone quarry. He probably felt he didn't measure up to the rest of the folks who'd attend the dinner.

Before Charlie could respond, Arran stepped forward.

"Not to fear," he announced, still using his prince voice. "There is one last gift I left in my carriage."

He held Charlie's gaze, his grin wonderfully crooked, as he ran from the house.

Charlie looked over at Kevin, whose attention shifted from Charlie to the door, as if Arran was a stone short of a full chimney. Within seconds, the door burst open, and Arran entered carrying a leftover Christmas bag they'd had in the truck.

"For you, Mr. Lindsey." He offered the bag with a bow. "Even a father needs a moment to dress like a prince for his daughters."

Kevin hesitated before taking the bag, likely imagining a similar costume to the one Arran wore waited inside. But when Kevin pulled out the folded clothes, his stoic expression softened. "This can't be for me."

Was that one of Arran's suit jackets, along with the clothes he'd been wearing before changing into the prince? He must have brought the jacket for Kevin and realized the man didn't have the rest of a suit to complete the look so . . . he added his own. Even his shoes.

Charlie's hand flew to her chest. It was the most beautiful thing she'd ever seen.

"Yes, sir." Arran's smile grew. "No one should be forgotten at Christmas, especially an everyday hero like yourself."

The slight wariness in the man disappeared. He stood taller, pulling the bag closer with a nod. "I thank ya."

"Now, princesses." Arran turned back to the girls. "I must sweep Lady Charlotte away so that she can transform into her princess dress for a special dinner tonight."

He swept into a low bow, cape flapping behind him, and then ceremoniously offered Charlie his hand.

Interesting how the former playboy and gallant gentleman blended together in such an enticing sort of way. He certainly deserved a few reward kisses after this performance.

She took his hand and walked to the truck.

"You were fantastic," she said once they'd started back down the mountain. "It's as if you've played the role of a prince before."

His mouth twisted up in a half smile before he spoke. "I'm afraid the role of good prince has been sorely lacking of late, but I believe I'm on the right track to reprise that part."

"You wear it well."

"I think my head, my heart"—he sighed, holding her gaze—"and my priorities are in the right place now."

She wrestled with her grin, her gaze roaming over his costume, before she spoke again. "You do realize we're going directly to our dinner date, right?"

"Of course. We have reservations."

"Mm-hmm." She nodded, losing the wrestling match. "So we don't have time to stop for extra clothes."

His brow crinkled in confusion, and then he looked down at his attire before bringing the truck to a stop in the middle of the dirt road. "Oh dear" was his only response, before tagging a grin on the end of a helpless shrug. "Well, my lady, I suppose you must make do with a princely escort tonight rather than your dashing assistant."

She glanced at him with his red and navy puffed sleeves, his red cape, and the perfect prince-wave of his hair, the result of his generosity and sacrifice for Kevin Lindsey to be a hero for his daughters.

And the wonderfully warm feeling in her face traveled down into her chest as she realized . . . she loved him.

Charlie had no idea how it was going to work out, or what their relationship would look like in a week or two. But right now she just wanted to show him how much he meant to her.

With a breathless laugh she grabbed him by the front of his tunic and pulled him toward her, her lips finding his. He chuckled against her mouth and then slid his hands to cradle her face before moving them into her hair.

She pulled back, one brow rising with her grin. "I think your role as prince is definitely growing on me."

"What time do you and Ellie leave for the airport tomorrow?"

Charlotte, looking lovely in a large green sweater and leggings, curled up next to him on her couch as the ending credits of *It's a Wonderful Life* rolled across the screen.

"You are lovely."

The words produced the desired effect as a blush filled her cheeks. "Okay, Romeo, you don't have to keep upping the charm. I already like you."

"The sentiment comes so easily because it's true." He placed a kiss on her cheek. "Luke drives us at noon."

Her brow furrowed as she rested her palm against his chest. "I'm not really sure how to process this whole thing, Arran. I mean, you say you want to try to keep up with our relationship while we're apart, but... your life drastically changes once you return to Skymar."

Ah, he'd wondered if she'd second-guess his intentions. Of course, some of her fears about the royal life were justified. But he didn't care to keep to the spotlight. If it meant her comfort, he'd gladly relegate himself to the background. His return to hard work and service over the past couple of months had reminded him that one of the most princely qualities he could possess was humility.

After all, weren't they celebrating the humility of a much more important Prince in the upcoming season?

A good reminder of what mattered most. Humility and love.

His gaze moved over her, those large, beautiful eyes staring up at him.

Love.

"My life changing doesn't mean my desires will." He cupped her cheek. "Charlotte, I have a very long-term view when it comes to us, and I'm willing to pursue it. My heart and intentions are fixed on you alone. But I don't suspect it will be easy on either side, so you must make your choice."

She hesitated before wrapping her arms around him and leaning her head against his shoulder, securing her decision. "I don't really know what to expect. But I'm willing to try."

"That's all I'm asking, darling." He pressed a kiss to her head, breathing in her scent of apples and relishing the overwhelming gratitude of holding her trust—and her heart. "That's all."

The Wish and her day job kept Charlie busy, and her newfound skills in style and confidence led to unexpected opportunities in navigating more of the business side of the carpentry industry, impressing both Luke and Dave. Who knew that having a bit of confidence in how you speak in front of businesspeople made such a difference in how they responded! Though knowing a lot of these guys most of her life probably helped.

Arran checked in daily, sending sweet or funny messages and memes. Their time zone differences and wildly different schedules made phone calls difficult, but they'd managed a few in the two weeks he'd been gone. Plus he'd sent her a bouquet of the most glorious flowers a few times "just because." She still didn't know how to embrace his sweet attention to her. It seemed too good to be true.

And she missed him.

More than she'd imagined.

Not some prince in a story, but him. The guy with the dashing grin and excellent couch-snuggling skills. The man who looked at her from across the room and somehow made her feel beautiful. The gentle prankster and heart-stopping flirt and devoted encourager and spellbinding kisser. Simply and wonderfully . . . him.

How had he become such a regular part of her life in such a short time? Not just a regular one but—she smiled as memories of him flashed through her mind—a welcome, sweet, and romantic one.

As she passed by the main department store in downtown Ransom, the red gown that Arran had pointed out to her still waited in the shop front window in all its glorious detail.

The simple blue dress she'd originally chosen for the Gala waited in her closet. Still she paused, studying the scarlet finery and resurrecting a smart part of the eight-year-old girl she used to be.

It couldn't hurt to see how the dress fit, right?

A half hour later, she left the shop with the dress in her arms, grinning like an idiot.

She laughed.

Ridiculous.

Her phone buzzed, so she pulled it from her purse.

Arran: I hope your day is going well. I wanted to tell you I miss you, but also to warn you of an unplanned interview that may be featured online. It happened about half an hour ago. It is only a trifle, but I wanted you to learn about it from me instead of finding yourself surprised later.

Charlie: I guess since you're telling me, it had something to do with me?

A few small tabloids had featured a photo or two of them together when Arran had been in North Carolina, but nothing too disturbing. Arran had tried to prepare her for it.

Arran: They asked about your mother. I deflected and tried to answer in a way that honors you.

Her mother?

As soon as Charlie made it to her house, she went to her computer and typed in her name and Arran's. A video popped up with the headline "Does Family History Matter to the Royals?"

She clicked on the link to find Arran, looking wonderful in a white shirt, blazer, and jeans, walking down the street as reporters approached him. One asked about his recent trip to the States. Another about the new woman in his life.

"We're not quite ready to discuss our relationship with the world, James, but there's a larger smile on my face for a definite reason."

The reporter laughed.

Charlie touched a cool palm to her cheek as her grin stretched wide. Prince Charming, indeed!

"Are your parents concerned about your girlfriend's history?"

To this, Arran stopped walking and turned toward the female reporter. "Pardon me?"

"Her mother's current prison sentence? Surely His Majesty finds the connection somewhat concerning, especially with his long and storied legacy of quality women in the royal line."

Charlie's palm pressed into her stomach. Why would anyone ask such a thing? And how did they even know about her mother?

"Clearly, you're not informed of the many radical royals in our family history." Arran's quick response garnered laughter, but the light in his eyes had left. "I should think us lacking in character, indeed, if we judged every person based on the actions of some of their family members. Wouldn't you agree?"

"From the long list of ladies you've dated over the past year, it certainly seems you enjoy women with more eclectic backgrounds. Wasn't one of them connected to recent embezzlement charges?"

The smile left Arran's face for a moment before he recovered and gestured toward the street. "Do you notice all the lovely decorations we have in this beautiful city? It's a reminder of the upcoming holiday season, isn't it? A time for reflection on how love reached down into our sullied, dark histories and brought hope and a fresh start. I, for one, am grateful for second chances and the opportunity to prove that, with faith, I can rise above the latest version of myself to be a better person for those dearest to me and this country."

Charlie closed the computer and rested her face in her hands.

What was she thinking? Her life could never fit his.

If he'd stayed a carpenter in North Carolina, then no one would have cared about her history. But this?

She couldn't change her past or connections. There was no way to expunge her family's history. Her mother's imprisonment for robbery proved yet another stain to add to her extensive list.

And it would always be a part of Charlie's life. Heaven forbid if Charlie continued a relationship with Arran and her mother found a way to scrape up some demand for money.

She squeezed her eyes closed. She couldn't spend her life in constant worry that one day her past would prove too much for his heart . . . too much for their future. With a deep breath, she reached for her phone. Seven p.m. It'd be the middle of the night in Skymar. He'd be asleep.

Tears burned in her vision, but she blinked them away, accepting her choice.

She needed to keep her heart safe.

And, in the long run, this would prove the best for Arran too.

Surely he'd see that.

Charlie: Arran, the interview got me thinking. I'm a simple country girl and certainly not royal material, no matter what kinds of nice clothes I wear. And my family's past can only lead to more trouble for your family. To be perfectly honest, I don't think my heart can handle being broken by you, once you see I'm not the right fit for your world. I think, once you're back home long enough, you'll realize how right this choice is for both of us. Please forgive me for sending this via text. Forgive me for not being brave enough to try. You are a wonderful man, and I am so glad I had the opportunity to know you. You've made me feel special in a very fairy-tale sort of way, and I am awed, humbled, and grateful to have held your heart.

She winced at her own words blinking back at her, but she didn't see any other way.

She didn't belong with a prince!

And there was nothing she could do to change that.

THIRTEEN

The mobile rang again for the third time with no answer.

Arran stared down at the phone screen, doing the time zone math again. Nine a.m. her time. Surely she was awake by now.

When he'd woken up that morning to Charlotte's text, he'd nearly booked the first ticket back to North Carolina.

He needed to talk to her. Reason with her. Convince her the past didn't matter to him or his family. But even more so, he'd made his own choice: if she *couldn't* be brave enough to enter his world, he'd choose hers.

"Are you alright, son?"

Arran looked over to see his father joining him on the private balcony of Perth Hall, the country estate hidden in the northern mountains of Skymar. A *family* home. Quiet and safe from the noise and bother of the outside world. If only he could escape the noise of his heart as easily.

Arran turned his phone toward his father, with Charlotte's message on display.

"I know her history isn't a simple one, but it doesn't matter to me—except for how it impacts her."

His father nodded and handed him back the mobile. "I never discount someone's history."

Arran's gaze shot back to his father.

"Our histories define us, for good or ill. There's no changing that fact." Father's smile softened beneath his close-shaved beard.

"From all you've said, this Charlotte of yours is a capable and deeply compassionate sort. Some of the very hurts she's known likely also contribute to her strengths."

"I will fight to keep her, Father." Arran looked out over the countryside, his hands fisting the railing. "To convince her we are worth a chance."

"The media will run its course on the story and find a more interesting one soon enough." Father placed his palm on Arran's shoulder. "But here is my question. If she is not willing to take a chance on you, on all this"—his father waved an arm toward the horizon, encompassing the grand vista over the Skymarian landscape—"are you stronger now from knowing yourself better—and, perhaps, from knowing her—to continue forward with a healthier head and heart than the last time?"

Arran stared at his father, taking in the question. "I am most assuredly stronger now than I was before I left. I'm more secure in who I am and what I want," he said. "Which is why I am also willing to consider . . ." He paused and pulled in a breath. "A simpler life. If that's what she requires."

"You love her."

It wasn't a question. His father saw.

"I do." The admittance sank deep, securing his decision.

"Ellie's life and marriage to Luke has taught your mother and me to hold our expectations for our children more loosely than we'd planned." He grinned. "Apart from the past two years, you have proven an excellent ambassador and supporter of Skymar, especially your patronage of Bredon and the Western Isles. But you have a freedom not as easily afforded to your eldest siblings, and it offers you a choice."

"I know."

"Love has the potential to give any home the splendor of a palace, son."

The choice ached through him, a ripping of two worlds and two loves. He knew he could find happiness in her world. And although he'd been without her for merely a couple of weeks, he realized his world held less luster without her in it.

"It's true. And I've learned so much about love from you and Mother." Arran released a long breath. "But if Charlotte doesn't choose me . . ." He swallowed through his tightening throat. "I'd like to renew my commitment to my patronages and service to the realm. My time in North Carolina reminded me I have the desire and ability to serve others well." His gaze found his father's. "But right now my plan is to stay in Skymar through Christmas, and then return to North Carolina and win her back."

"If she's as smart as you claim"—his father smiled and drew in a deep breath—"I have no doubt you'll succeed."

Charlie: I promise to call you back, but I need to make it through the Gala tonight first. I leave in a half hour. Can we talk tomorrow?

Arran: I'll be preparing for the Royal Christmas Dinner tomorrow evening, so timing may be tricky, but I'll make it work.

Charlie: Thank you.

Arran: Charlotte, you need to know that I plan to return to North Carolina after Christmas. I've already spoken to Luke, and he's given me leave to stay at his place during his and Ellie's Skymar sabbatical and resume my spot on the building team. That will give me time to sort out my long-term plans. But one thing of which I am certain: I want to be where you are. And if that means my world changes, then so be it.

Charlie reread his text. Was he saying what she thought he was saying? Give up his royal life? Move to North Carolina?

For her?

Emotion gathered in her throat as she reread the message for the third time.

He was crazy.

Princes didn't do things like that. And working in construction? Living in her small Appalachian town?

Unless he believes I'm worth the chance.

The thought wedged in between her doubts like a crowbar. Any of the residual concerns about the former women in his life crashed beneath his choice, his determination. Her eyes burned with pooling tears.

Could he truly leave everything for her?

A knock at the front door startled her from her thoughts, and she peered out her bedroom window. Luke's truck sat in her driveway.

What was he doing here? He should be packing for his flight to Skymar.

She fastened the faux diamond earrings in place and then gave herself a quick look in the mirror. Arran had been right. She barely recognized herself in the elegance of such a gown. And with a touch more makeup, applied with the help of a YouTube video, and a careful twist of her hair, also from a YouTube video, she wondered if this was what Cinderella felt like as she walked into the prince's castle.

A lady.

Her gaze trailed back to her phone at the thought.

Another knock at the door pulled her from her musings and down the stairs. Luke stood on the threshold of the door, holding a large square package in hand and wearing a tux. His dark brows rose as he took her in, from her head down to her shoes and back. "You look amazing."

"And you're wearing a tux," she responded with equal astonishment.

"The invitation said 'formal,' so I figured this would work."

She gave her head a little shake. "You *own* a tux?"

And his regular, lopsided grin fell right into place. "Only because I'm married to a princess. Otherwise, I'd have gone for something less obnoxious and more comfortable."

She barked out a laugh, which didn't fit the sophistication of her dress at all. "What . . . what are you doing here? Don't you leave for Skymar in the morning?"

"I'm already packed." He gestured toward himself with his free hand. "Man. It only took me thirty minutes."

She bestowed upon him her most impressive eye roll.

"But I promised Arran I'd escort you, so here I am."

She stepped back for him to enter. "You promised Arran?"

He nodded, taking the familiar trek to her living room.

She swallowed through the lump in her throat. "Have you talked to him today?"

"Yeah, when he couldn't get ahold of you, he called me." Luke looked over at her. "I get it, Charlie. Probably better than anyone else. The idea of the royal life is daunting and weird." He shrugged one of those broad shoulders. "And I had to decide if I was willing to risk all the discomfort and negative media and strange royal protocol things and living six months of the year in a foreign country, but the rewards were a hundred times better. Ellie's been worth it all." He tugged at his collar. "Even the tux parts."

"But you're *you*." She waved a hand toward him. "Your history isn't like mine."

"You're right, it's not. But if Arran wasn't worried about it, then maybe that tells you how much *you* should be worried about it too." He stepped closer, dipping his head a little to catch her attention. "Charlie, it took years for you to step away from your past." He drew in a breath. "I can't know the hurt you've felt, but there comes a time when we have to quit sitting in the stink of our past and embrace the hope of the future."

"That was equally poetic and frightfully Appalachian at the same time."

His grin angled with a wiggle of his brows. "I have a gift."

She chuckled despite the sting in her eyes. "I don't know if I'm brave enough, Luke."

He nodded and pushed the package toward her. "Maybe this will help."

With a curious look at her cousin, she took the red-wrapped package and slowly pushed back the paper. Her breath caught in her throat. Framed in silver lay the painting from her childhood, complete with castle, girl, lion, and starlight. A quote, embossed in silver, fitted to the bottom of the frame.

"Have courage, dear heart."

She blinked up at Luke, thoughts stumbling one over the other. "Arran?"

"Yeah." Luke offered a one-shouldered shrug. "It took him weeks to find it, and with his connections, that's saying something."

All the jumbled desires and feelings within her warred for a victor. Her eyes burned as she sniffled.

"Now don't go messing up your makeup." He pulled a handkerchief from his pocket and handed it to her. "You don't have time to fix it."

She took the handkerchief and gently dabbed at her eyes. "I can't believe this."

"Yeah, maybe a picture is worth a thousand words after all."

She nailed him with a humorless stare. "Does your poetic side rise to battle emotional women or something?"

"Maybe." He grinned. "Or maybe there's a Renaissance man beneath all this grumpiness, just waiting to get out."

She laughed through another sniffle and ran a hand down the frame of the painting.

"But seriously, Charlie, he's a good guy. Even if he's a prince." Luke's grin sobered. "And I think that if you don't fight for your own fairy tale, you'll regret it for the rest of your life."

The words reverberated through her, but she fought against the tug. "I can't even believe you said that out loud."

"I probably got it from one of those silly Christmas romance movies Ellie's had on replay for the past three weeks." His shoulders slumped with a sigh. "She's promised her TV consumption will go back to normal after Christmas, but I'm afraid the Hallmark chime has destroyed her common sense."

Charlie chuckled again, her attention dropping back to the painting. "I thought choosing love was supposed to be easy."

"Easy?" Luke stared down at her, his gaze turning thoughtful. "Which fairy tale says that?"

"You're right." She offered a helpless wave of her arms and smiled. "Love never came easily in the fairy tales, did it?"

"And it usually took a whole lot of courage to make it to the happy ending." Luke shook his head. "From what I hear. Not that I've read any."

"Of course not." She offered another eye roll.

With a grin, Luke offered his arm. "You ready?"

His question dug deeper than a simple step from her house to his car. It prodded a choice she didn't fully know whether she had the courage to make.

She glanced back at the painting and slid her arm through his, embracing the possibility. "I am."

❄

The turnout for the Mistletoe Gala proved the largest in Ransom's history. Three hundred folks filled the banquet room of The Avenue Hotel, the ballroom adorned with greenery and lights, and a massive Christmas tree in one corner.

Charlie had survived—and even *thrived*—as the coordinator for such a large event.

She wasn't the same person she'd been before.

And no, it wasn't the gown or the makeup, though she'd learned to appreciate those at times. The change ran deeper. And some of that change had to do with Arran.

As Charlie took the stage, familiar smiles greeted her from the crowd. Grace Mitchell and her family. Several of the top donors. The entire rowdy clan of Edgewoods. Then her attention fastened on Kevin Lindsey and his two girls.

Her vision blurred for a second, but she cleared her throat and stepped to the microphone. *Number one: gratitude and/or welcome.*

"This has been the best and biggest year of The Mistletoe Wish, and it is all because of you." She continued, calling out certain sponsors, donors, and volunteers, the joy among the crowd spilling over in laughter, smiles, and applause. But that's how gratitude seemed to work: in a contagious sort of way.

Number two: acknowledge the story.

"The Mistletoe Wish began as a Christmas fundraiser because of the season we celebrate this time of year—a season of commemorating how love came to earth and inspired a contagion of joy, hope, generosity, and love throughout the centuries."

She smiled at the crowd, bringing them along with her. "The volunteers of The Mistletoe Wish desire to bring joy through generosity to the families we serve, but more than anything, we hope to shine a little of God's love into their lives. Because love gives us a sense of worth, and that worth inspires courage."

Charlie paused on the phrase. She'd written it a week ago. Days before Arran's interview.

"As a child, it's difficult to believe people truly care about you when one of your parents chooses something or someone else over you. A sense of doubt in trusting people, or the fear of not being enough for someone else, can leave us in constant uncertainty about the choices we make and the people we *believe* love us." She chuckled. "I think that's why one of my favorite Bible verses is 'Be merciful to those who doubt.'"

A soft rumble of laughter spread through the room.

"But this charity brings people together to build hope and courage. Especially"—she shrugged and pointed to herself—"for those who doubt."

Charlie completely abandoned her notes, the message pouring from some place deep inside her scarred-yet-healed heart.

"The Wish reminded me of the very reason for this season. God thought we were worth a miracle." She laughed to herself. "Worthy of the impossible." Her gaze fastened on Luke, his knowing smile confirming the realization in her heart. "Because knowing you are loved changes everything."

Her breath burst out in a laugh.

She wanted to fight for her future.

"I used to let those hurts hold me back from being brave. I couldn't—wouldn't—believe what I had to offer was enough. I mean, he's a *prince*."

A rumble of voices spread across the room, and Charlie pulled her mind back to her task. Had she voiced that out loud? In front of everyone?

Heat rushed from her toes to her forehead, and she searched the room for an ally. Of course, Luke was no help at all. He stood there covering his grin with his hand, his shoulders shaking with his laugh.

She stifled a wince and cleared her throat, focusing back on her paper. "So if you want to continue being a part of The Mistletoe Wish story, we have cards at each table explaining ways you can get involved. Let's reach as many kids as we can with the message that they are worthy of love and a future."

Applause followed her across the stage and down to the bottom of the steps, where Luke already waited for her.

"Can you make room on your flight tomorrow for one more?"

Luke narrowed his eyes and looked up to the ceiling as if contemplating, then his grin took a tilt. "I have special connections now. I think we can make it happen."

In usual royal fashion, the decorations for the Christmas Banquet exceeded last year's in elegance and beauty, in part due to his eldest sister, Rosalyn's, involvement for the first time. As Princess Royal, she was slowly being trained to take over more responsibilities, and she took to the role with the seriousness and extravagance it deserved.

A string quartet played at the far corner of the room, filling the space with soft Christmas melodies and the promise of caroling later in the evening.

The entire ambience took on a different hue now that Arran planned to leave it all behind. He shook his head with a sad smile. After disregarding his title for a couple of years, to face possibly relinquishing it after resurrecting his appreciation felt strangely ironic.

But the more he considered his choice, the more certain he became.

He wanted to pursue a future with Charlotte Edgewood, and if that meant a redirection of his plans, so be it.

A new wave of visitors entered the room, a dignitary here and an honored guest there, each moving along the royal assembly line to receive a proper greeting before dispersing into the Dining Hall for dinner and dancing.

As the youngest son, Arran stood near the end of the receiving line with Ellie. "Wasn't Luke supposed to be here by now?"

Ellie shifted a step closer. "The flight was delayed, but he's upstairs changing and assured me he was on his way to the Reception Room."

"Do you think he created an excuse to keep from spending more time in a tux than necessary?" Arran asked as he tugged at his own bow tie.

"Very possible." Ellie smiled, nodding as another guest passed before them. "But I do so love him in a tux."

Arran pressed his eyes closed with a sigh to let Ellie know exactly how he felt about her expressed appreciation of her husband in a tux.

"Any news from Charlotte today?" Ellie asked.

Arran looked away, the answer dropping like a stone in his stomach. "Nothing."

"But you both have been busy."

"Never too busy to phone, if she truly wished to speak to me." He gave his head a shake. "I've got to find a way to convince her that we can fit in the world together, wherever that world may be."

"That sounds terribly romantic, Arran." Ellie's lips pinched in a smile. "It must be love."

He blatantly ignored her teasing. "As soon as I find another break in the evening, I'll attempt to phone her again. She needs to be assured of my intentions." He searched his sister's face. "And I wouldn't mind a little assurance of hers."

Ellie's attention flitted over his shoulder and her full smile released. "Oh yes, that. I think you need not doubt her sincere feelings, brother-dear."

"What do you mean?"

Ellie's raised brow and widened smile was her only response. Arran followed her gaze and turned toward a doorway that led from the private rooms of the palace. Two servants held the double doors open to reveal an entering couple. Luke stepped forward, and on his arm walked . . .

All the air left Arran's lungs in one burst.

Charlotte?

His gaze trailed down her, and he sucked in all the breath he'd just released.

She'd purchased the red gown.

His grin stretched in response.

It looked remarkable on her.

And she'd worn her hair down, just as he liked it best. Long and wavy.

She stared back at him, her expression serious, her gaze searching his as if she wasn't certain what to do next.

"You may want to actually move toward her, Arran." Ellie's voice broke into his shock, and she prodded him forward with a slight push. "That would be more romantic than standing here with your mouth hanging open like a codfish."

He snapped his lips together and blinked, forcing his feet into motion.

She was here?

She'd flown to Skymar.

For him.

He didn't trust his voice as he approached her, so without breaking his stride or uttering a word, he nodded to Luke, slipped Charlotte's arm through his, and walked right back out the doors from which she'd just come.

"Arran?"

Her voice proved her all the more real, her delicious apple scent another welcome confirmation. Without a word, he continued down the hallway until he pulled her into a private alcove out of sight of the others.

She looked up at him, brow creased. "Arran, I—"

His mouth caught her words, drinking in the taste of those familiar lips. Her body stilled at their contact, but then something like a gasp escaped from her lips. She wrapped her arms around him, burrowing deeper against him.

He drew back and studied her face, those liquid silver eyes, her flushed pink cheeks, those rosy lips. "You're here?"

She laughed and then shrugged her beautifully bare shoulders. "Merry Christmas?"

"*Merry* doesn't seem a big enough word. Extraordinary?" His palm traced her cheek. "Remarkable?" He took both her hands in his as his gaze roamed over her face again and again, certain if he looked away, she may disappear. "How . . . What changed your mind?"

Her smile faltered a little. "While I was giving my speech at the Gala, I realized . . . I realized that . . ."

"I love you?"

"Yes." She squeezed his hands. "Or rather, I accepted the truth that you loved me." She rocked on tiptoe and kissed him again. "I'd always hoped that my prince would come and find me. But when he did, I thought I wasn't brave enough to . . . *be* enough." She raised a timid palm to his cheek. "But love has a crazy way of bringing a whole lot of courage with it." She offered a helpless look. "So I thought it was my turn to come find my prince and let him know how much I . . . love him too."

"*Your* prince?"

"Well, if you want to be." She wrinkled up her nose in the most adorable way. "I *have* been waiting my whole life for you."

He laughed, capturing her face in his hands. "I'm yours, darling. All yours." He tasted her lips again, his eyes burning a little from sheer pleasure. She loved him. She'd come to Skymar to show him. "How long can you stay?"

Her smile took a playful turn. "Well, since my boss is already here and he thought I could use some time off . . ."

He captured her lips for another brief kiss. "Then I can introduce you to my world, and we can sort out the future together."

"That sounds like an excellent plan." Her smile wobbled. "Perhaps an ease of entry for this country girl into royal life would be a good idea for everyone involved."

"I have no doubt you will manage it all." He brushed a thumb across her cheek. "You look lovely, by the way." He breathed out the compliment around another astonished chuckle.

"Thank you." One brow teased high. "The dress came highly recommended by a prince I know."

"Smart prince. You should listen to him more often."

She laughed, a lovely light and wonderfully happy sound. "Well, since you're so smart *and* a prince . . ." She leaned in close, their breaths mingling. "What do you figure our chances are at a happily-ever-after?"

"Chance?" He slipped his arms more tightly around her. "There's no chance about it, Miss Edgewood, if you're by my side." He breached the distance between their lips for a brief touch. "You and I are a certainty."

And then, as if mistletoe surrounded every corner of the alcove, he kissed her long enough to convince her of their mutual certainty of a happily-ever-after.

SAY NO
TO MISTLETOE

Sheila Roberts

ONE

Mistletoe is my kryptonite. One kiss under it, and I go weak in the head. My last three mistletoe kisses resulted in relationship disaster. Which is why I, Hailey Fairchild, am swearing off it.

You'd think after three love fails, I'd hate cupid. I don't. I'm one of his loyal acolytes. I write romance novels. I'm a believer.

If you ask me, everyone should be. We need more love in the world. *I* need more love, but so far I'm only finding it on the pages of my computer screen.

On the screen is better than nothing. At least that's what I keep telling myself.

Consider this a public service announcement, a warning. Don't go under the mistletoe. It's hazardous to your heart. Here's what it did to me.

Mistletoe Disaster Number One

Gregory, as in Gregory Peck, a.k.a. Atticus Finch in the classic movie *To Kill a Mockingbird*. Tall and dark and noble-looking. My grandma made me watch the movie with her when I was a kid, and I was hypnotized by his deep voice.

Like the movie star, this Gregory was tall and lean with dark hair and brown eyes, and he had an air of brooding mystery. Which was appropriate, since he wrote mysteries.

I met him at a party thrown by a friend of a friend. I spotted him across the room, surrounded by drooling women dressed to kill in body-hugging holiday dresses and heels high enough to give their arches cramps, and I thought, *Don't even try*. I wasn't dressed to kill. *Dressed to maim*, I thought, in my black silk pants and red top with a black silk jacket.

I'm not so bad to look at anymore. I've shed some poundage. Lost the zits. And hey, glasses are in style, and I have great frames. I think they make me look smart and glam. But I knew I couldn't compete with those women. I mean, they were beautiful. So I tried for aloofness, thinking it might make me look mysterious and unattainable.

I got my Christmas punch and strolled around the room, trying to pretend I belonged. And sort of nudged closer to Mr. Gorgeous and his fans.

"I think it's so rad that you're a writer," one gushed.

A writer! I was a writer. I'd just sold my first romance novel to Heartfelt, my publisher's romance line.

"It's not easy," Gregory said. "Everyone thinks they can write a book, but most people never do, and half the ones who do just write drek."

Hmm. A bit of a snob. What did he think of romance writers?

I had to know, so I abandoned my mysterious vibe and inserted myself into the conversation. "And what would you describe as 'drek'?" I challenged.

He shrugged and looked down his elegant nose at me. "I suppose you want to be a writer?"

I lifted my chin just a little. "I already am."

"Oh, who's your publisher?" he asked, and the other women drifted away.

I couldn't help feeling a little superior since I'd outshone them. (Outshining never happened to me when I was younger.)

"Herald Publishing," I said, and his eyebrows went up in surprise.

"Really?" He motioned to the sofa. "Sit down. Let's talk."

And so we did. He seemed perfect. I gave him my phone number.

Before I left, well, there was the mistletoe, hanging in the doorway. He caught my arm and gave me a little tug. It was so cute and romantic, I stepped right up and let him kiss me.

It was an impressive kiss, heady stuff for a girl whose first mistletoe kiss at the age of fourteen had about scarred her for life. This man wanted to be under there with me. Oh yes!

Except . . . Gregory whispered something creepy after our kiss that tarnished it a bit. *Ding, ding, ding!* Went a little warning bell, but I was already lost in that heady mistletoe fog, so of course I ignored it and went out with him.

One time. By dessert I knew it wasn't going to work. I wanted sweetness and chivalry. I quickly caught on that Gregory wanted . . . well, not that.

Mistletoe Disaster Number Two

That was Edmond, as in Edmond Dantès, the Count of Monte Cristo. Sigh. He worked in the art department at Herald Publishing, and I'd met him when I visited and got a tour of the offices. Lo and behold, there he was at the publisher's Christmas cocktail party, dressed in a gray suit and his dark hair flopped over one eye. Ready for a *GQ* shoot.

My first book, *What the Heart Seeks*, had done well, and I'd just turned in my second novel, *What the Heart Needs*. Back then I was beginning to believe everything I wrote; I was sure I was starting to figure out the ways of love. And Edmond, with his soft-spoken voice and sweet smile, fit the bill perfectly. I prefer strong alpha males in my books, but they can be problematic IRL, so it was points for Edmond that he didn't fall into that category. He also got points for being interested in my budding career.

At the time I thought that was hardly surprising. We were both in the business, after all. It was only natural that he would want to talk about how I was doing. I was happy to brag that I was doing fine and expected to keep on doing fine. The romance genre captures nearly a third of the book market and generates over a billion dollars a year. You've got to respect that. He did. And I respected him for appreciating what I do for a living . . . well, *almost* living. (I've finally been able to cut my barista hours down to half-time. Yay, me! Another few books, and maybe I can finally write full-time and still afford to eat.)

Edmond lured me under the mistletoe with a shy suggestion that we should get into the spirit of the season.

It was such a sweet kiss, with the promise of happily-ever-after. Oh yes. It erased the memory of him mentioning how you don't choose a career in publishing to get rich, followed by a little quip about finding the next Nora Roberts and marrying her. Set for life that way. Ha-ha. I thought it was a joke.

It wasn't. Edmond was a mooch. It's not cheap living in New York, even when you have roommates, and heaven knows my roommate, Ramona, and I did our share of scrimping, so I understood Edmond's need to pinch pennies. But in my novels, men pull their weight. I want the same thing in life. Edmond wasn't even going near his weight, let alone pulling it. I wasted a lot of money on that man. Thank you, mistletoe, for blinding me to what should have been obvious.

Mistletoe Disaster Number Three

David. That's such a strong name, isn't it? I hear it and think of Michelangelo's famous statue. Sigh.

I met him last year, at yet another Christmas party. That had been a promising kiss and a promising relationship. Or so I'd thought. After I've turned in my work mess in progress—if I ever finish this mess in progress—my next book is going to be titled *Blind Love*. How's that for a great title? It was inspired by David.

That mistletoe mania night, he'd been flirting with women like he was auditioning to play Casanova in a movie. But when he got around to me, he said I was the most awesome woman there and, well, that's all it took for me to be put on the path to disaster. And when he got me under the mistletoe, kryptonite hit again. All my brain cells shut down.

I plunged into the relationship, a love diver going headfirst into shallow water, sure we were headed for an engagement by Christmas. I was ready. I was thirty-three and reaching the point where the snooze alarm on my biological clock refuses to be silenced.

It turned out his clock had a much later setting, and I wasn't the only one he was watching rom-coms with. We broke up on Halloween. How's that for scary?

So, there you have it. Now here I am, trying to finish this stupid book, *What the Heart Knows*, which, in my case, is nothing. Oh, and I'm dreading the holidays. I should have been coming home to Cascade, Washington, the mountain town in—wait for it—the Cascades, with a ring on my finger and Save the Date announcements in my purse. Instead, I'll be arriving with a bare finger and a chewed-up heart, all thanks to that love piranha. The dirty, rotten, cheating . . . never mind. I'm not going to think about it.

Or the mistletoe incident that started this sick cycle I've been trapped in—the one kiss that's lived in my heart since ninth grade and haunted me like one of Scrooge's ghosts. It was terrifying, wonderful, and mortifying. It has kept me both entranced by and vulnerable to that stupid mistletoe ever since. And, to be honest, my heart still longs for the kind of ending I like to write, where the man who was my first love falls for me and becomes my forever love.

I'm not looking forward to coming home a love loser, even though I'll get to see my family and my old BFF Scarlet. There will be baking binges with Mom and parties. And there is bound to be mistletoe. I must avoid it at all costs.

And I must avoid Carwyn Davies, the great unrequited love of my young life.

Carwyn is the stuff a girl's dreams are made of. He was a junior in high school when he gave me my first-ever mistletoe kiss, already playing on the varsity basketball team. He looked like a Viking, with that golden hair and those intense eyes that were blue. No, green. No, both.

Of course, even though we lived right next to each other, even though he and my older brother Sam shot hoops in his driveway, he never saw me. He was three years older and too busy dating cheerleaders with perfect skin and flowing blond hair to notice a pudgy freshman girl with glasses and boring brown hair. Heck, I didn't even notice myself.

THE KISS happened at the neighborhood Christmas party at the Davieses' house. Mrs. Davies had hung mistletoe right there in the living room archway. I'd paused under it, not because I wanted to be kissed—I was way too shy to go looking for something so public. I hadn't even seen it. I'd simply hesitated, looking around the room, searching for Scarlet and wondering where I could hide if she wasn't there to talk to. It was such a large gathering, and I felt conspicuous in the bulky red sweater my mother had knitted for me. I looked like a big, round Christmas ornament with legs.

My dopey brother had teased me about standing there. "Looking for a lip-lock, Hailey?" he'd asked. Then, before I could reply, he summoned Carwyn. "Hey, Car, come give Hailey a zap."

My heart went into overdrive, and the blood rushed to my head, setting my whole face on fire. I tried to back away, but there was Sam right behind me, and there came Carwyn. Gorgeous, smiling Carwyn. No glasses, not a zit to be seen anywhere on that perfect face of his. (I, on the other hand, had one blooming right on my chin.) He strolled up to me and, with a chuckle, pulled me up against him like we were going to start dirty dancing right there in his living room in front of his family and all our neighbors and God and all the angels on holiday patrol.

I still get hot and bothered thinking about it. He had the kind of hard body like those heroes in the romance novels I devoured. He touched my lips with his perfect masterful ones, and my world tilted. I could smell his spicy aftershave, and he tasted like peppermint.

My breath smelled like garlic and onions, thanks to the chips and dip I'd gotten into before we came to the party.

Of course, he wasn't into it. I knew that. Who would be into kissing an onion-infested Christmas ornament? With zits. It was a joke, and it was all so humiliating.

I pulled away as fast as I could, pushing my glasses up my suddenly sweaty nose. My whole face was sizzling so hot you could have broiled a steak over it.

One of the older women said, "Isn't that cute?"

No, it wasn't cute. It was mortifying.

"Hey, what's your hurry?" Carwyn teased as I bolted for the punch bowl.

I'd have liked nothing better than to crawl under the dining room table with its long, red tablecloth and stay there forever, but you can only pull that off when you're five. So I tried to act cool and put out the fire burning my face with eggnog punch and pretend that I didn't want to act like a five-year-old.

I kept my back to Carwyn and the party guests while the sizzle on my face died down. The sizzle on my lips subsided, too, and that was sad. Later that night, alone in my room, I put my fingers to my lips, trying to recapture that glorious sensational second. Kissed by Carwyn Davies—holiday magic!

I remained trapped in the throes of unrequited love clear through high school. To feed my sickness I read Jane Austen and the Brontës and every book Barbara Cartland and Georgette Heyer ever wrote. I devoured Debbie Macomber and Susan Wiggs and Susan Elizabeth Phillips. And sighed at the end of each book, envisioning myself and Carwyn as the hero and heroine of those stories. I went to every basketball game he played in, sitting in the bleachers with Scarlet and sighing longingly as I watched him in action, all muscled and gorgeous. I dreamed about him at night but hid in my room whenever he came over to game with Sam. I couldn't think of another guy, let alone date one.

Not that boys were banging on the door. Shy bookworms were not in high demand. Except as a cliché in a novel.

I know about clichés. My first stories were full of them— beautiful, snobby cheerleaders (I know there are nice ones out there, but I didn't know any, and I wasn't about to give a single one of my fictional cheerleaders a heart); handsome jocks who could never see when the perfect girl was right under their nose; mean girls who got what was coming to them in the end. And girls like me, who were always successful and beautiful by the end of the story. And wore contacts. Of course they got contacts.

Except I didn't. I've never been able to master sticking something in my eye. I tried. Heaven knows, I tried. Anyway, like I said, glasses are in style now. And I'm in better shape these days, thanks to regular visits to that torture chamber known as the gym. But here I am, still single.

It seems everyone else in Cascade is with someone now. Scarlet is engaged and living in LA. Her younger sister Billie, who never left town, is married and working on baby number two. And Mom tells me that even Sam has found a serious girlfriend.

I just learned this yesterday when we were talking on the phone. *"Maybe you know her,"* Mom said. *"Gwendolyn Payne?"*

Yes, I know Gwendolyn—snobby mean girl. I suddenly felt like someone whacked me in the face with a giant Christmas pickle. If there's one person I don't want to see ever again, it's her. She was one of my nemeses when I was in high school. And Sam has fallen for her? Seriously? Did she hypnotize him?

Of course, she'll be on the scene, all smooth and slick. And there I'll be, all . . . alone.

Earlier in the year, when I thought I'd finally found true love, I'd been looking forward to coming home for Christmas with bling on my finger and a perfect man in tow. Revenge of the Nerd Girl. Career success, romance success—I'd have it all. I'm happy I still have my career (so far), but coming back as a love loser really stinks. And frankly, right now so does writing romance novels. Which doesn't bode well for my career.

Part of me wants to hide here on the East Coast, but I wiggled out of going home last Christmas, and that got me in scalding-hot water. If I try it again, my parents will disown me, especially since they insisted on buying my ticket. Anyway, I do want to see my family. I just don't want to run into any of the women who made me so miserable. I especially don't want to see Gwendolyn. But there she'll be. And then there's Carwyn.

If I could just stay in the house, I'd be fine, but Mom has plans. She has plans upon plans.

Including an appearance at the local bookstore.

Mom is my number-one fan and has bought copies of my books and passed them out to all her friends. In honor of my return, she's talked Eloise Matthews, the owner of Mountain Books, into having me in for a book-signing party. (That probably wasn't hard to do.

After all, Mom's bought so many of my books there that I think she's single-handedly kept Mountain Books in business. Eloise owes her big-time.) I'm not wild about standing in front of a crowd and reading from my novels. I always find parts I could have written better, and it's sooo embarrassing to read those second-best sentences.

I'll have to smile and sign books and pretend I'm not a romance fraud who writes about love but can't get it right in real life.

I shouldn't have committed to coming home so early and staying clear through New Year's. That's too much time—too many opportunities for Christmas gremlins to get into my life and mess it all up even worse than it already is. I can only hope the Davies family won't host their annual Christmas party. If they do, there's bound to be mistletoe. My kryptonite. Santa, help me!

TWO

He was everything she'd ever dreamed of.
—Hailey Fairchild, *What the Heart Seeks*

I'm flying out tomorrow, a whole eight days before Christmas Eve. In addition to the bookstore appearance, Mom's expecting me to be part of her cookie exchange, which means baking and cookie temptation. And she's volunteered me to speak to Mrs. Wharton's freshman English class.

"Future readers," Mom had said. *"It's important to be visible when you're an author. Marketing."*

Mom used to sell candles on the party plan. She knows about marketing.

"Janet is delighted you're going to do this," Mom had added. *"And then there's the book-signing party at Mountain Books. Everyone's coming."*

"This is going to be a circus," I tell Ramona, my roommate, who's watching me pack.

"You need to face your demons."

Carwyn Davies is the first face that comes to mind. He's hardly a demon, but the few times I've seen him when I've been home (from as great a distance as I could manage), it's about given me hives.

Then there have been those encounters with mean girls who loved to make my life miserable back in high school. I was never even sure why. Because I was smart and that intimidated them?

Because I was shy and easily embarrassed, and that made me an easy target? Who knows. All I know is most of them haven't changed, and I don't care if I ever see any of them again. But it's Christmas. No matter where we've moved, everyone comes back home for Christmas, even the ones who ought to be taken captive by Krampus. And the worst of them, one of the ones who never left, is now with my brother.

"What doesn't kill you makes you stronger," Ramona says.

Like me, Ramona is pursuing creative success. In the theater. Which is why, like me, she has a side hustle as a barista. Unlike me, Ramona is gorgeous, with long dark hair and dark eyes. She never met a brownie she didn't like but still has the most perfect body on the planet . . . without enduring gym torture. When I get all jealous, she just shrugs and says she's got good genes. The gene pool is a rip-off, if you ask me. Still, I love her, and I know she's going to be a star on Broadway someday. She's already promised me free tickets.

If, for some crazy reason, she ever changes her mind about acting, she could be a life coach.

"What if this kills me?" I shoot back at her.

She gives a snort. Ramona is a snorter, which I love. Everyone should have one flaw, right?

"You're a successful author. Everybody's going to fawn all over you." She dives across the bedroom, which we share in our itsy-bitsy apartment, and pulls a gift bag from behind her twin bed. "Got you a care kit."

"Aww, really? Sweetness."

I dig into it, and the first thing I pull out is a Seattle Chocolates chocolate bar. Rainier cherry. My fave.

"Got it on Amazon," Ramona says. "Save it for when you're in crisis mode."

"I'll probably be in crisis mode the whole time," I say. "Why did I let Mom talk me into staying clear through New Year's?"

"Because it's family, and family is important."

She's right about that.

Next, I pull out a small pink journal.

"I know you're going to get inspired with ideas for book titles and characters," Ramona says.

I hope I don't get inspired to write a horror story.

Finally, I pull out an Anastasia Beverly Hills lipstick. Rose-colored.

"There's not enough of yours left to dig out with a toothpick," she points out.

What can I say? I make things last. I'm thrifty. Living in New York, you have to be.

Still, it's worth it. I love the energy of the city. I love spending time in the art museums and hanging out at cozy little dives with some of the other writers I've met.

"You are the best," I tell Ramona.

"Yes, I am," she agrees. "And I have a mantra for you."

"You know I don't do mantras," I say.

"Okay then, a slogan. Repeat it on the plane and when you land. Definitely repeat it if you go to any parties where there's mistletoe."

This should be interesting. "What is it?"

"Say, 'I am smart, I am strong, I can conquer any situation, and I can resist mistletoe.'"

I repeat the words, stressing the mistletoe resistance. "You're right," I say. "I've got this."

I give her a big hug and thank her. I feel like an ancient knight who's just been armored up. I am now ready to go to battle, er, home.

The next day I am up before any bird with a brain and Ubering my way to the airport. I should be used to getting up early. I work a morning shift at the coffee shop around the corner, and my shift starts at a time I used to consider nighttime. But I don't like it. I dream of the day when I'm making so much money as a writer that I can wake up when I want and set my own work schedule. (It's coming soon. I hope!)

I don't really like to fly either. Every little bump and dip sends my imagination soaring, and I can see myself trapped inside the plane with its tail on fire and its wings blown off, hurtling toward the ground. The dark side of imagination.

Happily, on this flight I am distracted by a friendly grandma–type who wants to yak. And when she learns I'm a writer, she wants to know all about what kind of books I write.

"Ah, love," she says after I tell her. "It's what makes the world go round."

It's made mine spin pretty crazily, but not in a good way.

Her parting words to me as we're leaving the plane are, "I hope some nice young man catches you under the mistletoe."

No, no, no! If I didn't have my hands full with my carry-on and my purse, I'd be plugging my ears. Too late. I've heard her and the first thing that swims in front of my eyes is a vision of Carwyn Davies coming up to me, moving like an elegant panther and holding up a sprig of mistletoe.

I recite the words Ramona gave me. "I am smart, I am strong, I can conquer any situation, and I can resist mistletoe." Yes, I can.

Both Mom and Dad are waiting at the cell phone lot at Sea-Tac International Airport to pick me up. Dad owns a masonry supply store, and he's taken the day off so he can, as he put it, "be with his girls." He and Mom have been married thirty-nine years, and they still like to hang out together. Now that's love.

I text them that I've arrived and make my way to the passenger pickup area. Within minutes, Dad's vintage Volvo station wagon is pulling up curbside, and he's out and running around the car to load my suitcase. Mom has ejected herself from the car, too, and is rushing to hug me like I've been gone for a million years.

Suddenly it feels like I have, and I'm so glad to see my parents. Moving away and adulting is all well and good, but their excitement over welcoming me back into the nest, knowing they love me and always will, no matter what? That makes me go all mushy inside and happy to have flown back.

Dad was a football player in college. The muscle has turned to flab, and he looks a little like a water heater with legs. And he's losing his hair, poor guy. Although Mom says that's okay because he has a perfectly shaped head for being bald. She made him shave his head because she said that ring of hair around his shiny top made him look like a monk, and she doesn't want to be married to a monk.

Good ol' Mom. She may be bossy, but she has a heart as big as Mount Rainier.

She looks great. Except for her hair, which she's dyed an alarming shade of clown-wig red. Yikes! But that's Mom. She likes to make a statement. I wonder what kind of statement this new hair color is supposed to be.

"Welcome home, Princess," says Dad, taking my carry-on.

I know he'd hug me, but Mom got to me first and has her arms wrapped around me like a python. "It's so good to have you back, baby girl," she says.

"It's good to be back," I say.

With Mom's arms around me, I feel the truth of it. Texts and Zoom are great, but hugs are the best.

"Everyone is excited to see you," she says.

Everyone meaning her friends, of course. I don't have many everyones left in town, other than my best friend Scarlet's little sister. Scarlet will be in town visiting, though, and I'm looking forward to seeing her. And, of course, I have my brother, Sam. But he'll be obsessed with his new someone. Who will probably be obsessed with making me feel gauche.

"Your brother's already talking about a Wii bowling marathon tonight."

"I'll lose," I predict. I always do.

She chuckles, then hurries on. "Then I promised I'd bring you by the bookstore tomorrow to see Eloise. She wants to talk to you about your book event. She's ordered fifty copies of that Christmas anthology you're in. I hope it will be enough."

"I hope there won't be a ton of books left over," I fret. Author humiliation when that happens!

"There won't be," Mom assures me. "Everyone's coming."

This is almost scarier than the idea of ending the evening with a pile of unsold books. Being the center of attention in a large group is not an introvert's idea of a good time. And remember how much I hate reading in front of people.

"Gram's knitting group alone is going to take up one row," Mom continues.

I can't help but smile at that. "Gram's the best."

She loves romance novels. She keeps begging me to write something super steamy. My grandma and sexy books—sometimes it's hard for me to make the connection.

"And the women's Bible study group from church will all be there," Mom adds, which makes me glad I'm not listening to Gram's advice. The last thing I want is the pastor's wife buying a book of mine and stumbling on a scene I've written where clothes are flying everywhere and my characters are too busy doing all kinds of stuff to each other to bother shutting the door.

"Then there's the talk to Mrs. Wharton's freshman English class on Monday," Mom hurries on.

More torture. I groan.

"They'll love you," Mom assures me.

According to Mom every girl at Cascade High wants to grow up to be me. "Glad I can inspire someone," I mutter.

I just hope none of them ask about my personal life. I'm not exactly taking vacays to Tahiti and dating celebrities, something I always envisioned successful writers doing. But we can't all be Danielle Steel.

"And we have the cookie exchange on Friday, the Davieses' Christmas party next week..."

Where there will be mistletoe. *Don't think about it!*

"And tonight Gwendolyn is coming over for dinner. She's looking forward to seeing you."

I'll bet. More like looking forward to looking down her perfect, pert nose at me and finding a way to make me feel like a loser.

I am smart, I am strong, and I can conquer any situation. I can certainly conquer sitting across the kitchen table from Gwendolyn Payne.

I half want to tell Mom what a horrible creature Gwendolyn is, but I keep my mouth shut. I mean, she *is* Sam's girlfriend.

"Gram and Grandpa will be joining us. Gram's already at the house, baking the gumdrop cookies."

"My favorite." Gram's motto is "Cookies say love." It's a great motto.

"Lasagna for dinner," adds Dad.

"We figured we could lure you back with your favorites," Mom says, and I know she's talking about more than Christmas.

But I can't leave New York. It's where I have a whole new life. A safe life. I know some people think big cities are dangerous, but let me tell you, small towns can be just as deadly when sharks from your past are swimming in the water.

As we head north on the freeway, the cities like Seattle and Lynwood fall away. Soon we come to farms and pasture, and then we bear east and we're heading toward the Cascades. Foothills, mountains, and the famous Seattle rain turning to snow. Trees are shrugging on a shawl of lacy white.

We come to the town of Cascade and it could be a movie set, with the snowy trees and the houses with colored lights strung along their rooflines, waiting for dark and their time to show off. And, in the background, the Cascade River.

Like a lot of the houses in town, ours is a Craftsman with a long front porch. Blue with white trim. Seeing it brings back memories of family movie nights complete with popcorn and root beer, of baking cookies with my mom and grandma, of sitting in that swing on the front porch with a bag of chips and a book. Of watching Carwyn from behind the pages as he and Sam shot hoops.

Surprisingly enough, Carwyn never left Cascade. He's now the principal at the high school. And I bet he looks as gorgeous as he did the last time I saw him, which was from a distance. For one crazy moment I imagine running into him downtown—not here at the house, that's too boring. No, I'm out by myself, having a cup of coffee that someone else has made and looking elegant in a sleek, red winter coat (I don't own one), looking like a modern-day Audrey Hepburn.

Not that *that* will ever happen. I'll never be as elegant as Audrey. And I probably won't have one minute to myself, not with all the things Mom has planned for me. But still . . . in my imagination it's a quiet, perfect moment. He does a double take and says, *Hailey, is that you? You look amazing.*

"Here we are," says Dad as we slide into the driveway. The streets are still icy, I can tell, but Dad's thrown rock salt around like birdseed, so we make it into the house without anybody going down. I'm going to have to bag wearing my cute shooties and dig out my trusty old winter boots if I want to stay upright around here. Not

very glam, though. I'll at least wear my good stuff when I'm out trying to look impressive. For sure when I go to the high school to talk
to the kids.

But here at home . . . I'm suddenly ready for jammie bottoms,
slippers, and a sweater.

The minute I walk into the house, the aroma of baking cookies
skips over to meet me. What is it about the smell of something
baking that says home?

Not so welcoming is the sight of mistletoe hanging in the front
hall. Really, Mom? Naturally, with Sam's new love there must be
mistletoe. I'm sure staying away from it, though.

"We're here," Mom calls, and a moment later my grandma is in
the hallway, short and round, wearing a red sweater to match her
red-rimmed glasses, coming toward me with arms outstretched.

"Look at you, all New York and elegant," she says. "You look
fabulous, chickie-boo."

Ah yes, family always sees through the eyes of love. "Thanks,"
I say.

"Give me your coat," Mom says.

"I'll take your bags to your room," Dad says.

"Come have a cookie and some peppermint tea," Gram says.

For a moment I do feel a little like Danielle Steel, like someone
important. Yep, it's nice to be loved.

Of course, once Sam comes over after work—he works with Dad
in the business—he does his brotherly duty and pops my fat head.

Mom and Gram have insisted I stay out of the kitchen, like I'm
some kind of visiting royalty, and he finds me reading in the living
room.

"Hey, geek-o," he teases and gives a me a brotherly punch in
the arm. "About time you came home. You better not have eaten
all the cookies."

"Ha-ha," I say.

He plops down on the couch and sprawls out his long legs in front of him. "Glad you're back. We miss you around here."

"You just miss having someone to bug," I tease. Heaven knows he did enough of that when we were growing up.

"There is that. Seriously, though, you know we're all proud of you."

"Thanks," I say.

Sam is such a good bro. We had our share of fights when we were kids, but he also got me through algebra, helped me practice for my driving test when I was sixteen, and always bought me romance novels for Christmas and my birthday. And, of course, bought copies of my books. He's a good guy. Way too good for Gwendolyn.

He clears his throat, a sure sign that he's about to step into an awkward conversation. "Look, I'm sorry about—"

I cut him off. "Don't even say the name."

"He didn't deserve you."

"You're right," I say and mean it. "But hey, New York's a big place. I'll find my perfect match." Just not under the mistletoe.

"New York isn't the only place with men, you know."

"I know."

"Lots of men around here."

I think of Carwyn. There's an impossible dream.

"Just sayin'. You could move back."

"Maybe someday," I say. Except I don't see that happening. New York is where my friends are. It's where I found myself.

Sam nods. Topic closed. "Guess you heard about Gwendolyn and me."

I try not to wrinkle my nose. "Yeah, that was a surprise."

"Ran into her at Pete's Pizza and we got to shooting some pool and"—he shrugged—"it just exploded from there. She'd broken up with that tool Denny Morris and needed comforting."

Reptiles need comforting? Who knew?

"You remember her, right?"

Do I ever? I remember her and her mean girlfriends hovering over me in the girls' bathroom, pointing out the big zit on my nose.

"Can you see it with your glasses on?" she'd teased, and they'd all laughed.

I could see it just fine. I could also see what a bucket of barf she and her friends were.

"I remember her," I say. I'm sure Sam's hoping I'll add something positive about the woman, but I can't.

Maybe she's changed.

Just like a leopard changes its spots.

"She's pumped to see you," says Sam.

Pumped to torture me, more like. But I've got to put on a brave face for Sam. *Come on, muscles, lift those lips.*

Sam's brows lower. "What?" he prompts.

"We weren't exactly friends in high school," I say. That's putting it mildly.

"Hey, high school. Everybody's awful in high school, right?"

"I wasn't."

He smiles at that. "No, you weren't. You were a good kid. Still are. And, man, look at you now. You're a star."

Twinkle, twinkle. I hope I can manage to shine just a little tonight when I have to face Gwendolyn.

THREE

She awoke that morning knowing something special was going
to happen to her.
—Hailey Fairchild, *What the Heart Seeks*

Gwendolyn arrives at the house looking like I'd love to look—stylin' and smilin', wearing that red wool coat I'd imagined myself in, along with black leather gloves and a black scarf around her neck. Her hair is long and perfectly cut and highlighted with silver and lavender, flowing onto her shoulders. Her makeup is also perfect—eyeliner that makes her eyes look feline and sexy, a flashy neon-green eye shadow, and fun little faux star tats scattered along her cheekbones like freckles.

Wouldn't you know I have to be the one to open the door and let her in. Sam's upstairs showering, Mom and Gram are in the kitchen, and Dad is making a last-minute run to the store for more eggnog with Grandpa as his wingman. So, it's just me and Gwendolyn, face-to-face. At least I don't have any zits she can point out anymore.

"Hailey," she says and gives me a smile that doesn't make it to her eyes.

"Gwendolyn," I say. Okay, now we each know who we are.

I step back from the door, and she slithers in and sheds her coat, handing it to me to hang up. Designer jeans, baby-blue sweater to match her eyes, great boots. I refuse to let myself feel jealous.

"Everyone's excited you're back," she says. Her tone of voice adds, *Heaven only knows why.*

"It's nice to come home for a visit," I say.

"Only a visit? Don't you miss home?"

"I miss my family." *But I sure don't miss people like you.*

She gives her hair a shake so it will fall just so. It shimmers. Gorgeous.

"I like your hair," I say. I hate to compliment her and feed her ego, but I can't help myself. Her hair *is* gorgeous. And anyway, I have to be nice since she's with Sam. *Oh, please, Lord, don't let this turn out to be permanent.*

She smiles. "We specialize in color at Hair Today. Did Sam tell you I'm a stylist there?"

"Uh, no." Not that I'd asked what she was doing. Not that I cared. One thing I know she's been doing—deceiving Sam into thinking she's nice.

Okay, she could be now. I could be imagining these adversarial vibes. I need to give her a chance.

"I love what I do," she adds, almost as if she needs to justify her chosen profession.

"Making beautiful women more beautiful," I say. Okay, that sounds envious and immature. "It's got to be fun."

"It is. Everyone's beautiful in her own way," Gwendolyn adds. "You should come in and let me do your hair, get you all glam for the holidays."

"Yeah?" What's her hidden agenda?

"Yeah. It can be my good deed for Christmas."

Was that supposed to come off as cute? It doesn't. It sounds condescending. I still can't believe my brother has fallen for this woman.

"Uh-huh," I manage. Not a yes, simply an acknowledgment that I heard.

Sam comes down the stairs, and the way he's looking at her says, *Ring by Valentine's Day*. It won't be the first diamond she's collected.

I can already see how their story will play out. She'll treat him like a cash machine, leave him watching the kids while she goes out on Friday nights with her girlfriends and flirts with other men. Eventually she'll divorce him and take him for all she can.

Maybe my imagination is running away with me. Maybe I'm wrong.

I doubt it.

The lasagna is beckoning us to the kitchen, but suddenly I don't have any appetite.

Mom has come out now. "Gwendolyn! You look lovely as usual."

I'm suddenly just a tiny bit jealous.

How pathetic is that? I don't need my mom to tell me I'm pretty. I'm fine. And I'm successful and . . .

Single. No ring in my future. No man. Nothing to brag about but a string of mistletoe fails.

Stop it! I scold myself. *You are doing fine. And you don't need a man to be happy.*

True. But I don't need to be wandering around Romancelandia alone all the time either. I mean, where's the fun in that? And what does that say about me? Those who can't have it settle for writing about it?

Dad and Grandpa arrive with the eggnog. Grandpa is thick like Dad. They have the same blunt nose and superhero chin, and it's easy to see they're related. Even their smiles look alike. They're both smiling now at the sight of Gwendolyn. Dad gives her a hearty hello. Grandpa compliments her on her outfit. It's like she's already a member of the family.

"She's a winner, isn't she?" Grandpa says to me as we all go down the hall toward the dining room. Grandpa-speak for she's awesome.

"She's something," I say, staying diplomatic.

At dinner talk turns to the many social obligations Mom has committed me to.

"You're like a celebrity," says Gwendolyn, giving me that almost-smile again. "You really do need to let me do your hair for the book party. My Christmas present to you."

"What a sweet offer," Mom says. "Gwendolyn is amazing."

I suddenly wonder if Gwendolyn did Mom's Christmas-stocking-red hair. If she did, what has she got against my mother?

Mom confirms it. "She did mine earlier this week. It'll fade, so we went extra strong so it will last through Christmas," Mom explains. "It will eventually turn pastel."

"Pastel," I repeat. So Mom's head can look like cotton candy.

"Although I already love it just as it is," Mom adds. Either my mom is lying diplomatically, or she needs to borrow my glasses.

"How about you come in tomorrow?" Gwendolyn suggests. "I can fit you in."

"I have to help Mom bake for the cookie exchange," I say.

"That won't take all day," Mom says.

Thank you, Mom.

"I can take you at one," Gwendolyn says.

"That would be great. Then you'll be all festive for Christmas," Mom says.

I picture myself at the bookstore event, my hair clown red like Mom's. "Oh, I don't think . . . ," I begin.

"Go for it," says Sam. "She'll make you look great." He really believes it.

"Oh yes," puts in Gram.

Crap, I think. "I like my hair the color it is," I lie. Actually, I'd love to do something glam with my brown hair, but I don't trust Gwendolyn to make it happen.

"You can trust me," she says.

"I'll think about it," I lie.

"She'll be there," says Mom.

❄

Later, after we've all watched a Christmas movie and played Wii bowling (I lost), Gram and Grandpa have gone home and Sam and Gwendolyn have disappeared to enjoy some time together. Now it's just me and Mom.

She brings up the subject of my hair. "I don't understand why you'd balk at doing something fun with your hair."

I love my mother, I really do. She's great. But like I said, she can get a little bossy. And sometimes she's clueless.

She's sure clueless about Gwendolyn, but that's my fault. I never shared about the high school bullying. Looking back, I wish I had, but I'd been too embarrassed. My parents were so proud of my smarts. I hated for them to see the loser side of my life. Mom, who'd always been popular in school, wouldn't have understood. When you like everyone and everyone likes you, you assume it must be that way for your kids too. It was for Sam.

"I don't think right before I'm going to do so much public stuff is the time to experiment," I say.

"Darling, I think you'll look adorable with some flirty colors in your hair. It might be exactly the pick-me-up you need after . . ." She pauses, looking for the right words. "After the disappointing year you've had."

Mom knows all about my breakup. I called her in tears, and she wrapped me in sympathy, told me what a fool David was not to appreciate me. Told me how wonderful I am. Then offered to hire a hit man. Good ol' Mom. She also said, *"Mistakes are the stepping-stones to happy endings. This puts you one more step closer to yours."*

It was a great line. I'm going to use it in a book someday.

"Take a chance, darling," Mom continues.

"I don't know," I say.

"You never win if you don't enter the contest. You did that with pursuing the career you want. Why not take the same attitude about the rest of your life?"

"That was different. I knew I could make it as a writer."

"You can make it as a lovely young woman too," Mom says gently. She lays a hand over mine. "I don't think you've ever looked in the mirror and really seen yourself."

Right.

I give her a look. *Really?* I know I look better than I did when I was young, but I'm no Gwendolyn. Hmm. I should probably be thankful for that.

"You're like all of us women," Mom continues. "You see your flaws and stop there."

"Mom," I protest. I can feel a mother lecture coming on.

Mom may not have known about the bullying, but she knew about my insecurity. She knew about my Cheetos addiction, too, but never guilted me over it. She did give me plenty of pep talks, though.

"One of these days you're going to see what we all see—a lovely woman with a smile like sunshine. You've worked hard to get fit these last few years, so why not gild the lily a little?" she says now.

Gild the lily. Such a strange expression. What does that mean, really?

"Have some fun. It's the holidays."

"Mom, I don't want bright-red hair," I protest. "Sorry," I add. The last thing I want to do is diss my mom.

She laughs. "A few washings, and it will be just the color I want. And you don't have to go so wild. I do think Gwendolyn wants to be friends. Why not give her a chance?"

"Who said I'm not giving her a chance?" I protest.

"Your body language at dinner," says Mom. "I take it you two have a past."

I shrug. I'm sure not spilling the tea now, not after all these years.

"You're both grown-ups now," Mom says.

I think she's going to say more, but she leaves it at that.

Which is worse than her saying more because I feel small, like maybe I'm not being fair to Gwendolyn. Maybe I'm letting my imagination take control and reading too much into her words and actions.

Maybe it would be fun to do a little something to my hair for the holidays. Get wild, get glamorous. Start living the life I always imagined successful writers live. Do I want to write about life, or do I want to experience it?

Oh, what the heck. Why not?

"Okay, I'll go," I say.

Once I'm in bed, I nibble on my candy bar, then pull out the journal Ramona gave me and write my first entry. *Every heroine faces challenges, both big and small. That's great in fiction, but who wants it in real life?*

Oh well. What doesn't kill me . . .

I close the journal, shut my eyes, and dream of myself walking next door into the Davieses' house, sleek and elegant with lavender highlights in my hair, which is twisted in a chignon. I'm wearing that famous black cocktail dress you always see Audrey Hepburn wearing in those old movie posters. No cigarette, though!

Anyway, there I am, strolling into the Davieses' house. There's mistletoe hanging in the archway to the living room. I pause for a moment to take in the chatting crowd. Christmas music is playing softly in the background.

And here comes Carwyn, wearing a tux. Oh, good grief, he is so droolworthy.

And he's staring at me as if he's seeing the *Mona Lisa* for the first time. "Hailey," he says breathlessly. "You look amazing. And what have you done to your hair? It's awesome."

"Just a little something for the holidays," I reply.

"We've missed you," he says.

"Have you?" I raise an eyebrow. I am so sophisticated.

"*I've* missed you," he says. His eyes are burning me. He lowers his voice. "Remember all those years ago when I kissed you under the mistletoe?"

I shrug. "I've been under a lot of mistletoe since then."

"And broken a lot of hearts, I bet." He takes a step closer. "I've never forgotten."

"We were just kids," I say.

"We're not now," he says and slips an arm around my waist.

I wake up before he can kiss me. *Nooooo.*

I squeeze my eyes shut and try to get back into a dream state. *Come on, subconscious, be a sport. Let me at least have Carwyn in my dreams.*

My subconscious is a tease. She refuses.

I wake up the next morning feeling like I've been hit in the head by the Grinch. It takes two cups of coffee and an extra helping of pancakes to make me feel better.

And that's only momentary. The feel-better ends when Mom says, "I left a message at the salon for Gwendolyn, so you're good to go." She smiles. "You'll look fabulous."

My mother is a force of nature, a sweet, well-meaning force. I remind myself that I'd already made up my mind. I'm going to do this.

Not just to make Mom happy, I realize, but because maybe it's time I took more chances. I'll be taking a big one on Gwendolyn, but like Mom said, we're all grown-ups now. And besides, Gwendolyn wants to win points with Sam. Of course she's not going to sabotage me.

But to be sure, I'm going to make it very clear that I want something super subtle. No clown-wig red.

I help Mom with kitchen cleanup, then catch up on my social media. I text Ramona.

Hailey: Bro's girlfriend is coloring my hair. Pray for me!

I get back a shocked face emoji.

Hailey: I know. Then there's the cookie exchange. Temptation!

Ramona: You can resist.

Hailey: And all the other stuff.

Ramona: You'll be fine. Stay strong and have fun!!!

Hailey: I will, I vow.

I'm going to have fun this whole visit, I decide. I will juice up my hair, I will be a rock star at the school, and I will proudly read from my book at the big book party and not feel even remotely self-conscious. Because I am smart, I am strong, and I can conquer any situation.

Okay, how am I supposed to conquer *this* situation?

I stare at my reflection. My hair is a startling shade of green. I am supposed to do a book signing looking like Daughter of Grinch? Even worse, go speak to high school kids looking like this?

Gwendolyn is standing behind me, smiling a Stinkerbell smile. Someone needs to sic Krampus on her.

"What do you think?" she asks, as if she can't tell from my horrified gawking.

My reflection has narrowed eyes and looks ready to hurt someone. "I think you did this on purpose."

Gwendolyn's fake smile vanishes, and she frowns at me. "I did not. I can't help it if your hair is extra porous."

"Aren't you supposed to know about things like that? Aren't you supposed to do a test first?" I demand. "And my scalp is itching like crazy."

She gives a snort. "You're allergic to looking good."

"I'm allergic to looking like a traffic light!" Okay, I'm getting a little loud, and everyone in Hair Today is staring at me. Or maybe they're staring at my hair. I lower my voice. "It was supposed to be pastel. You've got to fix this. Bleach it out or something."

"I can't. It will damage your hair. Anyway, a couple of washings, and it will be perfect," she insists. "Sheesh, you're so ungrateful."

I yank off the plastic cape, grab my purse, and head for the door. It's a good thing I'm not paying for this. Oh, wait. I am. I'm paying with a ton of humiliation.

"See if I ever do your hair again," she calls after me.

See if I ever let you. I don't say it. Trying to be mature here.

"It will look good eventually," says the receptionist as I march past her.

Sometime before death would be nice. I don't say a word as I push open the door.

I am so wishing I'd worn a hat as I leave the salon. What if I run into someone I know?

What if? There is no what-if. Of course I'll run into someone I know. This is a small town and I grew up here. Hopefully, whoever sees me will be someone I barely know.

It's snowing, and our little downtown looks like it should be inside a snow globe. All the shops have fir swags across the top of their windows and wreaths on the doors. The last of the late afternoon light is dimming, and the streetlamps, all wrapped in red plastic ribbon, have come on. So have the twinkle lights in all the trees along Main Street. A big banner that says *Happy Holidays* is strung across the street. For a moment I'm caught up in the charm as I walk toward my car.

Until I see . . . oh no. Please. Anyone but him.

FOUR

Her hair was so beautiful, like threads of gold spun just for him.
—Hailey Fairchild, *What the Heart Seeks*

Carwyn is coming out of the hardware store, just two stores down. If he sees me looking like a green-haired monster, I'll never survive the mortification. I am *not* that strong. I dash for my car, which is parked halfway between the salon and the hardware store. If I can just get in it, I can duck down and hide until he passes.

Dashing through the snow works fine if you're wearing the snow boots you packed and not the cute shooties you just had to wear to prove that you, too, could look like a social media influencer.

I almost make it to the car before I hit a slippery patch. My arms start to windmill, and my body waves back and forth like those tall, inflatable, yellow sausage people you see at car dealerships. I'm doing the holiday hula and making shrieky noises. And here goes my right foot out from under me. Down I go, hitting the sidewalk with an "Eeep!" *Oh no. Get up.*

I try, but I end up scrabbling around like I'm at a roller rink with wheels on my feet.

"Here, let me help you," says a deep voice.

I don't even have to look up to know it's Carwyn. I'd recognize that voice anywhere.

"Hailey," Carwyn says with a big smile as he lifts me to my feet. "Are you okay?"

"I'm fine," I lie, brushing off my coat. If you don't factor in complete mortification. I know my face is red. I can feel the flame burning through my cheeks. He's staring at my hair, making the flame hotter. A corner of his mouth lifts. He's about to laugh, I know it. I'd probably laugh, too, if it wasn't me.

He quickly pulls that corner back down and coughs to choke back the laugh. "It looks like you're getting in the Christmas spirit."

I could pretend I don't know what he's talking about, but since I'm not carrying any bags filled with goodies, there's no point in it. "I just got my hair done," I say, lifting my chin, daring him to laugh. Now there is a three-alarm fire on my face.

"It's . . ." He clears his throat. He covers a fresh guffaw with a cough. "It's . . . festive."

"It's awful," I say miserably, losing my bravado.

He goes from amused to pitying. "It's not that bad, really."

"Yes, it is."

"Okay, yes, it is. Who did that to you, and what did you ever do to her?"

I sigh. "Gwendolyn Payne. She and Sam are together now."

He nods. "Yeah, Sam told me. I'm sure she's changed."

I point to my hair. "You think?"

He lifts his shoulders. "Bad hair stylist day?"

I'm not laughing.

"Hey, it's no big deal, really. Lots of women do crazy things to their hair."

Not me. I never do anything crazy. I only get wild in my imagination. Although Gram might say different. She'd like me to get a lot wilder.

"I'm going to have to buy a wig," I say miserably. Yes, this is a memorable conversation I'm having with the star of my recent fantasy.

"How about a hat, instead?" he suggests. "Come on, I'll help you pick one out. I just saw some in Ray's." He takes my gloved hand and starts leading me toward the hardware store.

This is . . . strange. I'm holding hands with Carwyn Davies, and we're going . . . hat shopping. In the hardware store. The heroes and heroines in my books would come up with a better activity than this. Why can't I craft my real life to match my fiction?

"I heard you were coming back for Christmas. Welcome home," he says, and I try not to think of the glamorous reunion I'd dreamed of.

In the hardware store, he hands me various knitted hats to try on—long stocking caps, several in Seahawks colors and sporting pom-poms. I'm not into football, so I pass on those. Finally, I pick a gray wool hat with a turned-up brim that will hide the green.

"It's nice," he says in approval. "It shows off your eyes."

My eyes aren't all that exciting. They're hazel and too round for the current fashion. I know he's shoveling it on thick.

"And my glasses," I joke and push my glasses up my nose.

"Okay," he says after I've made my purchase (while keeping the hat on—made ringing it up interesting). "Now that you don't feel like you have to run for cover, how about going out for something to eat?"

"In public?" I squeak. It's liable to get hot in one of Cascade's handful of restaurants, and no way am I taking this hat off.

"Big Ben's Burgers. We can eat in my car."

Burgers with Carwyn, like we're . . . what? What are we? Two neighbors who ran into each other, that's all. I tell my imagination not to go romping off someplace silly.

"Anyway, I owe you."

I cock a questioning eyebrow.

"For almost laughing," he says and smiles. That smile could melt a snowman at twenty paces.

"Come to think of it, you do," I say, so off to Ben's we go.

We order peppermint milkshakes. I know I'm strong, but who can resist a peppermint milkshake?

"Everyone's talking about you being back in town," he says and crams a couple of french fries in his mouth. "You're like a returning hero."

"Hardly," I say.

"Local girl becomes famous author."

"I'm not that famous, and everybody writes books these days."

"Nobody around here."

I work up my nerve and ask, "How about you? Are you impressed?"

"Absolutely," he says. He shakes a fry at me. "But then I always knew you'd go on to great things. You were so smart, always with your nose in a book."

Hiding sometimes, if I'm being honest. Which I'm not, at least not now. "You've done pretty well for yourself," I say. "High school principal. That's an important job. What's next, superintendent of the district?"

He shakes his head. "No, I've got my hands full just taking care of things at the high school. And with my folks."

"Your folks?"

"I guess your mom didn't tell you. My dad's been diagnosed with Parkinson's."

I don't know what to say. This feels like a gut punch. If it feels that way to me, what must it have felt like to Carwyn when he first heard the diagnosis?

"He was beginning to slow down, joking about starting old age early. But then he started to complain about muscle stiffness. When the tremors began, we took him to a specialist in Seattle.

He's still doing pretty good so far, but we're bracing for things to get worse."

"I don't suppose your brother can come home," I ventured.

"From Burkina Faso? No, not right now. Anyway, he's doing important work."

"So are you," I point out.

"I'm already here. Anyway, we're managing. My parents will need more help over time. It's gonna be hard for Dad. Already is."

He looks so sad. I wish I could hug him.

He shifts gears, back into cheerful. "Mom's looking forward to your book signing," he says, signaling that the subject is closed.

"She's coming? That's nice," I say. I'm glad some people are coming—it's the ultimate humiliation to do a book event and have no bodies there—but I also don't want a huge crowd.

"Everyone's coming," he says.

"Everyone?" I squeak.

"Hometown girl makes good, remember?"

His phone dings with a text. He checks it. "I'm gonna have to cut this short."

"Oh." I sound disappointed. How pathetic is that?

It's a girlfriend, of course. Carwyn Davies isn't married—if that had happened, I would have heard about it—but he's got to have a girlfriend. He's too gorgeous, too nice, too . . . everything not to have one.

"I promised Mom I'd help Dad get the tree up," he says.

"Oh, I thought you had a girlfriend waiting for you," I say lightly.

He's suddenly serious again. "There's no one in my life, Hailey."

"There should be," I blurt. Great. Now I'm sure my face is as red as Santa's suit.

"I had a couple of almosts, but in the end they never felt right." He smiles. "Maybe, down the road . . ."

I'm imagining the way he's looking at me, I'm sure of it. "You'll run out of gas right in front of her house," I quip lightly. A perfect meet-cute.

"Or find her next door," he says, just as lightly. "What about you?" he asks. "You have to have someone."

I shrug. "I thought I did. It turned out to be a mistletoe mistake."

He half smiles at that. "Mistletoe mistake, huh? I can remember one of those."

"You can?"

"You were *my* first mistletoe mistake," he says.

"Me! No way."

He shakes his head and gives a rueful smile. "Talk about deflating a guy's ego. You couldn't get away from me fast enough."

"I had onion breath," I protest. "And it was all so embarrassing. I mean, honestly, Sam calls over the hottest guy in town and says, 'Kiss my sister.' I thought I'd die."

"Hottest guy in town, huh?"

Speaking of, can my face get any hotter? "You know you are," I say, disgusted over betraying myself.

He grins. "Did you have a crush on me?"

"Oh, who didn't?" I say irritably.

He starts his car. "This is interesting stuff. We need to continue this conversation."

"No, we don't," I mutter. I've humiliated myself enough for one day.

"I know you're gonna be busy," he says when we get back to my car, "but I hope you won't be too busy for your neighbor."

Carwyn Davies wants to hang out. Okay, am I dreaming this? "I might be able to fit you in," I say with a smile.

Then, once I'm back in my car, I pinch myself. *Ouch!* Nope, I'm not dreaming. I will have some pages to fill in that journal tonight.

❋

"Oh my," says Mom when she sees my hair. I'd forgotten about my hair for a while there. Now I frown, and she quickly adds, "It will fade after a couple of washings."

Right.

I move to a more important topic. "You never told me about Mr. Davies."

"I should have. I forgot."

"Pretty big news to forget," I say.

She sighs. "I guess there never was quite the right time to tell you. Whenever we texted or talked, we had so many other things to discuss."

Like my love fails. Or how I'm struggling to write this new book, thanks to my mistletoe disillusionment. My conversations with my editor, my concerns about cover art. There hasn't been much conversational room for anyone else. How humiliating.

❋

Sam comes home, takes one look at my green hair, and goes all *ho ho ho* hysterical.

"It's not funny," I say. "Your girlfriend did this on purpose."

He stops laughing and his brows pull together. "Gwen wouldn't do that."

"Of course she would. That's how she's wired."

He scowls. "Hey, you're talking about the woman I'm in love with."

I sigh inwardly and backpedal. "Maybe I'm imagining she did it on purpose."

"Of course you are. Gwen doesn't have a mean bone in her body."

Not one but a whole collection. And there's no escaping her. She will be the holly thorn in my side clear through to New Year's. Or longer, if she and Sam make things permanent.

Sam stuck with Gwendolyn—*there's* a terrible thought! Seeing my brother freed from her is now at the top of my Christmas wish list. That won't be easy. Santa's elves sure have their work cut out for them.

FIVE

Others looked at her and missed who she was. He didn't.
—Hailey Fairchild, *What the Heart Needs*

I am relieved that Gwendolyn is not part of Mom's cookie exchange. It's the usual suspects—Mom, Gram, Mrs. Davies, and their friends. There are so many plates of cookies spread across the dining room table that it makes my mouth water.

I can conquer any situation. I will not yield to cookie temptation.

"That is an interesting shade of green," says Geraldine Greer, who lives across the street.

She's raising an eyebrow, looking at me as if she's convinced that I meant to do this.

I can feel the face fire again. I never liked her very much. She was always stingy with her trick or treat candy at Halloween.

"It's supposed to fade," I say. Not that it has yet, despite two washings.

She shakes her head. "Dyeing your hair every color of the rainbow, such a silly fad."

Mom is standing nearby, the poster child for silly fads. "Oh, lighten up, Ger. You're just jealous 'cause you're not brave enough to do it," she teases.

Geraldine sniffs and helps herself to more punch.

"Never mind her," Mom whispers to me. "Your hair will look great by Christmas."

But what about the talk at the school? And the book signing?

As soon as the women leave, laden with cookies, I'm back upstairs in the bathroom, washing my hair again. I blow it out and check my reflection. Still traffic-light green. I am so not looking forward to displaying this hair at the book signing.

❋

"You look fabulous," Dad tells me when I come downstairs, dressed for my appearance at Mountain Books.

I look good from the neck down at least. I'm wearing a black sweater accented with a gorgeous Christmas-red scarf and jeans. And my shooties. Carwyn is coming to the signing and has offered to drive me. I really want to look glam for this, so I'm hoping he'll be able to keep me upright if we encounter any slippery spots. Hopefully, Eloise Matthews will have scattered rock salt in front of the store.

"Wow," he says when I open the door. "You look Gucci."

I push my glasses up my nose and roll my eyes. If I am looking good, it's got to be the lipstick Ramona gave me, because it's sure not the hair.

"Seriously," he adds. "And the hair makes you look like the new Beat Generation."

He is so full of frijoles, but never mind. I'll take the compliment. "You look pretty good yourself," I say. Understatement of the year.

He, of course, looks fabulous in his lined suede jacket, jeans, and boots—serious boots that will not slip under any condition.

"So, you ready?" he asks as I let him in.

"I don't know if I'll ever be ready," I admit.

Gram and her pals are already at the bookstore, and she's texted Mom that there's a crowd. I hope I don't stumble over my words when it's time to read from my book.

Dad greets Carwyn with a friendly slap on the back, then calls upstairs to Mom. "Come on, hon! We're not going to get seats if we don't move it." He turns to me and gives me a hug. "See you there, Princess. Break a leg."

"That's the theater," I say.

"Okay, then break a sales record," he amends with a grin.

Carwyn pulls his car up in front of the bookstore. I feel like there are gremlins in my stomach having a snowball fight.

"You've done these before, right?" Carwyn says, trying to calm my nerves.

"Not in my hometown." Where I was that shy little Fairchild girl (to the older generation) and the nerd (to mine).

"You'll be great. Everyone loves you," he says and wraps an arm around my shoulders.

Everyone loves me. Except for Gwendolyn, who is sitting in the front row next to Sam. He's smiling. She's sneering. I suddenly don't want to read from my latest novel.

But, of course, I have to.

My hair has changed drastically since Mom and I dropped by the store to check in with Eloise, but Eloise pretends not to notice. She introduces me and everyone claps. A teen girl, also in the front row, looks ready to give me a standing O. She looks a lot like I did at that age. Well, okay, kind of like I still look, with the brown hair and glasses. Except now my hair is green.

I smile at her, and she beams. She has no idea I'm not bestowing that smile on her. I'm thanking her for the confidence boost.

Carwyn is smiling, too, like what I'm doing matters to him. It's hard to believe it could after all those young years of unrequited love. I'm reading more into all this than I should, I'm sure. He's only being friendly.

After I'm done reading there is more applause, and this time my front-row fan is on her feet, along with Gram and her posse and Mom and Dad and all their friends. So far so good, but now it's time for the dreaded Q & A. It's the usual questions: *Where do you get your ideas? How many hours a day do you write? What music do you listen to when you're writing?*

Gwendolyn has a question. Oh, joy.

"You write romance novels, which aren't really literature, right?" she begins. Can she even spell *literature*?

"That's right, I write romance novels," I say. "Was that your question?"

"No. My question is, what's the difference between literature and what *you* write?"

I've heard this a few million times also. It's always meant to be an insult, and the first couple of times it was thrown at me I stammered and stuttered and blushed and said something about everyone having different taste. Now here it is again, from the same woman who bullied me in high school and who, only a few days ago, turned me into Daughter of Grinch. I'm past being intimidated by that question. I am smart, I am strong, and I can conquer any situation.

"I cry all the way to the bank," I say, deadpan.

Everyone laughs, and for once I'm not the one with the red face.

And I am loved. I spend an hour signing books and talking with people.

"Good job, sis," says my brother, and asks me to sign the book he bought for Gwendolyn.

I don't bother to write anything gushy in it, as I know it will wind up in her garbage can.

My admirer from the front row shyly asks if I'll sign the book she's holding "To Emily."

"Of course," I say. "Are you Emily?"

She nods and her cheeks turn pink.

"Well, thank you for coming tonight, Emily. It means a lot," I say.

"Really?" she asks.

"Yes, really," I assure her.

She produces my first book from her messenger bag and asks if I'll sign that too. "I love your books," she gushes.

"Thank you," I say. I sign both, and she clutches them to her heart and leaves smiling.

And I'm smiling too. Everyone (except Gwendolyn) was supportive, and I feel like a success.

And I feel all twittery when Carwyn, the last in line, comes up and says, "You were great." He hands me a book. "Sign it for me?"

"Who should I sign it to?" I ask.

"Me, of course," he says.

"You don't want to read this." I scoff.

"Of course I do."

"Well, thanks for boosting my sales."

"I want to keep you crying all the way to the bank," he replies with a wink. "Anyway, it's got a happy ending, right?"

"Of course." Every woman deserves a happy ending.

"I could use a happy ending," he says, and I suspect he's thinking of his dad.

I write in the book, *To my favorite neighbor*, and he reads it and grins. "How about your favorite neighbor takes you out for hot chocolate?"

❅

We drink that hot chocolate and debate over the best-ever Christmas movie. I insist on *Elf*, and he likes *National Lampoon's Christmas Vacation*. "The squirrel in the tree, man. That scene can't be topped."

I don't know. This one where we're sitting in Lulu's Diner, which is all decked out with tinsel garlands, drinking hot chocolate while snow is starting to fall outside the window rates pretty high in my book.

"I'm glad you came home," he says when he drops me off.

So am I.

"Got any more book signings you need me to drive you to?" he asks.

"I'm afraid that was my fifteen minutes of fame."

"I guess I'll have to think of some other excuse to hang out, then," he says with a smile.

I smile back. "I guess you will."

I'm still buzzing when I get back in the house, and not simply from my successful signing and my parents' proud gushing.

Back in my room I text Ramona.

Hailey: Carwyn Davies is more addicting than peppermint lattes.

Ramona: Your first mistletoe kiss? Oh no. Have you???

Hailey: No. I don't want to ruin things.

Ramona: Hey, you're not under the influence of mistletoe this time. It's all good.

I hope she's right.

SIX

It's easy to be brave when someone believes in you.
—Hailey Fairchild, *What the Heart Needs*

It's Monday, and I've borrowed Mom's car and am off to Cascade High to speak to Mrs. Wharton's freshman English class. Under my coat I'm wearing a beige cashmere sweater over black leggings. This time I'm wearing my boots. I don't want any more close encounters with the pavement.

Even though my book signing was a success, the gremlins are back in my stomach, churning the eggs I had for breakfast. There's nothing to be nervous about, for crying out loud. According to Carwyn, I'm returning like a conquering hero. And didn't I prove that at the signing? I park the car, square my shoulders, and walk into the school. The same school where I was once the shy bookworm, bullied by Gwendolyn and her gang of pirates.

Those days are gone. Carwyn was right. I am a conquering hero. Mrs. Wharton greets me like I'm Taylor Swift.

"This is so sweet of you," she gushes.

Mrs. Wharton was never really a gusher. She was more of a frowner. A tall frowner who, I think, felt like fashion and literature couldn't co-habit. Today she's wearing a pea-green top under a stern black jacket to match her outdated black slacks. Her hair was starting to go gray when I had her in school; now it's arrived at its destination. I remember once overhearing her tell my mother that her students were going to turn her hair gray. It looks like they succeeded.

But this seems like a mellow class. They're all quiet, smiling, and looking at me expectantly. Waiting for pearls of wisdom to tumble out of my mouth. Which is suddenly very, very dry. But there's Emily, my fan from the book signing, looking adoringly at me. The gremlins settle down.

"Everyone, here's the surprise I promised you. Hailey Fairchild, one of our own Cascade High graduates, has graciously agreed to tell you about her life as a bestselling author."

Who has had three love fails and is stalled out on completing her next book.

I clear my throat. "It's not easy getting published."

My number-one fan's smile falls from her face. I've just told her the writer's equivalent of "There is no Santa."

"But that doesn't mean you can't do it," I hurry to add. "You have to keep trying, and you can't give up. And you have to write every day, no matter what is going on in your life." Says the woman who hasn't written a word since December 1. "Get out there and get under the mistletoe." Oh no. Where did that come from? The sizzle is hitting my face. "Metaphorically speaking," I quickly add.

I babble on for what feels like a century but is only ten minutes, and then it's time for questions.

"Do you ever get writer's block?" asks one girl.

"Every writer does at some point," I say and then wonder if that's really true. Maybe there are authors out there who are sailing happily through every book they write, who never run out of ideas.

"When is your next book coming out?" asks my younger twin, Emily.

"June," I say. Although the manuscript should have been turned in by October. I block out my last conversation with my editor. It won't be pretty if I don't hand it in by January 3.

This is not the time to think about that. I need to focus on ... oh no. What is Carwyn doing slipping into the room? He smiles and gives me a thumbs-up, and my brain switches off.

"Did you always want to be a writer?" asks one of the boys.

How else do you work out your fantasies about Carwyn Davies? "I guess so," I say. "I've always loved stories and reading. Every time you open a book, you open the door to a whole new world."

"Wow," Emily says under her breath, as if I've just said something profound. Maybe I have.

The kids continue to pepper me with questions until the bell rings, signaling the end of class. Also, since it's the last class, the bell means it's the end of school until January. The room explodes with energy as the kids rush for the door and freedom.

"We're all so proud of what you've accomplished," Mrs. Wharton says to me as the students stampede past. "Thanks for coming today. I think we have some budding writers in this class. I hope you've inspired them."

"Me too," I say.

"You inspire me," Carwyn says as he walks me to my car. "How about dinner tonight? Do you have plans with your family?"

Just as he's asking, a text comes in from Sam.

Sam: Pool at Pete's Pizza at 6?

I love spending time with my brother, but I hate to not see Carwyn. "How do you feel about pizza with Sam tonight?" I ask.

"I feel great," he says.

Hailey: Kk. Carwyn's coming with.

Sam: Kk

I drive home happy. This will be fun.

Or not. It turns out that Gwendolyn is coming too.

She and Sam have already staked out a table when Carwyn and I arrive a little after six, and as we join them she greets me with her famous fake smile that never reaches her eyes. Ugh. The smile warms up when she turns to Carwyn. I've lost my appetite.

"I already ordered pizza," says Sam. "You're on your own for drinks."

Gwendolyn is already halfway through her drink, a large glass of beer. Carwyn orders one and she asks for a second. I stick with my usual diet cola.

"Come on, let's shoot some pool," says Sam, so off we go to the pool table. It beats sitting across from Gwendolyn, trying to find something to say to her.

She teases Sam and flirts with Carwyn the entire time we're playing. I fade into the background along with the eighties music. Bonnie Tyler is singing "Total Eclipse of the Heart." I feel her pain.

The pizza has arrived, and we return to the table where Gwendolyn starts on her second beer and leers at Carwyn. She leans on her elbows and shakes a finger at him. "Bad you."

He raises both eyebrows. "Bad me?"

"You used to be so cool. What happened?"

Sam frowns. "He's still cool."

"Naw. Look who he's with. Oops. Sorry. It's your sister."

"Yeah, it is," Sam growls, "so lay off."

She holds up both hands. "Whoa, pardon me for hurting you with the truth."

My face is totally on fire, and my brain is frozen. I sit rooted to my seat and stare at Gwendolyn. How much beer has she really had? Probably more than two, because she's getting sloppy with her bullying.

"You should have stayed with me," she says to Carwyn.

Wait. Carwyn dated Gwendolyn? When was that?

"If I had, you wouldn't have wound up with Sam," he says. His face is red. It's probably not as red as mine, though. He shoots Sam an apologetic look.

"Pfft." Gwendolyn dismisses Sam with a flick of her hand.

"Thanks," Sam says and frowns.

She leans into him. "It's okay, baby. I'll settle for you."

Now Sam's face is red, too, and his lips are pressed together so hard they're white around the edges. "Okay, that's it. I'm taking you home."

"Ooh, good idea," she purrs. "We can have a lot more fun without these two."

Sam doesn't look ready to have fun. He stands up and throws some bills on the table. "Let's go," he says to Gwendolyn, his voice terse. He turns to Carwyn and me. "I'm sorry, guys. She had a beer before you got here."

"Truth serum," says Carwyn, and Sam nods.

"This doesn't look good," I say as Sam stalks off with Gwendolyn trailing behind at a stroll.

"One can hope," says Carwyn. "She's bad news."

"If you knew that, why didn't you warn Sam?" I demand.

"A man doesn't diss another man's woman. It's a good way to ruin a friendship. Anyway, I figured she'd show her true colors."

"I guess you saw them first," I venture. "I don't remember you two dating in high school." I remember every girl he dated.

He nods, grabs a slice of pizza. "It was after you moved to New York. It lasted about a minute. She's got a mean streak. And I've seen puddles deeper than her. She wasn't what I'm looking for."

"So what *are* you looking for?" I ask, and I realize my leg is bobbing up and down as I wait for his answer.

"I want someone who's smart and kind." He abandons the pizza, smiles at me, and traces a hand up my arm, making me quiver like a little girl in front of the Christmas tree. "I want you, even if you are out of my league now."

This is all so fantastical. If it weren't for the goose bumps, I would swear I'm dreaming. "I've never been out of anyone's league," I mutter.

He shakes his head. "Why do you do that?"

"What?"

"Put yourself down."

Because it's hard to see past my geeky teen years, and even harder to see past all my mistletoe mistakes. This can't work out. I shrug.

"Hailey, you're great. And I'm loving hanging out with you."

"Really?" I study his face, looking for some sign that he's feeding me malarky. I can't see any.

"Really," he says. "I always thought you were a cute kid. Even if you were a snob," he teases, making me snort and shake my head at him.

"I was never a snob," I tell him. *Just shy and awkward and in awe of you.*

After the pizza is long gone, Carwyn takes me back home. He walks me to the door.

"So prove you're not a snob," he says.

He draws me to him and smiles down at me, and I smile back up at him, trying to hide the fact that I'm on the verge of a love heart attack.

And then it comes. THE KISS.

I light up inside like a string of Christmas lights meeting electricity for the first time. The feel of his lips on mine, the warmth of his body—oh my! Every sensation I've imagined for my heroines cascades over me, and I want it to go on forever.

He ends the kiss and grins. "That was a lot better than the last kiss we had."

"Yes, it was, and I'm glad there was no mistletoe involved."

He gives me a teasing frown. "What's wrong with mistletoe?"

"It's bad luck," I inform him and kiss him again.

"Oh, man, that one was even better," he says.

He's ready for thirds but I pull back and tease, "Don't be greedy," which makes him chuckle.

"See you tomorrow at Mom and Dad's party," he says.

He certainly will. I am so very, very glad I came home for the holidays.

When I walk into the house, I find Sam camped on the family room sofa, gaming and scowling at the TV, shooting imaginary enemies. My poor brother. I set aside my own happiness and plop onto the couch next to him and ask what happened.

"We're through," he says tersely.

I'm relieved, but I still feel badly that he's hurting. "I'm sorry."

"Don't be. I guess I've known all along what she is. I just didn't want to admit it. Lucky escape, really."

He's not smiling like a lucky man, but I hope his heart will catch up with his brain quickly.

As for me, my brain is pulling hard on the reins, telling my heart to slow down. Two kisses do not a relationship make. Plus, we live on opposite coasts. How can that work?

My heart's not listening.

SEVEN

*Was it possible that someone like her could attract his attention?
It was what she'd dreamed of for so long that she was almost
afraid to hope.*
—Hailey Fairchild, *What the Heart Seeks*

I meet my old bestie Scarlet and her sister Billie for coffee at Cora's Coffee House. This place hasn't changed. It still looks like a giant living room, with oversized chairs and sofas grouped around scuffed wooden tables. A wreath is hung on every window, and Mariah Carey is singing about all she wants for Christmas. I can smell coffee and the aroma of baking goodies, something with a heavy hand of cinnamon, floating from the kitchen. Cora's mom is eighty now, but she still bakes all the cookies and pastries for her daughter. Even though it's late afternoon and coffee rush hour has passed, the place is packed, with people getting their eggnog and gingerbread latte fixes.

The sisters have snagged a small table in a corner by the front window. Scarlet waves at me as if I don't see her, but I'd recognize that auburn hair and big smile anywhere. Her sister smiles, too, and waves as well, and I hurry over to hug them.

Billie is sporting a baby mountain, and I have to bend over it to hug her. "When are you due?" I ask.

"February," she replies.

"And she'd better not go into labor right in the middle of my wedding," jokes Scarlet. "I hope you remembered to save the date," she says to me.

"I wouldn't miss it," I say.

I hurry to order my drink, yet another peppermint latte (What? They're seasonal!), and a slice of gingerbread. There will be a ton of food at the Davieses' party tonight, but I'd be a fool to pass up on Cora's mom's gingerbread.

I can feel both sisters staring at my green hair as I settle in at the table. Still green after eight washings. Not quite as bright as it was at first, but it would still be hard to lose me in a crowd.

"Is this a new look?" asks Billie.

I scowl. "Gwendolyn did it."

"Gwendolyn!" exclaims Scarlet.

"She's with Sam now," Billie says. "I forgot to tell you."

"Everyone forgot to tell me," I say and take a sip of my drink. "But thank heaven, they just broke up."

"Good. I'd hate to see Sam stuck with the likes of her," Scarlet says, then moves on to new conversational territory. "I'm sorry we missed the book party. My plane was delayed."

"And I was stuck waiting at the airport forever," adds Billie, rolling her eyes.

"But I hear you packed the place," Scarlet continues. "I'm so proud of you, girl. I read your last book. It was epic."

"Your whole *life* is epic," puts in Billie. "A famous writer living in New York, so glamorous." She sighs.

I think of my mistletoe fails and my writer's block, neither of which I've shared with Scarlet. Yep. So glamorous.

"It must be pretty boring here compared to that," Billie says.

I think of Carwyn and smile. "You'd be surprised."

"Scarlet told me about David, but I bet you've already replaced him. So, who are you with now, some big mover and shaker back there?" Billie asks as I cut into my gingerbread.

It almost feels too good to share, but I have to. "Actually, someone here. Early stages, though."

"Here!" both sisters exclaim in unison.

"Who?" Scarlet demands.

"Carwyn," I say, and her eyes about pop out of her head.

"Carwyn," she repeats. "*The* Carwyn?"

I nod. Simply thinking about him makes my heart start dancing around like those eleven lords a-leaping in the old song.

"How did this happen?" Billie asks.

"We ran into each other, and things took off from there," I say.

"We need deets," Scarlet says, leaning forward, her flat white long forgotten.

I fill them in. They giggle and sigh in all the right places.

"A real-life happy ending," says Scarlet. "Now you've come full circle from that first mistletoe kiss."

"Well, we haven't kissed under the mistletoe," I confess.

"What? It's Christmas!" protests Billie.

"Trust me, it's my kryptonite. If we kiss under the mistletoe, it will ruin everything," I say.

"Don't be so superstitious," scolds Scarlet. "It's Christmas. You *have* to kiss under the mistletoe."

"No, I don't," I insist.

And to prove it, I avoid every single piece of mistletoe all during the party that evening. Carwyn keeps trying to lure me under it, but I resist. Instead, I make the rounds and visit with neighbors. It's amazing how much you can find to talk about when people suddenly want to talk to you.

Speaking of talking, it's hard to visit with Carwyn's dad and not tear up. This kind man doesn't deserve the future that's waiting for him.

On the surface, everything looks fine. He stands with his

hands in his pockets, a happy smile on his face telling me it's nice to have me back.

Mrs. Davies joins him. "We're all happy to have you back, Hailey."

It feels like a parental blessing to me, and I smile at them both and thank them.

The party winds down. Eventually the last guest leaves, and Carwyn suggests a walk in the snow. It's a perfect night for it. The air is crisp and the night is clear, the sky a jewel box filled with stars. Colored lights line snowy rooftops, and inflatable Santas wave at us as we walk past.

"I bet you don't see this in New York," he says.

"No, but we have the holiday displays on Fifth Avenue and the Rockefeller Christmas tree and the skating rink," I say. "New York at Christmas is amazing."

"I wouldn't mind seeing it," he says. He wants to see New York. There's proof that everything will work out.

"I wouldn't mind showing it to you," I say.

"Still, there's no place like home," he adds.

I feel a twinge of *uh-oh.* "Home is where your heart is," I counter.

"Yes, it is," he agrees, and I decide that I imagined that *uh-oh.*

"Is it okay if I come over after the Christmas Eve service?" he asks as we finally circle back toward my parents' house.

"Absolutely," I say.

"You still owe me a kiss under the mistletoe."

"I don't think that's a good idea," I say.

"I do."

"How about a kiss in the snow instead?" I suggest.

He smiles. "I guess I could settle for that."

He slips his arms around me. His body is hard, and his arms

are strong. He tastes like peppermint pie and smells like the outdoors. Living a happily-ever-after is so much more satisfying than writing one. I'm filled with holiday happiness.

Once inside the house I float up to my room. I text Ramona that I hope she's doing great. It's party season, and I know she's probably still awake.

Sure enough, she texts back minutes later and assures me that she is and asks how things are going.

Hailey: Perfect.

Ramona: Have you kissed under the mistletoe?

Hailey: No way. Don't want to ruin things.

Ramona: You won't. True love can't be ruined.

I smile. I must find a way to use that phrase in my novel.
My novel.
Suddenly, I'm inspired. I text bye to Ramona, pull out my laptop, and start writing. It's the best love scene I've ever written. I might finish this book by January 3 after all.

I finally get ready for bed, shut off the light, and snuggle under the covers. Once asleep, I dream that Carwyn and I are in New York, looking at a condo on Park Avenue. It costs $3 million, and the real estate agent informs us that the HOA fees are $3,000 a month.

"No problem," I say. "I can afford it." Of course I can. This is a dream, and in it I'm richer than Danielle Steel.

I wake up with a smile. Surely the dream is a sign of wonderful things to come. Not the richer than Danielle part. I don't care about that. Only the part where Carwyn and I are together.

Mom greets me when I come into the kitchen to help her with breakfast. "Did you sleep well?"

"Great," I say.

She opens the oven to check on our breakfast casserole, and the aroma wafts over to me. Eggs, cheese, and green chiles. My taste buds can hardly wait for the meetup. I grab the bread and start making toast.

"Your hair's looking better," she says.

It is. Finally, after yet another washing.

"So's yours," I say as I help myself to a cup of coffee.

"I guess Gwendolyn knew what she was doing after all," Mom says with a smile.

Obviously, Sam hasn't told Mom that he and Gwendolyn are done. "I don't think we can count on Gwendolyn coloring our hair anymore."

"Oh? Why?"

"Sam broke up with her."

"What? When did that happen?"

"When we went out for pizza."

"I thought they were so good together." Mom sounds perplexed.

"He's lucky to be rid of her," I say and tell Mom about Gwendolyn's behavior. "She's always been a bully," I add.

Mom's eyes narrow. "Did she bully you in high school?"

I shrug.

"You should have told me."

"You know there are some things kids have to work out on their own," I say.

"Still, lucky for her I didn't know," Mom says, eyes still narrowed.

"Oh well. You know what they say. Living well is the best revenge."

She smiles at that. "And you are. It looks like something's going on with you and Carwyn."

Now I'm smiling. "I think so."

"Good. He's a first-rate man. Unless there's something I don't know about him," she adds.

"No, he is."

"You could have a good life with him. And it would be so great to have you back here," Mom continues.

Back here? I don't say anything, but inwardly I'm thinking, *But I'm a New Yorker now.*

"If it's meant to be, it will all work out," she adds.

"Yes, it will," I agree.

Of course it will. True love always finds its happy ending, right?

That evening at the Christmas Eve candlelight service, Carwyn and I exchange smiles across the pew as we sing "Joy to the World." I love the profound and overwhelming message of Christmas. To be here with my family and see the man I've adored all my life smiling at me with love in his eyes adds to the joy.

Gram, who never misses anything, links her arm through mine as we leave the church. "That one's a keeper. Don't let him get away."

"Not planning on it," I say with a smile.

We're all gathered around the dining table, eating our Christmas Eve snack of chips, cheese, and crackers and artichoke dip, washed down with eggnog, when the doorbell rings.

"I bet I know who that is," says Grandpa, winking at me.

I hurry to the door and open it, and there stands Carwyn in jeans, boots, and that mountain-man suede jacket of his. It's lightly snowing now, and some of the snow has dusted his hair. He's holding a wrapped present.

"Come on in," I say, and he steps inside and hands me the box.

"Merry Christmas," he says.

"I don't have anything for you," I protest.

"Oh, I think you do," he says, and points to the mistletoe hanging above us.

Here it is, the moment of truth.

EIGHT

At last she would be his. He was sure of it.
—Hailey Fairchild, *What the Heart Needs*

I set the box on the hall table and turn to face him. My heart is galloping faster than Santa's reindeer on takeoff. *Don't let this be the beginning of the end.*

It's a beautiful kiss, tender and sweet, with his hands on my cheeks. None of those other mistletoe fails started with a mistletoe kiss like this, so packed with respect and kindness and . . . love? Is it possible? It sure feels possible.

"That wasn't so bad, was it?" he murmurs.

"No, that was fantabulous," I say and come back for more.

We're still standing there, going at it, when Dad comes out and says, "Hey, you two, knock it off and get to the kitchen. The artichoke dip's getting cold."

Carwyn chuckles and takes my hand, and we move to the table where everyone is discussing what holiday movie to watch.

"Not *Elf*," says Sam, giving me a stern look.

"And not *Die Hard*," I shoot back.

"*Family Man*," suggests Mom.

"We have to watch *It's a Wonderful Life*," Gram insists, and everyone groans. "It's tradition," she argues.

We've all watched that movie every year at Christmas for forever. I can say all George Bailey's lines right along with him. And I can't stand Zuzu. Sam is rolling his eyes, and I bet now he's sorry he voted down *Elf*.

"That's a great movie," says Carwyn, earning points from Gram.

"Of course it is," she says and plunges another cracker into her dip.

We watch *It's a Wonderful Life*, everyone all comfy in chairs and couches, Carwyn and I sharing the big overstuffed chair. It *is* a wonderful life, and as we watch it, I can't help thinking how much Carwyn is like George Bailey. He's such a big part of this community, and so good to his parents. Would he ever want to leave it all behind and live in New York with me?

I push the thought away when Carwyn kisses me good night. It's a forever kind of kiss, for sure. I'm so inspired, I must write!

And write I do, sitting up in bed and tapping away at my keyboard into the wee hours of the morning. I'm on a roll. I can't quit. And I don't until all I have left is the ending scene, where my heroine and her hero embark on their happily-ever-after. Success! It's the perfect way to end a perfect day.

I text Ramona early the next morning before breakfast.

Hailey: The book is almost done!

Ramona: Yay! Where did you find your inspiration?

Hailey: I kissed Carwyn under the mistletoe. It was amazing.

Ramona: Ho ho ho! I know this one's going to work out.

Yes, it is. I wish her Merry Christmas, give her a pep talk to help her get through Christmas Day with her dysfunctional family, and then sign off.

The grandparents arrive by midmorning the next day, and we settle in around the tree with our coffee and pastries and begin to open presents. Mom hands me the one from Carwyn. I open it to find a collection of hand-blown ornaments. *Think of me when you hang them,* says the note he's included.

I'm already thinking of him. All the time.

❄

Carwyn and I spend every day together between Christmas and New Year's Eve. It's all so perfect. Walks in the snow, a Wii bowling tournament with Sam, an evening with Carwyn's parents, and dinner for two in a quiet corner at Cascade House, the fanciest restaurant in town.

The menu isn't much by New York standards, but they do have linen tablecloths on the table. And candlelight. Dining by candlelight—it feeds my romance writer's soul. I still haven't written the end of my book, but I'm not worried. I'll write it on the flight home.

On New Year's Eve he invites me to his house for dinner—steaks on the grill and French bread. I insist on at least bringing the salad. He's ordered cheesecake from Cascade Bakery and put champagne on ice. "You have to have champagne on New Year's Eve," he says.

After dinner we settle on his looks-like-leather-but-isn't couch and gaze at the flames in the fireplace. It's all so romantic. It's like he knows instinctively what feeds my soul, and I tell him so.

"I want to make you happy," he says.

"You are," I tell him. "I've never been happier."

When it's almost midnight he pours the champagne and raises his glass. "To us," he says.

"To us," I repeat, and we touch glasses and drink.

"This last week has been epic for me," he says.

"Me too," I say.

"Is it too soon to ask if you want to keep this going?"

"Oh, Carwyn." I'm so thrilled I can barely breathe, let alone get out the words. "I'm all for that. I can hardly wait to show you New York," I add.

"I can hardly wait to see it. And I can hardly wait to get you back to Cascade. I bet your parents will love having you back."

"For visits," I clarify.

He nods thoughtfully. "So, long-distance relationship?"

"Well, I do live in New York."

New York is where my life is. Even though it's where my mistletoe mistakes haunt me like Scrooge's ghosts, it's where I've formed friendships, where I've found myself, and where I feel comfortable. I'm not sure why, but I assumed if we reached the point of talking about rings and weddings, our story would end with us in New York. I'd be back in my world, with my kind—writerly types—and with my perfect man.

But my perfect man isn't saying anything, and there's the *uh-oh* again.

"We can find a way to work this out," he says finally.

Can we? He's the principal at the local high school, for crying out loud. And his family's here. His dad.

"I can come to New York during spring break. Maybe you can come out for the summer."

"And what if this gets serious?" Oh, crud. I didn't mean to say that out loud. It's too early to say things like that out loud.

"We'll work it out," he says, but now the *uh-oh* is looming over us like a giant Grinch.

The clock starts to chime. It's midnight. Now I know how Cinderella felt. The ball is over.

NINE

*Her heart sank. Was this one small thing going to tear them apart,
just when they'd finally found each other?*
—Hailey Fairchild, *What the Heart Needs*

L et's get you home," says Carwyn.

Home to my parents' house, or home to New York?

Have I just blown it big-time?

No, I can't have. Real heroes keep trying until they win their
woman.

He doesn't say anything on the ride home, and I have no idea
what to say. On the front porch, he kisses me again, but it doesn't
feel the same as those other kisses.

❄

"Happy New Year! Did you have a great New Year's Eve?" Mom asks
when I drag myself into the kitchen the next morning.

I'm glad it's only the two of us. I'd hate to announce to the whole
family that I'm about to mess up my love life again. I shake my head.

Her smile falls. "What happened?"

"I don't think this is going to work," I say, and my lower lip begins
to wobble.

"Why not?"

"He can't leave here."

"So you'd come back to Cascade. That sounds like a good thing." Mom studies me. "Why wouldn't you?"

I hate to say it. It sounds foolish, but it's how I feel. "I don't belong here anymore."

Her brows furrow. "Why on earth not? I don't understand."

How do I explain something I'm having a hard time explaining to myself? "I've moved on. I belong in New York."

"Why?"

"Because my publisher is there. My friends, my life."

"You can have a life here too," Mom says gently.

"I have no past in New York."

Actually, I do. I have three love fails.

I think of how my stories always end. The hero gives up everything for the heroine.

But none of those heroes have a sick father. Carwyn is needed here.

Sam ambles into the kitchen and makes himself some coffee. "Why are you two looking so serious?"

"Your sister's trying to sort out her life," Mom says.

"Trying to figure out how to spend your next big royalty check?" he teases.

He knows that's still a long way down the road. If ever. Because now my writer's block is back, and I can't even think about the book, and my editor is going to kill me, and I'll never get another book contract again. Then I'll be a love loser and a career loser. A life loser.

I haven't said anything, so he pushes. "Something go wrong with Carwyn? I thought you were into each other."

"We are," I say. "But he's here, and I'm in New York."

Sam holds out both hands and gives his head a little shake. "So move."

"I don't want to live in Cascade." That sounds so . . . snobby. Ungrateful. Immature.

He frowns. "What's wrong with Cascade? We're all here. You'd pick a big impersonal city over the town where your family and friends live?"

"I don't have any friends in Cascade," I snap.

"You have Billie," he suggests.

Billie is fine, but it's Scarlet I'm friends with.

"And how about Eloise at the bookstore?" puts in Mom. "You could start a writers' group and meet there."

Sam downs half his coffee and shakes his head. "I guess you're not that into him."

"I am!" I protest.

"No, you're not. Otherwise, you'd be willing to do whatever needs to be done to make things work. He's got real reasons for staying put. You don't, sis."

I don't know what to say to that, so I say nothing.

A moment later, Dad's in the kitchen. "What's for breakfast? I'm starving."

"Waffles," Mom says and gets busy with her waffle iron.

I set the table and Sam gets more coffee.

"Everybody sure is quiet," Dad observes.

Yes, we are. Because now it feels like there's nothing left to say.

Until Mom and Dad inform us that come summer, they are going to take a world cruise. Sam will be in charge of the store while Dad's gone.

"About time you guys did something interesting," he says to Dad.

"Our entire life has been interesting," Mom says firmly.

Dad nods. "Yep. Good friends, good times. Good kids."

"The best place to find gold is in your own backyard," Mom says and looks at me. I don't think she's talking about New York City.

Carwyn comes over and hangs out. Holds my hand while we all watch the Rose Bowl. Then his parents call, and he has to take off.

His dad has had a fall. "Nothing serious, but I'd better go," he says. And that's that.

He texts me the next day when I'm at the airport, waiting for my flight.

Carwyn: Gonna miss you.

I sigh. Is this what our future will be, lots of *miss you* texts? I'm never at a loss for words ... until now.
Five minutes pass and another text comes in.

Carwyn: ????

Okay, I can't keep ignoring him.

Hailey: How's this going to work?

There are the little bubbles. He already has an answer. Then come the words.

Carwyn: I don't know.

Not what I was hoping to see.
More words follow.

Carwyn: But let's not give up. We've started something great. Let's not be quitters.

I thumb my brilliant response.

Hailey: OK.

I'd planned to finish my book on the flight home. Instead, I stare at the computer screen, and the flashing cursor mocks me.

Back at the apartment I have a therapy session with Ramona. We go over the whole trip and how I felt about every moment of it, and we talk about where my relationship with Carwyn is now probably not going.

"You did survive Gwendolyn," she points out. "And unlike my family, yours is together and great and you love them."

"I do."

"You had a good time. And most important, you started a romance for the ages. This one isn't a mistletoe fail. Unless you make it one," she adds. "Do you love him?"

"I do."

When I was young, I loved the idea of Carwyn, the unattainable boy next door. Then I loved the one-dimensional, hunky, fantasy version of him. But now I love the real him—the kindhearted, trustworthy man whose kisses promise a life of commitment and contentment. It's the best version of all three.

"Then, really, what's holding you back? It's not New York and your life here. Don't give me that. It's such a bunch of beans."

I press my lips together, rub them back and forth, searching for the reason behind the excuses. "I don't know."

"Yes, you do," she says.

Yes, I do, really.

"Say it."

"I'm afraid," I blurt. "I'm afraid this will end up being just another mistletoe failure. I'll give up my life here and go home, and it will all crumble before my very eyes."

She scoots over on the couch and puts an arm around my shoulders. "Don't be a goof. Your past is, well, your past. You got a mistletoe do-over this year. Take advantage of it. You deserve the kind of happy ending you write."

I bite my lip. A tear is trickling down my cheek. Do I?

Ramona has been reading my mind. "You have the power to write your happy ending. Think Nike and just do it," she adds with a grin.

Just do it.

I take a deep breath and nod. Can't bring myself to say I will, but maybe I can move in that direction.

She runs a hand through her long dark hair. "I'm pooped. I'm going to bed." She gets up and starts for the hallway. But she turns before she vanishes into the bedroom. "First, finish that book. Let your heroine tell you what to do."

I frown at her retreating back. Let my heroine tell me what to do. Stupid. My characters never talk to me. I talk to them. I'm the one in charge.

Maybe that's why this last book hasn't been going so well. I'm in no condition to be in charge of anyone's love life, even if she's fictional.

I decide to talk to my heroine, just like Ramona suggested.

"What should I do, Augusta?" I whisper.

Get me out of this forest, she demands. *I need to find Henry and claim my happy ending.*

Claim my happy ending. There it is—what both of us need.

I do get Augusta out of that forest. She finds a horse and rides all night, dodging bandits and wolves and things that go bump in the night. By dawn she has found Henry, and they've vowed never to be parted.

"I know now that love is worth any risk," Augusta says as Henry holds her in his arms. He's looking at her, but I can feel her looking over his shoulder at me.

I email the manuscript to my editor and then grab my cell phone and call Carwyn.

"Hailey," he says in surprise. "What time is it out there?"

"It's time for me to show that I'm all in. I won't be a quitter," I say.

I can hear the smile in his voice when he says, "All right. You just made my day. No, my year."

Maybe I've made mine too. We'll have to see what happens next.

TEN

Seeing him standing there, she knew she had to trust her heart
this time.
—Hailey Fairchild, *What the Heart Knows*

Carwyn sends me flowers for Valentine's Day. He calls and we talk for hours.

He comes to visit over Presidents' Day weekend, and we do all the tourist things—the Staten Island Ferry, the Statue of Liberty, the Empire State Building.

We wind up at the September 11 Memorial & Museum. It's a sobering reminder of how short life is and how quickly we can lose those who are important to us. I don't want to lose Carwyn. And I don't want him to lose precious time with his father.

We talk every day after he leaves, and by the time I fly back to Cascade to spend spring break with him, I know what I need to do to get my happy ending. In all my stories it's the hero who sacrifices for his woman, but in my real-life story, I realize I need to be the one to sacrifice. After all, heroes aren't the only ones who can give their all for love.

Anyway, I'm not sure this is that great a sacrifice. I can write anywhere. And really, what's to fear about moving back? Gwendolyn? Pfft. Who cares if I run into her in the grocery store? I certainly won't be seeing her at Hair Today. As for her posse, most of them have moved away. All that remains are their ghosts, and I'm not afraid of ghosts. I'm not afraid of anything. My time away, even my mistletoe fails, forged me into a new woman, and that new woman can thrive anywhere. Thriving with the people who love me best—what's not to like about that? And New York will always be there.

For visits.

On the last night of my spring break trip, I go to Carwyn's place and cook dinner for him. And make my big announcement. "I'm moving back to Cascade."

He looks at me, hopeful and yet afraid to hope. "Seriously? Are you sure?"

I nod.

Now he looks like he's just won the lottery, with a big grin on his face. "Oh, man, Hailey," is all he gets out before he wraps me in a python hug and kisses me so hard I see stars. I'm so happy I feel like I've caught a whole galaxy in my hands.

He pulls back. Studies me. "Are you absolutely sure? You love New York."

"I really want this," I assure him. "I love New York but I love you more, and this is where I belong. In Cascade."

"And in my arms," he says and kisses me again. "You'll never regret coming back. I'll make sure of that," he promises.

I know I won't. This is the happy ending I've wanted all my life. I made a new start in New York City, but my big finish is right here, where my story first began.

ELEVEN

Love is worth any risk.
—Hailey Fairchild, *What the Heart Knows*

I haven't regretted coming home for one minute. I've been living with my parents for the last couple of months, but I spend most of my time with Carwyn, and that gets better every day. I catch sight of Gwendolyn and her one remaining evil lackey once in a while. They sneer or whisper, but it bounces off me because love has become my shield. I don't have time for their pettiness anyway. I'm too busy working on my next book, *When Love Wins*.

Today Carwyn and I are going ring shopping. We're planning a December wedding, and Scarlet and Ramona will be my brides-maids, with Ramona flying out to do the maid of honor duties. Mom is talking about baking the wedding cake, and Billie wants to do the flowers. Not sure what those will look like yet, but one thing I do know. There will be mistletoe.

ACKNOWLEDGMENTS

Kathleen Fuller

Dear Reader, thank you for visiting Mistletoe, Missouri, and meeting Emmy, Kieran, and their families. I hope you enjoyed reading the story as much I did writing it. A big thank you to my editors Becky Monds, Amy Kerr, and my dear friend and fabulous critique partner, Amy Clipston. With your help I was able to bring *Return to Mistletoe* to life. Merry Christmas!

DISCUSSION QUESTIONS

Return to Mistletoe

1. When Kieran returns home, he finds that things have changed, but they also remain the same. Have you ever experienced returning home or going back to a favorite place, and how did that make you feel?

2. Jingle Fest is one of the Christmas activities Emmy and Kieran enjoy. Do you have a favorite Christmas activity or tradition you do with family and friends?

3. Maggie tells Kieran that he can't outrun grief or a broken heart. What advice would you give him to help him with his grief?

4. Kieran knew he was being a coward when he left Mistletoe right before Maggie's party, and he had to find the courage to return and make things right with his family and Emmy. Discuss a time when you made a mistake and had the courage to fix it. Where did that courage come from?

A Mistletoe Prince

5. What was your favorite scene in the story?

6. Arran dresses up as Prince Phillip from *Sleeping Beauty*. Do you have a favorite movie "prince"?

7. What were some of the internal struggles of Arran and Charlotte? What were their insecurities?

8. In what tangible ways do we see them overcome those insecurities in the story?

9. "Have courage, dear heart" is a beautiful quote not only of encouragement, but "dear heart" is an endearment. How has being loved and loving others helped you have courage?

10. Since this is a Christmas story, how does Arran's "redemption" and Charlotte's realization of who she is show us some truths from the Bible?

11. In *The Mistletoe Prince*, mistletoe is described as a symbol of resilience, protection, and love. How do we see these characteristics shown in Arran and Charlotte throughout the story? How have you seen them in your own life?

Say No to Mistletoe

12. Hailey Fairchild was nervous about coming home for the holidays and looking like a failure. Do you think she was justified?

13. When was the last time you shared a kiss with someone special under the mistletoe?

14. Who was your first crush?

15. Hailey felt like a love failure. What would you have said to encourage her?

16. Gwendolyn Payne did a good job of hiding her true character from Hailey's brother. Have you ever known someone who is good at putting up an impressive front that hides who she or he really is?

17. Once Hailey got home there were lots of Christmas traditions to enjoy and plenty of parties. Does your family have a favorite tradition?

18. Do you think Hailey was justified in her belief that Carwyn should give up his life and move to New York with her? What advice would you have given her?

19. Have you ever been in love with someone who you felt was out of reach?

20. What's the most romantic Christmas you've ever had?

21. Ramona gave Hailey a positive affirmation to quote when she was home visiting. Do you have one? If so, what is it?

LOOKING FOR MORE GREAT READS? LOOK NO FURTHER!

THOMAS NELSON
Since 1798

Visit us online to learn more:
tnzfiction.com

Or scan the below code and sign up to receive email updates
on new releases, giveaways, book deals, and more:

@tnzfiction

ABOUT THE AUTHORS

SHEILA ROBERTS

USA TODAY and *Publishers Weekly* bestselling author Sheila Roberts has seen her books translated into several different languages, included in *Reader's Digest* compilations, and made into movies for the Hallmark and Lifetime channels. She's happily married and lives in the Pacific Northwest.

Website: sheilasplace.com
Facebook: @funwithsheila
Twitter: @_Sheila_Roberts
Instagram: @sheilarobertswriter

Photo by Robert Rabe

KATHLEEN FULLER

With over a million copies sold, Kathleen Fuller is the *USA TODAY* bestselling author of several bestselling novels, including the Hearts of Middlefield novels, the Middlefield Family novels, the Amish of Birch Creek series, and the Amish Letters series as well as a middle-grade Amish series, the Mysteries of Middlefield.

Visit her online at KathleenFuller.com
Instagram: @kf_booksandhooks
Facebook: @WriterKathleenFuller
Twitter: @TheKatJam

PEPPER BASHAM

Pepper Basham is an award-winning author who writes romance "peppered" with grace and humor. Writing both historical and contemporary novels, she loves to incorporate her native Appalachian culture and/or her unabashed adoration of the UK into her stories. She currently resides in the lovely mountains of Asheville, NC, where she is the wife of a fantastic pastor, mom of five great kids, a speech-language pathologist, and a lover of chocolate, jazz, hats, and Jesus.

Michael Kaal @ Michael Kaal Photography

You can learn more about Pepper and her books on her website at www.pepperdbasham.com.
Facebook: @pepperbasham
Instagram: @pepperbasham
Twitter: @pepperbasham
BookBub: @pepperbasham